J. N. Chaney

www.jnchaney.com

1st Edition

STAY UP TO DATE

Chaney posts updates, official art, previews, and other awesome stuff on his website. You can also follow him on Instagram, Facebook, and Twitter.

Search for **JN Chaney's Renegade Readers** on Facebook to join the group where readers can come together and share their lives and interests, especially regarding Chaney's books.

For updates about new releases, as well as exclusive promotions, sign up for the VIP mailing list. Head there now to receive a free copy of *The Other Side of Nowhere*.

https://www.subscribepage.com/organic

Enjoying the series? Help others discover the Variant Saga by leaving a review on Amazon.

BOOKS BY JN CHANEY

The Variant Saga:

The Amber Project

Transient Echoes

Hope Everlasting

The Vernal Memory

Renegade Star Series:

Renegade Star

Renegade Atlas

Renegade Moon

Renegade Lost

Renegade Fleet

Renegade Earth

Standalone Books:

Their Solitary Way

The Other Side of Nowhere

HOPE EVERLASTING

BOOK 3 IN THE VARIANT SAGA

J.N. CHANEY

CONTENTS

For S.M. Boyce,
who pushed me through
the looking glass.

PART I

A ship is safe in harbor,
but that's not what ships are for.
– William G. T. Shedd

The fair breeze blew, the white foam flew,
The furrow followed free:
We were the first that ever burst
Into that silent sea.
– Samuel Taylor Coleridge

PROLOGUE

Somewhere in another world, deep within the forests of a planet known as Kant, two men walked together, each on the verge of collapse. One, a former servant to the Temple of the Eye, husband to a warrior priestess and father to a missing child. The other, bred and trained as a soldier, genetically engineered in an underground society, and the first human to travel to another living world.

Each of them, a fugitive.

Each of them, starving and afraid.

"How long before the border?" asked Terry, the younger of the two.

"Several days," said Ludo, clutching his wounded side. "We must first look for Talo in Capeside, then go north."

"Your family is from Capeside," remembered Terry.

"My grandmother has a house near the market. Talo knows. He will have gone there by now."

"We'll find him," said Terry. "We'll find your wife, too. Both of them."

When the twin suns had set, the two men slept under a clear night sky, blanketed with stars, no cloaks or furs to keep them warm. They had only their prison uniforms, ragged and torn—a reminder of what came before.

Terry awoke several times to the chilled air of the countryside. What he wouldn't give for a bed and a soft pillow, a warm bowl of soup to calm his aching stomach. Instead, he had only the brush and dirt beneath him.

But he was still alive…and he had Ludo by his side.

Lying on the dirt, and with his friend asleep, Terry closed his eyes and concentrated, quieting his mind until everything went dark. He imagined an empty blackness, never-ending and eternal, and he let himself fall into it. The void washed over him, surrounding his mind and bringing tranquility. A wave of peace.

He forgot his worries, forgot the field and mud around him, forgot the freezing cold. Everything faded and dissolved, and suddenly he was elsewhere, far and away from the place he had been.

A bath of light broke through the night, touching his face, replacing the shadow. A vast and violet sky stretched beyond the horizon as two suns beat down against his cheeks, warming his skin. Now, at last, he stood atop a wide plain, a mountain range in the distance.

A bird chirped behind him, near the edge of the forest. Flapping its wings, the blue and yellow creature squawked excitedly. It leapt forward into the air, and all at once a flock emerged from deep within the trees, scattering.

They filled the sky like stars. They filled the sky with wings.

Before him stood a building, a familiar, inviting farmhouse. Several lots of tilled land surrounded it, encased within a fence. Ludo's home, or so it had been, back before the soldiers came and burned it to the ground. In the real world, nothing remained of this place. Nothing but ash and dust and memories.

But not here. Here it stood preserved, pristine and untouched, an eternal memory stuck inside the mind of a young, human man.

Terry had created his own little universe and filled it with grass and sky and *things*. Birds and bugs and animals, each living separate lives, with goals and personalities. In this place of make-believe, he felt the warmth of the suns, the pressure of the wind, and the wetness of the river. The whole wide world remained as he'd made it, another reality in his imagination.

As long as he was here, it was real in all the ways that mattered.

Terry placed his head against the grass, and the afternoon heat relaxed him.

He closed his eyes, suddenly tired. Now, he could finally sleep. He could rest.

When he awoke, he found himself once again lying on the wet dirt, freezing. "Welcome back," said Ludo. "I feared you would never rise. The light is new and we have far to go. Let us leave before the second sun rises."

Terry blinked, then rubbed the sleep from his eyes. "Sorry. I must have been tired."

"I am certain that is true," said the farmer, helping Terry to his feet.

"Will we reach the village today?" asked Terry. He wiped some mud from his hands.

"Tomorrow or the day after."

Terry examined him. Ludo seemed stronger than yesterday. There was more strength in his posture. "Do you feel better today?"

Ludo nodded his agreement. "The wounds are healing. Soon they will be gone." His gaze drifted toward the direction of the prison. "Though, I will not forget."

Terry remembered the look on his friend's face when he stood over a dying tyrant, back in the compound. A man named Gast Maldeen, the Lord of Three Waters, had tried his best to kill them—an act which Ludo had managed to reverse. Gast was dead, and the two of them had fled, but the memory would never fade.

Terry had expected a battalion of soldiers to come running, calling for their heads. You killed our Lord, they would cry. We will chase you forever.

Yet, somehow, days had passed and here they stood, no army at their backs. Only the wild country around them, forests and fields and rivers, as though they'd marched to the far edge of the world where none could follow.

With so much behind them, the two men looked forward. First Capeside, and then north to the border to Everlasting.

Everlasting, thought Terry. *The glowing city on the hill. The place where everyone flies.*

A hundred questions darted through his mind, circling endlessly. How large must such a legendary city be? What were the people like who lived there? Were they like Ludo…or somehow different?

He'd never find the answers, but it hardly mattered. The only mission now was finding Ludo's family. Terry owed the man his life, and he'd follow him to the edge of oblivion if that's what it took.

Right to the bitter end.

S.O.F.T. Mission Report
Play Audio File 13
Recorded: February 4, 2351

FINN: *We found the entrance to this place, finally. Big old staircase going to the surface. I haven't poked my head out yet, but I could see light shining in from the door.*

CURIE: *Do you think it's a good idea to go up there already? You still haven't finished exploring the facility.*

FINN: *We've seen enough. Looks like it's been abandoned for years. If you don't mind, Mei, I'd rather get on with the real reason we're here.*

CURIE: *I know. It's okay. I'll have Zoe send the flippies and we'll map the rest of it. You focus on finding Terry.*

FINN: *I wonder what's waiting for us up there. Think we'll find something cool?*

CURIE: *Like what?*

FINN: *I don't know. Maybe zombie robots from Planet 9. I could use a pet zombie robot. He'd make a good sidekick.*

CURIE: *I'm sure you could. I have no idea what you'll see, but I'd say anything's possible. Be careful, though.*

FINN: *Awesome. Don't worry about me, babe. I've always been the careful type.*

CURIE: *Says the guy who rushed into a portal to another planet without so much as a second thought.*

FINN: *Always the critic.*

End Audio File

Bravo Gate Point
February 4, 2351

John munched on a protein bar, gobbling it down and wiping the crumbs from his jacket. He and his team had spent nearly two days exploring this underground facility and they still hadn't found anything useful. Oh, sure, some scientists back home would probably end up obsessing over every little detail of his reports, every frame of recording, every picture taken, but none of it brought him closer to the true purpose of this mission: to find his oldest friend and bring him home.

Ever since they found Terry's pack in the room with the portal, John had hoped for more. Another clue as to his friend's whereabouts, but so far there was nothing. Only an underground cave with some fancy machines here and there. No signs to point his way.

But today his team had found the exit. A way to leave this empty place and see the real world. Surely, if Terry was alive, he'd be out there somewhere, waiting. John could almost imagine it. He'd climb those steps and reach the top, walk into the light, and see his old friend waiting. "What took you so long?" Terry would ask, and John would shrug and together they'd laugh.

"Boss, you good?" asked Hughes.

John blinked and looked at his teammate. Mason Hughes was smaller than most, coming in at around 157 centimeters, but what he lacked in physical strength and stature, he more than made up for with skill. Hughes could shoot the wings off a fly from two kilometers away. "Yeah, I'm fine," said John, a second later. "What about you, Hughes? You ready to head topside?"

The marksman nodded. "Been itchin' for a chance to see what's out there."

"We all have," said John. He got to his feet. "Tell the boys to rally. We're leaving in a few."

"Yes, sir," said Hughes.

John thumbed the side of his rifle as it rested gently

along his leg. The process of finding Terry would probably take some time, so he'd have to wait, but patience was never John's strong suit. *Hopefully soon*, he thought, digging his fingernail into his stock.

His team convened quickly, gaggling together a few yards in front of him. "Ready, sir," said Hughes.

John nodded. "Alright, folks. Here's the plan. Most of us are going topside, but I need two of you to stay here and guard the gate. Any volunteers?" He paused. "No? Okay. Mickey and Track, you're up."

The two men released a short sigh, but didn't complain. The protest had been involuntary, almost reflexive, so John couldn't fault them. If he wasn't a genetically engineered hybrid with superhuman senses, he never would have noticed. "Once we're on the surface, we'll have to set up some signal repeaters. Which one of you has them?"

"I do, boss," said Brooks, standing near the edge of the group. She reached into her pack and held one of the boxes above her head. "Got six of these from Bartholomew this morning."

"Good. While you're doing that, we'll need to scout the area. I'll assign once we get there. Everyone ready?"

"Yes, sir!" said the group in unison.

"Alright, Blacks. Saddle up your gear. It's time to see what's out there."

JOHN and his team traveled through the tunnels of the underground compound, each of their weapons at the ready. Despite having already explored most of the surrounding area, particularly the main tunnel, they stayed on their guard. It took nearly two hours to traverse the massive subterranean path on their way to the exit, but they eventually found the end.

John stared beyond the staircase and into the distant, beaming light of the outside world. He couldn't help but wonder what awaited them there. If his time chasing razorbacks had taught him anything, it was to always be prepared for the worst. Monsters and enemies might be waiting around every corner, through every open door, foaming at the mouth for a chance to chomp on human bones and rip apart their flesh.

Then again, maybe this planet was different. Maybe he'd find a litter of puppies up there, playing in a field of daisies. It certainly wouldn't be the strangest thing he'd ever seen.

John grinned. *Here's hoping*, he thought.

The Blacks reached the bottom of the staircase, and John gave the signal to move. Privates Meridy and Short took the lead, while the rest follow two at a time. John stuck to the rear—his job as the squad leader.

The air grew warmer as he climbed, until the light of the outside world finally touched his skin, bathing him in light and heat. He felt suddenly relaxed.

The light hit his eyes, and he flinched. It was bright.

Was this common here? He had no way of knowing yet, having been outside for only twelve seconds.

Near the entrance to the cave sat a couple of domed buildings, cracked with age and neglect. John peered into one of the windows, only to see an overgrown garden of weeds inside, covering most of the floor. Useless. "Whatcha think, boys?"

"Lots of purple, same as home," said Short, one of only three females on the team. "And I'm not a boy."

Hatcher snickered. "Careful boss. Don't wanna set her off. Short just broke up with her girlfriend."

"With Michelle?" asked John, glancing at Short. "What for?"

"Cheated on me with a Collector," said Short, fanning her hand. "Dropped her ass as soon as I heard."

John laughed. The Collectors were one of the other squads working under Colonel Ross's new SOFT program. They'd received their name after an early expedition where the team had stumbled into a den of Otters—a species of giant rodents found mostly in the southern caves, far from the city. After killing a few of the animals, the team decided to bring a few home. They turned one of them into the Science Division for studying purposes, but kept the other as a sort of trophy, stuffing and mounting the head in their command hall. The Science Division was thrilled with the new discovery, and requested the team continue bringing them any new species they encountered. A few dozen kills later, and with a wall of trophies under their belt, people started calling them the Collectors, and it stuck. They also had a rather morbid reputation.

"A Collector? Gross," Hatcher remarked. "You're better off. Anyone who screws with a Black deserves to get dumped."

"She's lucky she didn't get a beating," said Short, narrowing her eyes. "Took everything in me not to kick her teeth in."

"Always the lady, this one." Hatcher grinned, pointing his thumb at her.

Short glared at him. "Want to test me, Hatch?"

He held his arms up, but kept smiling. "No, ma'am. I'm good."

John glanced around the field. "If you two are about finished, what say we get on with it?"

"Yes, sir," said Short and Hatcher.

"Hot damn, would you look at that?" barked one of the soldiers. Hughes, by the sound of it.

John jogged to where the young sniper was, several yards away, near the edge of the rock wall. The kid was facing the other direction, looking beyond the ridge. John expected to find something outrageous, like a pack of wild animals.

No such luck.

"What is it?" he asked, seeing nothing.

Hughes stared into the sky, wide-eyed, and he pointed. "Look, boss!"

There, hanging far above the horizon, two suns rose

steadily beneath thin clouds. One was deeply yellow, while the other had a touch of red in it. John didn't know what to say.

"Looks like we really are on another planet," muttered Hatcher.

"Hot damn," said Short.

John cleared his throat, then turned so his back was to the light. "We can gawk at everything later, once this mission's done. Form up!"

"Yes, sir!" said several of the Blacks.

In a matter of seconds, the squad convened before him, standing in formation. "First things first," barked John. "I need those repeaters in place. Brooks, you hear that?"

"Yes, sir!" she snapped. Brooks was John's second-in-command as well as the resident techie. "Got three left, after dropping one at the gate room and two in the hall."

"Right, better get to it," said John. He watched as Brooks took off to plant the repeaters. "Next, I want eyes up. Hughes, you hear me?"

"Loud and clear, boss," said Hughes, glancing at Short. "Ready, spotter?"

She gave him a nod. "Good to go."

The two of them left the gaggle, heading to the base of the cliff, preparing to climb.

"Everyone else, we've got three CHUs to set. I want them up within the hour," said John.

"We can do it in half," said Hatcher.

"Alright, let's go. Dismissed!" barked John.

The Blacks dispersed, and John jogged toward the Capsular Housing Unit equipment, along with several others. They unlatched the first CHU and began assembling it. The process didn't take long, since it was mostly automated. The oxygen tanks and seals still had to be physically set up, however.

The CHUs were a huge priority, given the Variant in the air. John's team wouldn't be able to migrate back and forth through the portal every day like they'd been doing, so an oxygenated shelter had to be erected to allow for certain activities. John could survive here indefinitely, but most of his squad had to wear breathers so they didn't suffocate on Variant. They had to eat and sleep, after all, and while it might be possible to do both of those things with the devices over their mouths and noses, it certainly wasn't safe.

According to Captain Thistle, John's superior back in Central, the Science Division was in the process of working on an injection or a pill to give them the ability to breathe Variant for a temporary amount of time without suffocating. Unfortunately, they'd heard nothing about it so far, which probably meant it was a failure. Still, if the labs ever managed to manufacture them, there would be no need to worry about filtration systems or breathers. It would extend their ability to explore, and it would make John's job a lot easier.

"Tech Shop. Huck," radioed Brooks.

John tapped the side of his ear, pressing the embedded

communications device beneath his skin. "Tech Shop, go for Huck."

"The repeater is functional. You should be able to reach the gate room now. Over."

"Good work. Over." Using his pad, he switched frequencies. "Huck. Zapper."

A short burst of static. "Zapper copies," said Mickey, responding to his call sign. "Everything alright?"

"Fine. Just checking the signal," said John.

"Roger that," said Mickey.

John tapped the pad again, then put it away.

"Huck. Door Nail," radioed Hughes. "I'm in position."

John turned and craned his neck, spotting Hughes above the rock wall. Thanks to his exceptional eyes—a product of his genetically engineered genes—he could see further than any regular human. He gave Hughes a short wave, and the sniper returned it. "Look for any signs of movement Track anything larger than a finger. Over."

"Whose finger?" asked Hughes.

John flipped him off.

Hughes grinned. "Say no more."

ONCE THE TEAM had the CHUs erected, John ordered them to start combing the local forest. "Make sure your pads are in constant scan mode so we can chart the area," he told them. "I want a square kilometer fully detailed within the hour. You hear me?"

"Yes, sir," said the Blacks.

As they began their sweep, they made certain to stay within line of sight of each other. The Blacks did this sort of thing constantly back home. Given the nature of their missions—to seek out and destroy any and all threats, particularly razorback nests—it was prudent to have procedures in place when exploring new and potentially dangerous areas. They'd spent close to three years going into caves, forests, and more than a few abandoned old-world buildings, all without a single casualty. By now, they knew how to get the job done.

John monitored his pad, watching it slowly fill with detail as his team progressed. With every step his people took, a little more of the map revealed itself. It wouldn't be long before they had most of the surrounding area, giving him a fair read on the land.

They found the vale in the middle of the woods in under an hour. Hughes spotted it in the distance, using his scope, and radioed John to let him know. The team proceeded carefully, never dropping their guard.

At the center of the field within the woods, they found a building. Another dome, like the two others near the cave, only it was double their size and mostly unfinished. John checked upstairs and found some rags on the floor, almost as though someone had been staying here at some point. Probably not for a while, though.

Before they could explore further, a call came in from Mickey at the gate room. "The portal's set to come on in ten minutes, sir. You want me to patch you through once it's ready?"

"Sure thing, Mick," said John. The signal clarity was clearer now, a sign Brooks had placed a few more repeaters. No need to head back, unless he had to. He could speak to Mei right here.

Too bad he wouldn't have much news, not about the real mission. Sure, they'd found a few buildings, but nothing to point them in the direction of their missing friend. For all John knew, Terry could be long gone...or worse.

He shook his head. *Better not to think like that,* he reminded himself. *Gotta stay positive.*

The call came in a few minutes later, and Mickey patched him through to Mei. "John?" she asked, almost immediately. "Are you receiving me?"

The sound of her voice made him relax. "I'm here. I've got you loud and clear."

"Hey, goof. Have you found anything? Did you make it outside?"

"We did," he said. "Spotted a couple of buildings, too. Haven't been used in a while, though."

"Buildings? What kind?"

"Houses, maybe. I'm not sure," he admitted. "Don't worry. I'll have one of my guys take some pictures."

There was a short pause. "Is the site secure?" she asked.

"We're still working on it, but so far so good. Got most of the local area mapped and logged."

"What's the next step?"

"Sensors for movement. We'll place a few around the cave entrance, a dozen along the outer ridge, and then a bunch more in the surrounding woods."

"I want pictures of everything you find," said Mei.

"I've already got someone scanning the two near the cave. I'll send them during the next transmission," said John.

"Well, it sounds like you've got it under control over there," she said.

"Hey, this is what I do," he said with a big grin.

She laughed. "Just be careful, and keep your eyes open. Let me know if you find anything strange."

John glanced up at the two suns. "Strange, huh?" he said, still smiling. "Hold on a sec. I'm gonna send you a picture."

2

S.O.F.T. Mission Report
Play Audio File 16
Recorded: February 5, 2351

FINN: Sensors are in place around the camp. If anything bigger than a gopher passes by, we'll see them.

CURIE: *How do you know what size a gopher is? They've been extinct for two hundred years.*

FINN: Hey, give me a little credit, would you? I went to the same school you did.

CURIE: *There's no way you got that out of a book. You always skipped the reading, then copied Terry's homework.*

FINN: Okay, fine. I saw them in an old movie. Happy now?

CURIE: *I knew it.*

FINN: Anyway, the sensors are in place, and my team's working in shifts to keep watch. If there's anything out there, we'll know pretty soon.

CURIE: *I should think there is.*

FINN: *Why's that?*

CURIE: *Those buildings you found were built by someone. Same with the technology in the gate room. If intelligent beings once existed on that planet, there must also be lower lifeforms around. You have to have animals before you have people.*

FINN: *What if they wiped out everything? What if they killed their whole world and that's why nobody's here?*

CURIE: *Even after Variant struck Earth, life kept going. It changed and it evolved, but somehow it just wouldn't die. Never underestimate adaptability.*

FINN: *So, you think there's something still out there?*

CURIE: *Almost certainly.*

End Audio File

Somewhere on Kant
February 5, 2351

A cold drop of water touched Terry's nose as he and Ludo walked along the road to Capeside.

He stopped, glancing skyward, and noticed a small gray cloud. In the distance, several more had appeared, floating high above the horizon. "Looks like rain," he said.

Ludo nodded his agreement. "Keep moving. We'll look for shelter on the way."

A moment later, a drop of water grazed Terry's neck, and soon another on his forehead. It wasn't long before a shower arrived, dousing the two men completely. Terry didn't mind, once it started. After so many days in the countryside, he needed the bath.

But Ludo spotted something in the woods, near the edge of the road. A small dome building with a faded red door, large cracks running through the wood, and weeds sticking out of the roof.

The old building was empty, not a soul to be found. Terry closed his eyes and listened for any sign of movement, but there was only the rain falling everywhere, beating the ground like drums.

Ludo collapsed against the wall, near the open door. "The storm will last a while. We must wait."

"How long?" asked Terry, joining him.

"All night," he said, closing his eyes. "Rest until morning. This storm will go for hours. No use walking through it."

Terry sighed, wiping the rainwater from his cheeks and forehead, pulling his long hair behind his head. He eased his back against the wall, feeling the soft, aged planks behind him. The scent of the rain consumed the little house, blending with the dank smell of rotting wood and filling his lungs. He closed his eyes and took it all in, instantly transitioning into his other state, the place he drew his strength. The world slowed, and instead of a storm, the rain came down like cannonballs, thudding and stomping into the dirt. He ignored them, concentrating on the body of the house, searching and exploring with all of his combined senses. He could hear the rain hitting the roof, falling through the cracks, dripping into the rafters overhead. An air current passed through the cracked door, touching his face, cooling him. A rodent, hidden in one of the walls, scurried down a plank and through a burrowed out hole.

Terry lingered there a while, absorbing the building, taking in the sounds and smells of the architecture as well as the natural world surrounding it. Somehow, it relaxed him, slowing his pulse and calming his mind. He felt the tug of sleep, allowing himself to drift, and soon the melodies of the rain and the voice of the building faded, and he fell away.

When he opened his eyes, the air tasted cleaner, thinner. The thick moisture of the storm had gone. A beam of light pierced a nearby crack in the wall, hitting him in the eye. The new dawn had arrived, fulfilling the promise of time.

Ludo stood on the other side of the round room, sorting through debris. He hoisted a tattered cloth bag above his head, examining it. Spotting several holes, he tossed it to his side and continued rummaging.

"You're always awake before me," muttered Terry.

"You sleep longer than most," said Ludo. "More than a single period."

When Terry had first met Ludo, it took him a while to get used to the term *period*. It was about double the length of an hour. For the longest time, he had to do the calculations in his head, but now it came second nature to him.

"I used to get less than one, but now I like to sleep in," said Ludo. He slapped his chest. "I'm getting old and lazy."

Terry knew Ludo was an early riser, but couldn't imagine getting less than two hours of sleep every night. "You're as young as ever."

Ludo laughed, bending and pushing a crate out of the way. He retrieved another bag, this one in decent condition. After briefly examining it, he placed the strap across his shoulder and neck, twisting it to sit on his back. "How long do your people need to rest?"

"Several periods," explained Terry.

"Truly?" asked Ludo.

"Three to four periods is typical," said Terry. "I only need about two."

"So much," said Ludo, gawking. "But you do not sleep this long. I have seen it."

"I used to, a long time ago," he explained, and it was true. Before his exposure to Variant, he was weaker and needed more rest. After the gas chamber and eventual visit to the surface, something had changed in him, and he'd found a well of energy he never knew existed. When Terry arrived on Kant, he felt even more energized than before. Something about the purity of the Variant, he guessed.

These days, he could only sleep, at best, about four hours or two periods. Anything more was useless.

When Ludo had finished scavenging, he and Terry left the abandoned dome behind and made their way toward the west to Capeside. With any luck, they would find Talo, Ludo's son, and proceed to the border soon afterward.

They could do with one tiny victory. Was it so much to ask?

CAPESIDE LAY on the edge of where the Thirsty River met the Living Sea. Ludo had explained the village had existed here for nearly a hundred years. After discovering a rich supply of fish along the coast and river, a tribe of wandering hunters had founded the settlement, quickly growing into one of the more dominant trading outposts in the region. Capeside now contained a large harbor for ships to dock and rest, providing a means of travel to distant lands, such as Tharosa and Lexine. Ludo had never been to either of those places, but he'd heard tales from traveling merchants and soldiers during his time living at the Temple of the Eye.

Tharosa, he had learned, was far to the northeast, covered in snow and ice. It was said the people there lived in great castles carved into mountainsides, and from there they mined beautiful jewels and precious metals. Their traders often came to Capeside with trunks of intricately designed rings and necklaces, selling to the wealthiest of local families. Many of the statues in Ludo's old temple had been built by Tharosian artisans, in fact.

As for Lexine, he'd explained, far less was known, though the rumors spoke of vast deserts and devices capable of carrying a dozen passengers high into the sky. "I do not believe such things, though," said Ludo. "One can only fly with the mind, not with any machine."

But Terry knew better. He'd read about how humanity built airplanes and blimps, rocket ships and space shuttles. If his people could do it, so could Ludo's, though they might be different in design. Still, the more Ludo told him of the great, wide world, the more fascinated he became. He wanted to see these places, to explore their cultures. Perhaps he could, someday, when all of this was over.

They reached the top of a hill overlooking Capeside sometime in the afternoon. From here, Terry could see throngs of people moving through the narrow streets, talking and laughing. Hundreds of buildings dotted the landscape, more than he'd expected, while dozens of tents took up a large portion of the docks, near several anchored vessels. Terry had never seen ships before, except in his childhood textbooks. These were different from the pictures, but not by much. They appeared to be made of wood, mostly in the same shape, and used wind sails to move.

Very few trees stood near the village. Instead, far-stretching fields of different crops lay adjacent to the river.

A large herd of animals gathered near the gates, their shepherds talking together. Birds cawed and cooed overhead, lightly touching down on the stone walls before gliding into the air again.

The whole scene was unlike any Terry had ever seen, like something from a storybook. Had his own people lived this way before the Jolt? Were they sailors, shepherds, ranchers, and fishermen? The great civilizations of Earth evolved from humble beginnings much like this. Did any of them predict the end result? Did any foresee the cost of progress? How lucky they would have been to live like this forever, never building cities of metal and glass, never playing God with portals, genes, and children.

But there was no looking back, not to his home. Not anymore. Only this world with its strange new people...its civilizations.

"Almost there," said Ludo, pulling him from his thoughts. "Talo is waiting for us."

Terry nodded. "Right."

Ludo took the cloth he'd found in the abandoned shack the night before and handed it to Terry. "Put this on."

Terry looked at him, confused. "On what?"

"Your head. Cover what you can."

Terry opened his mouth to ask why, but stopped, finally understanding. He looked quite different from Ludo and the other people of this world. No doubt, many would stare and ask questions. They couldn't have anyone growing suspicious. Their previous captor, the Lord of Three

Waters, had told Terry as much during his stay in the prison. "You will fetch a good price," he had said. "Exotic slaves always do."

Terry glanced at Ludo's long ears and flattened nose. "Okay," he finally said, placing the bag over his neck and scalp.

Ludo frowned. "I am sorry, my friend."

Terry smiled. "We have to find your family, right? This is no big deal."

"Thank you," said Ludo, placing his hand on Terry's shoulder, then began his descent along the hillside.

Terry followed after him, and together they made their way through the valley, toward the bustling seaside town.

TERRY AND LUDO ENTERED CAPESIDE, suddenly finding themselves surrounded by stone buildings and passing natives. Local chatter filled the streets, coming from all around them. Terry could hear a variety of dialects and languages, if he listened closely, erupting from all across the village.

The scent of the sea floated in the air, filling his nose and lungs. The taste of salt water lingered, and for a moment he felt reinvigorated, and a sudden urge to go swimming.

They passed by several shops, curving along the path between the many buildings. Several were selling various foods, and their scents hit Terry quickly. Baked goods, fish, and broths. All of them culminated into a fresh aroma, making his stomach growl. He was suddenly ravenous.

Ludo motioned for him to hurry, so Terry doubled his pace, and together they rounded a nearby alleyway, finally stopping before a faded green door at the side of a thin building. Ludo knocked twice, and someone shuffled on the other side, hurrying to answer. When the door swung open, they were met by the face of an aged woman with thin black hair and frail hands. Ludo smiled and bowed his head. "Grandmother."

The old woman's eyes appeared to focus, lingering on the man in front of her, before finally widening into realization. "Grandson?" she asked. "Is it you?"

Ludo smiled warmly. "It is!" he exclaimed, opening his arms to embrace her.

She laughed and fell into him, disappearing briefly behind the farmer's large torso. Letting go of him, she giggled, spiritedly. "It has been too long. Have you come for your son?"

A look of relief washed over Ludo's face. "So, he is here?"

"Oh, yes," she told him. "Little Talo arrived several days ago. I was so pleased to see him. He looks exactly like your father did at that age."

"Where is he now?" asked Ludo, quickly.

"At the docks, fetching tonight's dinner. Had I known

you were coming, I would have told him to get more," she said, laughing. "Oh well. He can always go back."

Ludo glanced at Terry. "I need to find him. Do you mind waiting here?"

Terry removed the bag from his head. "Not a problem."

"Who is this?" asked the old woman, finally taking notice of him.

"I apologize," said Ludo. "This is Terry, my chakka-kin."

Terry cocked an eye at the term. What was a chakka-kin? He'd never heard Ludo say such a thing before.

The old woman nodded. "Any chakka-kin of my family is welcome here," she said, warmly, extending her hand to Terry.

He took it. "Thank you."

She led him through the door, shutting it once they were inside. Ludo remained in the street, no doubt to go look for his son. Terry wondered how long it would take to find the boy and return. He knew nothing of this place, and this elderly woman was a stranger to him, despite being Ludo's grandmother. "Please, rest in the sitting room. Be at home."

The sitting room, as she called it, was similar in many respects to Ludo's farm. Large and circular, with a small fire pit in the center, though it wasn't lit at the moment. Terry took a seat on one of the cushions, relieved to be off his feet.

The old woman brought him a cup with steam coming

from it. He recognized the smell. Ludo had made this drink for him several times before, back on the farm. "Fissin?" he asked.

She smiled. "You have had it before?"

"Yes," he said, accepting the drink. He took a sip, and it warmed his mouth and throat, relaxing him.

"It is our family drink," she explained. "Not for outsiders."

"Outsiders?" he asked, pausing to look at the cup. "Isn't that what I am?"

"You are chakka-kin to Ludo," she said, matter-of-factly, as though this should tell him everything.

"What's that mean?" he asked.

She tilted her head, blinking. "You don't know?"

He hesitated. "I'm…from far away," he answered, quickly. "Another country."

"Ah," she said. "I wondered about your accent and appearance. That explains a great deal. So, you are unfamiliar with our customs."

He nodded. "Where I come from, it's very different."

She took a sip of fissin. "A chakka-kin is someone who has become like family. This can happen in different ways, but it always means the same thing." She motioned at the cup in Terry's hand.

He looked at it, nodding slowly, and drank from it. He hadn't known it at the time, back on the farm, but when Ludo had shared this drink with him, it had been a great honor. He felt embarrassed now that he finally understood.

She smiled. "He trusts you as he would a brother. For what reason, I do not know, nor should I. A chakka-kin is not made easily, and the bond must be respected. For this reason, I shall look at you the same as my own grandson...a member of my family and this house."

"Thank you...I..." He paused, not knowing what else to say.

She smiled warmly. "Let us drink now, Terry, my new grandson, and talk about the outside world. It has been too long since I last saw it."

LUDO ARRIVED in less than an hour, his son close behind him. "We are back! We are here!"

The grandmother rose to her feet with trembling knees and headed to greet them.

Terry lingered in the sitting room, letting the old woman go ahead of him, and then followed. Ludo had his arm around the boy, a wide smile across his face. "Talo, look! Terry has come, too."

Talo beamed a smile. "Terry! It is good to see you!"

"You, too," said Terry, smiling.

"We must give thanks to the Eye for this reunion today," said Ludo. "Truly, we are blessed!"

As the evening stretched on, Ludo spent time talking with Talo, and Terry listened while trying not to interrupt the pair. The farmer and his son seemed more than happy, as though their home hadn't been burned to the ground and everything was normal. Terry admired their joy, and before long he found himself longing for a reunion of his own.

But such a meeting would never take place, he knew. There could be no going home. He had accepted that hard truth, and he understood the reality of his situation. He would never see John or Mei again, nor his mother and sister, and that was okay. He was certain they were alive and well. He refused to believe otherwise.

It helped that he was no longer alone. He'd found a new family, however long it might have taken, here on this distant world. Ludo, Talo, Ysa, and now this old grand-mother, too. They had rescued him from himself, and he would do everything in his power to protect them.

Whatever the cost.

3

S.O.F.T. Mission Report
Play Audio File 24
Recorded: February 7, 2351

CURIE: Tell me you didn't kill it.

FINN: Babe, I'm telling you. I didn't have a choice. That thing was out for blood!

CURIE: Did you do something to startle it?

FINN: I don't know. We were scouting out the woods when we ran into it. Damn thing was pissed.

CURIE: Was anyone hurt?

FINN: No, as soon as it charged, we opened fire. Everyone's fine.

CURIE: Except for the animal you killed.

FINN: Hey, I said I'm sorry. What do you want me to do?

CURIE: We have no idea what kind of effect that will have on the other wildlife.

FINN: Judging by the size and look of it, they'll probably thank us. Damn thing had swords for teeth.

CURIE: Did you at least secure the body?

FINN: We left it there. No one's carrying that thing. It weighs more than a dirt cab.

CURIE: Any pictures, then?

FINN: Oh, yeah. Don't worry, babe. I've got you covered.

CURIE: Thanks. I'd like to examine it before it begins decomposing.

FINN: Are you planning on sending someone?

CURIE: I was thinking I'd go, personally, but not for too long. A day at the most. Can you watch the body until I get there?

FINN: Sure thing. I'll put Brooks on it.

CURIE: Thanks. In the meantime, if you encounter another animal, please just try not to kill it. I know your job is basically monster hunting, but do me a favor and try to make an exception.

End Audio File

Bravo Gate Point
February 7, 2351

John stood beside a large tree, staring curiously at the glowing blue foliage. He plucked a leaf from one of the branches, twirling it in his fingers. He bent it in half, breaking the film and smudging his skin with the guts of the leaf. He'd done this before back home, and he was always fascinated by how long the glow would last on his fingers. It usually faded after a minute or two, sometimes less. He couldn't help but wonder why. He was certain the scientists in Central knew exactly the reason behind this strange phenomenon, so all he really had to do was ask, but doing so would take all the fun out of it. He enjoyed the harmless mystery of it.

His com clicked on, and a voice came through. "John, I'm about done over here," said Mei. "Do you want to meet me at the CHUs?"

He wiped his hand on the side of his jacket, smearing the plant matter, which had already stopped glowing. "Sure thing. Get everything you needed from the animal?"

"I could spend days examining the body, but I have enough samples to keep me busy for a while. It's been productive."

"So, you're having fun?" asked John.

"I suppose you could say that," she said. "It's not every day you get to travel to another planet."

"Hard to get used to the idea," he said, glancing at the two suns overhead.

"I suspect we'll adjust eventually."

John ended the call and made his way through the woods, back toward the camp. He'd come this way to check out a malfunctioning scanner, which only had to be turned off and on. He could have sent one of his troops, but why should they get all the fun? He enjoyed taking walks, and this world was so much more lively than back home.

His pad beeped, and he stopped to check it. The screen showed another malfunctioning scanner a short distance from him. He was the closest to it. "Better check it out," he muttered.

After radioing the team to let them know, John set off toward the scanner. Birds, or what he assumed were birds, chirped in the treetops overhead, and he listened to them intently. The native animal population seemed sparse on this planet, a stark contrast to Earth. He wondered what kind of creatures there were beyond this forest. How large were the oceans, rivers, mountains, and jungles of the world? How many types of insects and animals waited there to be discovered? How many monsters?

Back home, Central had only catalogued about sixty different species of wildlife to date on the surface. Many had been scattered. Half of them, he recalled, were pretty tough to find, except in caves and underground tunnels. But here, the world was so alive and teeming with animals and crawling things. It was all a bit overwhelming.

John found the scanner soon. Like the one before, he only had to reset the power to get it going again. What could be setting them off like this? He didn't see any animals around, and wouldn't the scanner pick them up?

Must be malfunctioning, he thought. *Better have Brooks check them out before anything happens. Something might—*

The ground trembled beneath him, and he wavered. He cocked his eye at the sudden motion. Could it be a tremor like the kind they used to get in the city back home? Maybe—

Another earthquake, only this time stronger, and John lost his balance. He fell against a nearby tree, snagging a branch to catch himself. His fingers clutched at the bark so hard they stung.

Dirt sprayed up from the ground before him, going everywhere and floating in the air. A creature appeared, snarling from within a fresh hole. It towered over him, wearing a coat of brown fur, with a dozen black eyes on each side of its head, all of them staring at John. The beast let out a series of fast clicks, opening its mouth to reveal several moving teeth, all of which seemed to be rattling. The animal's body stretched far into the earth, like a snake.

John stared at it, amazed at its size. "Don't you look friendly," he muttered, wide-eyed. With one hand on the tree, he gripped the rifle on his side, tilting the barrel toward the creature's head. "Come on, monster. Don't make me have to kill you. Mei will be pissed."

The animal stood there, staring and looming, rattling its teeth. Its gaze seemed curious more than anything else, and for a moment John wondered if it might move on.

"That's it," he whispered. "Nice bug demon. Nice—"

The beast lunged at him, leaving the hole completely. Screaming wildly as it leapt into the air. John didn't hesitate, pulling the trigger and unleashing a storm of bullets.

The life in its eyes disappeared, but its body continued to fall toward him. He dodged to the ground, rolling away from the heavy carcass to avoid getting crushed. As the lifeless body fell, yellow blood poured from the fresh bullet holes in its flesh, pooling in the dirt and grass.

The clicking in its mouth continued for nearly half a minute, though it was most certainly dead.

John nudged the side of its head with his boot, then activated his communicator. "Tech Shop, Huck."

A moment later, Brooks answered. "Huck, this is Tech Shop. What's up?"

"Might have a problem with where we placed the sensors," he explained. "Over."

"They not picking up a signal? Over."

He stared at the dead thing on the ground. "Seems like they're having some unexpected side effects."

Capeside
February 7, 2351

Terry wandered around the docks, taking in the sights. A saltwater breeze carried through the marketplace, blending with the bakery and butcher, becoming something both delicious and relaxing.

He took a deep breath, staring across the water, observing each of the ships, some of which were newly docked and still loading and unloading cargo. He wondered where their travels would take them...or where they had been.

Grandmother had given him a shawl to wear around his head so he didn't have to use the old bag Ludo had found. It was a nice alternative since it felt fresher and didn't make him look like a vagabond.

A small girl came running past him, carrying a basket of goods from the market. Terry spied some fruit, bread, and something resembling cheese. Whatever they were, he wanted them. Thankfully, Ludo had given him a few coins to buy whatever he wanted. Maybe he'd start with some of that.

"You there!" called a voice from one of the docks. He had a strange accent.

Terry turned to see who it was, only to find a large, bearded fellow standing near one of the ships. He had several piercings on his face and neck, with a wide variety of reflecting jewelry ranging from hoops to gauges. Terry didn't know what to say, so he only stared at the stranger.

"You, the one with the thing on your head! Come here!"

"You mean me?" asked Terry.

The sailor nodded, grinning.

A moment later, Terry had found his way to the dock and approached the odd man. "Yes?"

The man examined him, bending a little, as though he were trying to see beneath the shawl. "Ah, just as I thought," he muttered. "You mind taking that off for a second?"

"Sorry, but I can't," said Terry.

The sailor furrowed his brow. "Where are you from, child?"

"What's that matter?" asked Terry.

The man stared at him. "My name's Hux, friend, and I've been all over the world. I've seen a wide range of people here and there, but never one like you."

Terry turned to leave.

The stranger leapt at him, snatching Terry's shawl with his fingers. Terry slid the man's hand away, preparing himself to fight. As he did, the cloth around his forehead fell, revealing his face.

The man with the beard laughed. "I knew it!"

"What the hell is wrong with you?" Terry demanded to know.

"You're not from around here, eh? I've sailed the world and never seen a face like yours. Tell me, where do you come from?"

"None of your business. I'm a traveler from a faraway country. Don't concern yourself with specifics." He flipped the shawl back over his forehead.

Hux stroked his thick beard. "No specifics, you say?" he asked, curiously.

"None," said Terry.

"Then I apologize, little traveler. I didn't mean to show you any disrespect. I've just never seen anyone like you."

"We're very good at hiding."

"Interesting," said Hux. "So, why are you here, so far from your home? This village has nothing in it, besides a few hundred fishermen and shepherds. Perhaps you are a merchant, come to sell your wares?"

"I'm here with a friend, helping him recover something that was lost. The details are my business, if you don't mind."

Hux smiled. "Of course, little traveler. I shall ask no more of it."

"If you'll excuse me, I have to get back now," said Terry, knowing the longer he stayed here, the more he risked revealing the truth. He had to be careful.

The stranger let out another laugh, deep from his belly. "Don't worry, little traveler. Your secret is safe with old Hux. I've got a whole book of secrets rattling around my head."

Terry left without another word. He'd made a mistake in coming here, thinking the shawl could hide him. If anyone realized who he was—that he and Ludo had escaped from the prison and killed one of the high priests—there could be hell to pay.

He had to tell Ludo about this quickly, before anything came of it. If the sailor decided to tell someone, especially a visiting soldier, about this encounter, word would spread and the military would soon be after them.

They would have to leave here soon, in any case. Ysa

needed help at the border, and as long as they lingered in Capeside, she would still be in danger.

LUDO LISTENED with attentiveness as Terry told him the details of his encounter with the strange man known as Hux. Once he had concluded, Ludo sat in silence for a moment, appearing to contemplate the words.

"We should leave," said Terry. "Don't you think?"

Ludo bowed his head, tilting it slightly, the way he did when he was thinking. "We could go," he started. "But it would be without a plan of action."

"What do you mean?" asked Terry.

"Everlasting is far to the north, sitting high atop the mountains. The border waits below, running from the sea to the Temple of the Eye. It would take weeks to walk there. I had hoped to secure passage with one of the caravans as they passed through here."

"A caravan?"

"A group of traveling merchants who carry supplies from one village to the next. The temple is on their route."

"So, let's do that," said Terry.

Ludo shook his head. "They have only just arrived here and will not leave again for several days."

"There's no way to encourage them to leave early?"

"I have tried, but it is no use. Either we wait for them… or we walk."

"Then we have no choice," said Terry. "We have to wait. If this is the only way, we have to take it."

"Yes, but I do not want to cause this place trouble. Grandmother and Talo must be kept safe," Ludo insisted.

Terry placed his hand on Ludo's shoulder. "They will. I'll stay inside while you take care of things around town. We won't take any more chances. I never should have left in the first place."

"You would do this?" asked his friend.

"I've gone longer than a few days without the outdoors. Believe me, I can handle it."

<hr />

Bravo Gate Point
February 7, 2351

JOHN WATCHED as Mei poked and prodded the dead animal he'd killed a few hours ago. "I know you're probably mad about this, but would it help if I said I was sorry?"

She bent down next to the creature's head and tilted it to get a better look inside the mouth. "I'm not mad," she said, turning to look at him. "Just disappointed."

He frowned. "I know you're joking, but it still hurts."

She smirked and continued examining the animal, poking one of the teeth. "Considering how scary this thing is, I can't blame you for killing it. These teeth are big enough to skewer a grown man. I'll take some samples and head home, same as before."

"Brooks says the sensors are moved, so hopefully we won't piss off any more of them," said John.

"I'm sure you'll find a way," said Mei, giving him a look.

When Mei had enough samples from the animal, John escorted her to the CHUs. The day was nearly done, so she would have to leave soon. Her people needed her on the other side of the gate, which meant he wouldn't see her again for several days.

John told his team to stay topside while he and Mei went to the portal room alone. It was a long walk and she'd need help carrying the supplies, even though a flippy could've easily done the job. Truth be told, John simply wanted the time.

"Any updates from Central?" he asked, once they were in the main tunnel.

"About what?" she asked.

"What we're doing here," he said. "The portal. This planet. The aliens."

"I haven't told them about the animals you killed yet, but I will when I get there," she said, winking. "Everything else has been in my reports. They haven't said anything, though."

"Not even that Tremaine woman?"

Mei shook her head. "Not a peep. Not since the last call when she told Sophie she'd have me shut down."

"Isn't that a little weird?" asked John.

She considered this a moment. "It could be the board," she said. "They might be getting pressure from Ross and Echols. I'll have to make some calls." She leaned in and hugged his arm, sliding her fingers along his wrist and into his hand.

He smiled at her. They walked through the dark halls with only the occasional artificial light to guide their way. They strode quietly together for a while, until they reached the final door—the one leading to the portal room. He stopped her there and waited.

She glanced up at him, staring into him, her eyes reflecting the light from the lamps.

He kissed her, long and deep, and when it was over he felt warm all over.

"What was that for?" she asked, her voice soft and gentle, as though she were suddenly tired.

"I figured we wouldn't see each other for a few days. Wanted to make it count."

"Are you sure it's not because you wanted to be the first person to kiss someone on another planet?" she asked, laughing.

"You got me," he said. "I'm in it for the history books."

The light on the wall flickered suddenly, and they both glanced at it. John opened his mouth to ask if she thought there was an electrical problem, when the lamp went out, leaving them in darkness.

The tunnel wasn't entirely void of light, but he could

barely see her face. Before he could say anything or move, he felt her put more weight against his chest, and he froze.

Mei got on her toes, raised her hand to his cheek, and brushed his ear, cupping the back of his head. In a gentle, easy moment, she pulled him down toward her, embracing him again.

They stood there together, deep in the tunnels of a forgotten civilization, holding one another in the dark.

4

Ortego Outpost File Logs
Play Audio File 845
Recorded: February 9, 2351

HARPER: Doctor Curie, I hope you'll pardon me if I'm a little surprised to hear from you. I don't usually talk with people in the field.

CURIE: I'm sorry to contact you directly, but no one else is picking up the com. Whenever they do, it's only a clueless intern. My team is supposed to file weekly reports, and as far as I can tell, no one is receiving them.

HARPER: Doctor, I assure you we're seeing your reports. I read one just the other day, actually.

CURIE: Then why hasn't anyone answered my calls?

HARPER: *I answered, didn't I?*

CURIE: *After six other board members refused to. Is there something going on that I'm not aware of?*

HARPER: *They might feel a little uneasy about speaking with you after that business with Tremaine.*

CURIE: *What about it?*

HARPER: *Haven't you heard? Oh no, I suppose that's the whole reason you're calling, isn't it? Not knowing what's going on. Well, because of the friction she was causing between the three divisions, Tremaine has been relocated to a more appropriate position.*

CURIE: *You mean she was fired?*

HARPER: *Exactly so. Yes. I'm afraid the board decided it would be best to side with the Motherhood and the Military in order to avoid conflict. Tremaine provided too much resistance, which we believed to be driven by an emotional investment in the project thereby preventing her from maintaining true objectivity. As you well know, the rules are clear on this sort of behavior.*

CURIE: *So you're saying she was fired because of how she treated me?*

HARPER: *Not exactly. Had it only been an issue with your team, we might have ignored it, but once the other branches got involved…well, you know how politics can be.*

CURIE: *I see, but this still doesn't explain why no one is responding to my team's reports.*

HARPER: *There's a lot of chaos right now. Papers are getting shuffled. It shouldn't take long. Once the board figures out who to fill Tremaine's seat with, everything will go back to normal.*

CURIE: *What happens in the meantime? If my people need supplies or have to make some sort of request, what do we do? Who do I report to?*

HARPER*: I couldn't say. Like I told you, people don't know what to do with you, Doctor. Your project has become something we didn't intend. No one's ever purposefully opened a hole to another world, and now we're sending people through it. Imagine if something goes wrong. I've read Tremaine's notes on all of it. So has the rest of the board. Her reservations were well placed, though I can't say I agree with her methodology. Nonetheless, before Tremaine was demoted, you worked in conjunction with Doctor Prescott, didn't you?*

CURIE: *That's right.*

HARPER: *As I understand it, he was also relocated. You have a history of losing other people's jobs, Doctor Curie. When someone talks to you, their career takes a nosedive. You can't blame people for recognizing a pattern when they see one.*

CURIE: *If that's true, why did you answer the phone?*

HARPER: *I guess you'd call it curiosity. A chance to see what new horizons might be waiting for us. A chance to see the future.*

CURIE: *I didn't think the board cared about that sort of thing anymore.*

HARPER: *Give me a little credit, would you? I didn't always live behind this desk. In fact, I used to be a scientist.*

End Audio File

Bravo Gate Point
February 9, 2351

John's team had mapped a great deal of the forest in mere days. More than a few kilometers' worth. Various members of his group had come across a variety of animals during that time, most of which had to be killed, due to their aggressively carnivorous nature. Brooks did actually manage to capture one, however—a small creature which seemed to live in the nearby trees, displaying little aggression. These animals had pale, white eyes and yellow fur, their teeth extending well beyond their bottom jaw. Mostly harmless, as far as anyone could tell, but John's experience had taught him to be cautious of wild animals, both large and small alike.

Years ago, when the Variant children had arrived on the surface of the Earth, they'd found a new world unlike anything imaginable. For a long time, John believed his life would be spent exploring it, scouting and hunting, trying to rebuild. In all that time, he never dreamed his work would take him anywhere beyond it. Yet here he stood, the same as he had all those years ago, ready to venture across the foreign landscape, no map with which to guide him, no compass at his side. He was a stranger in a strange land, and so he had always been, from the day of his birth until this moment. He had been built for this.

A hard breeze blew against his cheek as he leaned

against a massive tree. Built, he thought as he stared into the woods. He used to wonder what it meant to be engineered—an experiment in a lab, put together by a scientist and injected into a womb—but what was the point in dwelling on the beginning? There was so much more to life than that. Better to live for today, and be hopeful for the future. Build a life he could be proud of, and fill it with the people he loved.

"Hey Sarge," said a voice from behind.

John swung around to see Brooks approaching him.

"Sorry to interrupt," she said. "I would've used the radio, but it's not working. That's actually why I came to get you."

John leaned his back on the nearby tree, facing her. "What's wrong with it?"

"I'm not sure. One minute, it's working fine. The next, I'm picking up some strange kind of static."

"You think something is interfering?" asked John.

"At first I did, but I've checked everything I can think of." She pulled out her pad. "Here, turn yours on and try calling me."

He did as she asked, pulling up the com. "Testing, testing," he said, only to be met with feedback so loud it hurt, causing him to recoil. He turned it off. "The hell was that?"

"It's like this for everyone," Brooks explained.

"What's causing it?"

"I'm not sure. I can't find any damage on our end, so

my only guess is that it's coming from something on the planet. It could be a certain kind of metal in the ground, maybe some old machine inside the caves." She shook her head and shrugged. "Who the hell even knows?"

"Can we switch to another kind of frequency?" asked John.

"Possibly, but until we know what's causing it, I can't promise anything. It's almost like there's another signal overlapping ours, jumbling it."

John scratched his ear. "You mentioned the caves. Think you can run some signal tests down there? Maybe see if the old tech near the portal room is doing it."

"Sure," she said. "I'm no expert on alien tech, though."

"Get in touch with Mei's team and ask Bart and Zoe to help out."

"You got it, Sarge," said Brooks. She turned to leave, but paused. "Are you coming back to camp soon?"

"Yeah, I've had enough solitude for the day." His stomach suddenly growled.

"Sounds like you could use some dinner, too," she said. "I'll have Short put on some grub."

John grinned. "Now you're speaking my language, Brooks."

Capeside
February 10, 2351

TERRY AWOKE in the middle of the night, a shadow looming above him. His eyes adjusted quickly, allowing him to see the entirety of the room, including the person squatting over him. "Ludo, what's going on?" he asked, smacking his lips.

Ludo touched Terry on the shoulder. "Soldiers are here," he whispered. "They are going door to door, searching every home."

"Soldiers?" muttered Terry, still dazed, but growing more awake.

"They came from Three Waters. I recognize the uniforms."

Were they looking for them? Of course. What other reason would they have for raiding houses in the middle of the night? Terry and Ludo had killed Gast Maldeen, the Lord of Three Waters and one of the sacred high priests. There was no way they'd let a couple of murderers go free. Not if they could help it. "What do we do?" asked Terry.

Ludo helped him to his feet. "We must leave," he whispered. "We'll climb the western wall and hide for a day, then return once the soldiers have moved on."

"What about the caravan?" asked Terry.

"They leave in two days. We will return before that."

Terry got to his feet, gathering his blanket. He couldn't leave it here for the soldiers to find. A used but empty bed could spell disaster for Grandmother and Talo. Ludo seemed to understand, and quickly helped. Together, they stuffed the sheets and pillows into an old chest, locking it.

Grandmother shuffled into the room with a small bag in her hand. "I packed you some food," she told them, and handed the sack to Terry. "There's bread, cheese, and some meat."

Terry accepted the gift. "Thank you."

She smiled, then turned to Ludo. "You stay safe out there, Grandson."

"I will, Grandmother," he said, and hugged her.

Three loud knocks erupted from the front door, echoing through the house. "Oh, my," said Grandmother.

"There is a window in the rear alley," whispered Ludo.

Terry nodded. "Following you."

The curtain to one of the side bedrooms opened, revealing Talo. He rubbed his eyes, yawning. "Father? What's going on?"

Ludo paused at the sound of his son's voice, as though he hadn't expected to see him. Was he hoping to leave without saying goodbye to him?

"Who's at the door?" asked the boy.

"Soldiers doing their job," said Ludo. He bent down so their eyes were level. "No need to worry."

"Are you leaving?"

Ludo frowned, but forced a partial smile. "Terry and I must go and find Ysa. We will bring her back soon. Grandmother is going to look after you now."

Talo's eyes sank. "Will it be long before I see you again, Father?"

Ludo hugged him. "Not if I can help it."

Another knock at the door, followed shortly by an order to open it. "We had better go," said Terry.

Ludo got to his feet. "Very well."

As the farmer made his way to the adjacent room, Grandmother caught Terry by the wrist. "Hold on a moment," she said, quietly.

Terry paused, a little surprised. "Is something wrong?" he asked.

She leaned in. "You are a part of this family now, yes?"

He took her hand, placing it between his own. "Of course."

"Then look after your chakka-kin," she told him. "Protect your family."

"I will," he promised her.

She smiled and turned toward the front door. Another knock came. "One moment, please!" she yelled.

Terry disappeared into the back of the house. Ludo already had the window pried open, with his legs hanging out the other side. When he was finally through, Terry handed him the supplies. With Ludo's help, he hoisted himself to the window, sliding easily through the opening and landing outside.

The alley had little light to speak of, but Terry didn't mind it. He focused his thoughts, allowing him to see the world as clearly as if the suns were out. He could also hear the guards as they questioned Grandmother, asking if she knew of any questionable individuals.

"I couldn't say on that," said Grandmother, sounding

very clueless. "I never leave my little house these days. Too much hustle in the city for my old legs. You understand, don't you? Oh, it's all so much…and the noise from the streets is so loud. Do you think you could tell the neighbors to keep it down out here? I can barely sleep at night with so much chattering going on."

"Yes, thank you," interrupted one of the soldiers before much longer. "We only need to search your house and we'll be on our way."

"Search my house?" asked Grandmother. "Oh, by the Eye, is that truly necessary, sir? I'm so embarrassed by the mess. It's so much trouble to clean at my age. You understand, don't you?"

"We apologize, but it must be done," he said.

"Oh, alright, sir. Can I fix you some drink? How about a nice mondew? I get them from the finest vendor, and he gives me a good deal. You'll like them, I'm sure."

Terry smiled, turning his attention to Ludo. "Let's get going," he whispered.

Ludo motioned his agreement. "This alley comes out at the docks. We'll follow that until we reach the outer wall."

They crept together through the darkness, staying low, stopping at the slightest sign of movement. Getting caught would do them no personal harm, for they were more than capable of handling themselves, but the same could not be said of Talo and Grandmother, who would still be here when Terry and Ludo left. No one could know there was a connection between them, so they would do well to keep quiet.

Terry kept his ears on the soldiers, minding their movements. When he closed his eyes, he could almost see them, their feet pressing against the aged floorboards of Grandmother's home, their quickened breaths as they look through every room. Terry listened and saw without seeing that there were two soldiers walking along the street, passing by their position in three...two...one...

The guards appeared on the other side of the houses, just as he'd anticipated. They stopped in front of a nearby home, knocking on the door. A man answered, asking what they wanted. They gave him the same response the others had given Grandmother, and so he let them in. "Let's go," Terry said, once it was clear.

The two friends made their way along the stone walkway toward the harbor, doing their best to stay out of the lamplight. As they neared the marketplace, which now stood quiet and empty, Terry heard a tapping sound in the distance, and he paused, listening intently. "Wait a second," he told Ludo.

The noise grew louder—something was drawing near. Whatever it was, they'd have to hide. It was too easy to get caught, here on the edge of the street. Terry peered around the corner to the harbor, but saw nothing there but boats. It seemed clear enough.

Terry and Ludo crept through the marketplace,

heading to the wall, though it was still far. They made it to one of the docks, about a third of the way through, and Ludo stopped, pointing in the direction of the sound, indicating he could finally hear it. "We must leave!" said Ludo, quickly.

"Why?" asked Terry. "Do you know what that is?"

"An animal. The soldiers use it. Hurry or it will find us."

"Where do we hide?" asked Terry. "The sound is coming from the direction we're going."

Ludo looked around the docks, as though he were considering every option. He stopped soon, his eyes landing on the nearest boat. "There!"

They fled along the dock and boarded the ship, taking a position near the back, behind a pile of covered boxes. Terry noticed a vile smell and covered his nose and mouth. What sort of cargo was this ship carrying? "Gross," he whispered.

"Jungleberries. Good for wine, but terrible for the nose," Ludo remarked.

"Now what?" asked Terry.

"Under this," answered Ludo, taking the cloth from atop the boxes and placing it over their heads.

The smell overwhelmed Terry and he gagged, spitting onto the deck.

Ludo lifted the edge of the cover so it was slightly above their eyes. "Try to breathe through the mouth," he said.

Terry did, but the scent was powerful, so much he could taste it.

They waited there, listening for the guards. The ticking sound was still there, somewhere in the distance, drawing closer with every passing second.

Terry and Ludo watched from beneath the cloth, waiting for whatever was about to come.

Then, at the edge of the market, a soldier appeared, strolling calmly through the square. Behind him, a few more followed, talking amongst themselves. "Bring the feeler here," said one to the others. "Check the tents before we leave."

"Yes, sir," said another, running back behind the street corner. When he returned, he brought a handful of other soldiers with him. One of these had a leash in his hand, followed by an animal. The creature, which they had called a feeler, had a fat snout and thin eyes. Its hairless body showed several scars as well as a branded image on one of its thighs. Terry couldn't decide if it looked more like a pig or a dog, but either way it was certainly uglier.

The animal sniffed the nearest tent, hugging it close as it strafed the side of it. Every few meters it would stop and sneeze, shaking its snout. The soldiers watched, each with a bored expression, as the one with the leash led the animal from one spot to the next.

One of them, a larger heavyset man with thick eyebrows, stretched his arms and yawned. He went to the edge of the dock, staring into the water, glancing at the various vessels in the harbor. For a moment, his gaze lingered on Terry's position, as though he'd taken notice of something. Did he see them, hiding there beneath the blanket? The soldier tilted his head, as though something had just occurred to him. He turned to the others, motioning at them. "We should look on the ships," he told them.

"Won't it take too long?" asked the man with the leash.

"No, he's right," said another. "We have orders to search the whole city, and those ships are no exception."

The man with the leash tugged on the animal, eliciting a squeal from the beast. He led the feeler to the docks, and it sniffed the air. The creature stopped and yelped loudly, pausing to sneeze a few times. "Quiet," ordered the beast's master.

A sudden, loud thud vibrated beneath the deck. Terry and Ludo flinched, looking at one another but saying nothing. A few seconds later, it came again, followed by several more. Someone was down there, moving around the ship. Terry wasn't sure what to do. He couldn't get up and leave, but the person inside might draw the attention of the guards, and they might notice them.

The door to the lower deck flew open and a tall, bearded fellow appeared wearing nothing but a pair of shorts. "What's going on out here?" called the sailor. It was Hux, Terry quickly realized, the same man he'd met on the docks a few short days ago.

The soldiers took notice immediately. "Stay where you

are!" said the heavier man. "We need to search your vessel."

Hux went to the edge of his ship, bringing him within a few yards of Terry and Ludo. "For what purpose?" he asked.

"Fugitives," said the soldier. "Two runaways wanted for murder. We have reason to believe they are in this village."

Hux raised his brow. "And you think they've come aboard my ship?"

"We are looking everywhere," said the man with the leash. "A village holds many secrets. Many places to hide." The feeler yipped and sneezed.

This wasn't good. If Hux allowed these soldiers onto his ship, Terry and Ludo would be found. Not captured, no. A handful of soldiers wouldn't be enough to subdue the two of them. Terry would have to hurt them, though, and Hux might get caught in the middle.

But what other options did they have? Terry swallowed hard and breathed, darting his eyes between both Hux and the soldiers.

Hux leaned on the side of the boat, specks of moon-light flickering on his many piercings. "I assure you, there is no one onboard my ship. I would stake my reputation as a wavemaster on it."

"Still, we must perform our duty," said the soldier.

"And if I refuse you?" asked Hux.

The soldier paused. "We would have to forcefully search

your vessel, and you would be arrested for impeding us. It would be unfortunate."

"I see," said Hux.

"If the fugitives are not hiding in there, then you have nothing to fear."

Hux smiled. "I do not suppose you are familiar with the traditions or values of my people, but let me say simply that we value our privacy."

"Your people?" asked the guard.

"I am visiting from Chald," said Hux.

The soldier looked at the other men. "A wavemaster from Chald."

"The ambassador's ship?" asked the heavyset man.

"I heard he was docked here," said another.

"That's right," Hux responded. "And as I have told you, my people value our privacy. To search this ship would be an insult to the Chaldian people. Who knows what sort of problems would come from it?"

"An insult?" said the man with the leash.

"I suppose we can make an exception for the Chaldean ambassador," said the heavyset soldier. "We still have half the village to search."

The man with the leash nodded. "Very well." He turned to look at Hux again. "We will leave you to your business, sir. Please tell the ambassador that we mean no disrespect."

Hux smiled. "Think nothing of it. Good night!"

The soldiers began to leave, taking the feeler with them,

though it seemed to want to stay, wheezing and sneezing toward the boat.

Hux watched them go, waiting until they had completely vanished into one of the adjacent streets. When they had gone, he turned to look at the place where Terry and Ludo were hiding. With a slight grin, he said, "You can come out now, Little Traveler."

5

Ortego Outpost File Logs
Play Audio File 852
Recorded: February 10, 2351

CURIE: *With the addition of the latest sample, we now have a total of six foreign animals—four deceased, two alive. After spending the bulk of the morning examining the genetic structure of the newest specimen, a slug-like creature taken from the bark of a tree, I can confirm a genetic overlap between not only these various species, but also with those found on Earth.*

To clarify, each animal native to Earth shares a certain percentage of identical genes with one another, with growing variations between species and genus the further removed they become. For example, ordinary humans are largely identical to one another, sharing approximately ninety-nine point five percent of their DNA. The now-extinct chimpanzees once shared roughly ninety-eight percent of its genes with that of human beings, since they were the closest living animal on the evolutionary ladder at the time. Most mammals, including the common field mouse, were slightly less similar at ninety-two percent, while a fruit fly, an almost alien-looking organism, only shared about forty-four percent.

That was centuries ago, however, and now nearly all of these species have gone extinct, with the exception of humans. The Earth's native species have been largely altered, replaced almost entirely by Variant hybrids, which has only widened their genetic divide from standard humans. A kitobora, for example, only shares approximately fifty-six percent of its genetic structure with that of a standard human, despite having originated on the same planet. This is far lower than the overlap found in the pre-Jolt mammals, but still larger than what one would find in a mosquito.

Naturally, the same cannot be said of the Variant humans, of which I am included. As a hybrid, I share approximately eighty-four percent of my DNA with a kitobora, which is clearly far greater than the previously mentioned fifty-six percent. Such an overlap should not be surprising, of course, due to the method in which I was conceived.

Now, I state these facts for a reason, which is to show how a species and genus on a single planet are naturally similar to one another, and how the introduction of Variant can so drastically alter them. I also show these statistics with the hope that the meaning and importance of what follows is not lost.

As my colleagues and I have continued to dissect and map the biology of these new alien species, we have found there to be an unusually high overlap between their genetic makeup and those of the Variant *hybrids found on Earth. The similarities are so strong, in fact, that if the observer did not know any better, they might never suspect these species had come from another world at all. Samples taken from the trees on Earth share about ninety percent with those found on the other side of the portal, which is far higher than we would have ever expected. Similarly, a kitobora shares close to eighty-five percent of its DNA with one of the six animals we recently analyzed. It's as though, somehow, the two have a shared history, and while it could certainly be argued that Variant is the cause of such an overlap, I would be remiss if I didn't point out the fact that at least half of the kitobora's DNA is composed of non-Variant sequencing, and yet much of it is still found in these new species.*

In short, the native fauna of Earth and those found on the other side share a surprisingly large genetic base. The chances of such an overlap existing on two separate ecosystems, even with the shared influence of Variant, defies existing evolutionary theory.

The discovery gives me pause, and I'm left with far more questions than I ever expected. If the portal truly does lead to another planet with a separately evolving ecosystem, how can there possibly be so many genetic similarities? Is life so exceptional that it can only form in this particular way, or did the portal just so happen to take us to a planet almost identical to our own? If so, what are the chances?

More than that, however, my thoughts circle back to the beings who built the city underground. If I can have so much in common with an alien tree slug from across the stars, what of those who made the gate? Would they be like the fly, similar in the basic sense, but far removed in nearly every other way?

Or would they be as we are, with verbal language and emotion and a sense curiosity? Would we look at them and see ourselves, I wonder, as distant brothers from across the sea?

End Audio File

Tower of the Cartographers, Everlasting
February 10, 2351

Lena Sol sat in Master Gel's office, waiting to receive her next set of orders. She'd spent the last few weeks preparing for her first field assignment, which would begin early tomorrow morning. She was supposed to be in Medical, but instead had been called to this office at the last minute. For whatever reason, the Master Analyst wished to see her, and it simply couldn't wait.

The door opened, and in walked Gel with an odd look on his face. He was moving very quickly.

Lena jumped to her feet, waiting for him to sit before doing the same.

"Analyst," muttered Gel as he took his seat. "Thank you for coming."

"Of course, sir," she responded.

"Things are rather chaotic this morning, so I'm sure you understand my delayed arrival. There was an insurgent attack in sector seven only an hour ago."

"An attack?" asked Lena, immediately concerned.

There hadn't been any incidents of that nature in over six weeks.

"We are still determining the source of the explosion, but three citizens are now deceased. One was a member of this department. Jinel Din."

The name gave her pause. Jinel had been on the roster for tomorrow's mission, but it was not the first time she had encountered her. Lena had met Jinel approximately one year ago, exactly two floors below this one. Jinel was a records manager back then, tasked with filing assets and determining personnel placement. She'd since transferred to one of the cartography analysis divisions, much the same as Lena.

She didn't know what to say. Lena had never known someone who was murdered. Violence was forbidden in Everlasting. The Leadership called it an uncivilized act, punishable by permanent stasis, meaning you'd get locked in a box and forced to sleep for the rest of your life. No dreams, no nothing. Only blackness.

The idea that anyone would harm another citizen was simply unacceptable, no matter the reason.

"If you should require a memory cleanse, please let the department know," said Master Gel.

"Thank you, sir," she answered. "Do you think there will be another attack?"

"The suspect is in custody, so there is little reason to worry. The Leadership does not believe this attack is connected to the others."

Lena wanted to believe him, but there were always rumors saying otherwise. Talk of a terrorist organization engineering each of the attacks over the last decade. No one knew the validity of such claims, but they'd nonetheless planted seeds of doubt in people's minds. Whether it was true or not, Lena couldn't say. All she knew for certain was that the attacks were becoming increasingly more frequent.

What truly baffled her was why anyone would ever do such a thing in the first place. What good could come from killing agency members, or any citizens for that matter? Did these people not understand the importance of workers like Jinel Din? They were gears in a well-organized and functional machine—one that kept Everlasting safe and secure against outside threats. How would anyone survive without the protection of, say, the engineers who maintained essential systems throughout the city?

Imagine the chaos if the outer shield fell. What a disaster it would be! Toxic atmosphere would flood the city in less than a few minutes, killing every single citizen in the process. *Fools*, thought Lena. *Every last one of them...and cowards, too.*

"Are you sure you wouldn't like a memory cleanse, Analyst Sol?" asked Master Gel.

She snapped out of it, correcting her demeanor. "Oh, no, sir. Thank you. I was only reflecting on my work."

"Excellent," he said, a little distant. "You do your department proud. Analyst Din's death is a tragedy, especially given tomorrow's mission. I wish I could say I had a replacement for her, but there simply isn't enough time."

"Will there be a delay?" asked Lena.

"We are but one of many departments participating in this mission, and the consensus is that the loss of a single analyst is not enough to hinder performance. While it will require you to take on more responsibilities, I believe you are competent enough to handle the workload. Do you agree?"

"Of course, Master Gel."

He nodded. "Very good. Report to your next location as soon as you can. Remember, Analyst Sol, you do this not for yourself, nor even for this department, but for the city as it lives and breathes. There can be no higher calling than to go beyond the shield and serve your people. Do you agree?"

"All is for the good of Everlasting," said Lena, reciting the popular slogan used by the Leadership for the last thirty years. "I promise not to let you down."

"See that you don't," said Master Gel. "The Leadership will be watching."

Capeside
February 10, 2351

"So you mean to climb the coast?" asked Hux as he bit into a piece of yellow fruit, spilling juice and foam into his thick beard. He had taken Terry and Ludo into the cabin of his ship immediately after finding them on the upper deck.

Terry sat beside Ludo across the table. Moments ago, Hux had invited them into his ship, eager to understand what sort of trouble the two of them had gotten themselves into. As Terry told the story, Hux's smile grew wide and excited. "Ludo's wife was taken to the border," Terry explained. "We're going to get her back."

"And you killed the Lord of Three Waters," Hux said, like it was a joke.

"There was no other way," said Ludo, firmly.

"Your eyes are true, Little Traveler. I'm inclined to believe you. Though, if you're planning on heading north, why take the caravan? I've talked to them in the market. They mentioned the routes they use. There's at least two military checkpoints along the way."

"Small outposts," said Ludo. "No more than a few guards to inspect passing travelers, and the caravan is well known by them. They rarely give them trouble."

"Rarely is not the same as never, my stout friend," said Hux.

"It's our only option," Terry interjected.

"Is it?" asked Hux, taking another bite of fruit.

Terry leaned forward. "Do you know another caravan with a better route?"

"I'm all out of those," said Hux, chewing and swallowing. "But I do have a ship."

Terry glanced at Ludo. "Would that be faster?"

Ludo considered the question. "I am no sailor, but—"

"It's faster, Little Traveler. I assure you," said Hux. "If I were to take you north toward Edgewater, you could cut several days from your journey. I was heading to Tharosa after this, anyway, so the extra stop would be no trouble."

"What about the ambassador?" asked Terry, assuming that Hux must have other duties.

"There is no such person," said Hux with a grin. "At least, not on my ship."

"Oh," muttered Terry.

"What of the military?" asked Ludo.

Hux shook his head. "There are no checkpoints on the open seas."

Taking a ship along the coast certainly seemed like the better alternative. The countryside would be a risky venture, with so many enemies out to find them. Instead of moving through the chaos, perhaps they could simply go around it. "Ludo? Would you be okay with this?"

Ludo looked at the sailor across the table, then again at Terry. "Do you trust this wavemaster?"

"He risked his own safety to keep the guards from finding us. I trust him."

Ludo gave a soft smile. "Then I shall as well."

"Wonderful!" Hux grinned, wiping the juice from his beard. "We leave in a few hours."

Hux's ship, called the *Waveguard*, was a mid-sized vessel with a crew of thirteen. Apparently, his men had spent their night at the local inn, drinking and feasting as they often did when visiting harbor towns. According to Hux, it was custom for the crew to leave and rest while the captain remained to watch the ship. It was his property, after all, and he had too much invested to leave it in someone else's hands for the duration of the night.

Shortly after the two suns had risen above the horizon's edge, the crew gathered on the deck of the Waveguard to begin the next leg of their journey. They loaded supplies, including packaged spices and ointments from the local market, which would be taken to Tharosa for selling. Hux was a trader, Terry soon discovered, whose routes took him all over the known world. Sometimes this meant Capeside and Edgewater, but other times he found himself along the desert coasts of Lexine and Free Harbor to the west. "You should join us sometime," Hux told Terry while they waited for the crew to load the last of the cargo. "Once your journey is at an end, that is."

Before the market had even opened, the crew of the *Waveguard* lifted its anchors and unfurled its green sails. The ship left the harbor, curving into the wide sea, and a breeze of salted air blew through, stimulating Terry's senses.

The waves grew stronger and the water more pristine the further out they went, until at last they found themselves far from the shore. The shadows of what must have been fish swam a short way below the water's surface, dispersing into flickering silver daggers as the vessel floated by. Facing Capeside, Hux raised his outstretched hand, closing his left eye and hiding the town behind his thumb.

"When will you come back here?" asked Terry.

Hux lowered his hand. "My route takes me all over the world. It'll be a year before I come this way again."

"And your home?" asked Terry. "How often do you go back?"

Hux glanced at him sideways and grinned. "The sea is my home, just as it is for every wavemaster."

"What's a wavemaster?" asked Terry, having heard the term several times by now.

Hux raised his brow. "You've never heard of us?"

"Should I have?"

Hux laughed. "Everyone knows of the wavemasters."

"I don't," Terry admitted, shrugging.

"You must truly be from far away, Little Traveler, to not have heard the stories they tell." Hux ran a finger through his mangled beard. "The wavemasters control the four seas. We travel all over the world. Some are traders, like me. Others explore, both above and below. You would be surprised at the wonders resting far beneath your feet."

"So, wavemasters are sailors?" asked Terry.

Hux let out another chuckle. "Don't be absurd, my friend. A wavemaster is much more than a simple sailor. They're a force of nature."

"Captain," called one of the crew, motioning for him. "One of the barrels is leaking. Should we toss it?"

"Excuse me," Hux said, dismissing himself. He stepped away to join the crewmate.

Terry stood alone, watching the distant town of Capeside grow smaller by the second. It would still be a while before his gifted eyes could no longer see it, but eventually it would be lost to the horizon, replaced by a sea of dancing waves, Glittering in the light.

Bravo Gate Point
February 11, 2351

JOHN WAITED inside the portal room for Mei to arrive with her team. Brooks had spent the last day trying to fix the com system, but it only grew worse with each passing hour.

John placed his pack on the floor near the entrance, then leaned against the wall, scratching a small hole in his jacket with his index finger.

Mickey and Track stood to the right of the gate, tossing a tiny ball around. The toy had originally belonged to Track's sister, who gave it to him the last time he left Central. John didn't mind him having it. Anything to keep the boys busy and their minds occupied while they sat down here, essentially doing nothing.

A slight vibration ran along the wall. The beginning of the activation process, no doubt, as the machines kicked on and began receiving Mei's signal.

In seconds, the space between the giant ring filled with darkness, fluttering like a curtain in the wind, morphing into a clear and present image—a door to the other side.

The portal's sudden appearance surprised Track, who fumbled with the ball and let it go. The toy bounced high, falling onto the raised platform nearby, and finally into the gate itself. John watched as it continued to bounce, disappearing to one side, out of view.

A woman's laugh soon followed. "Who's throwing things?" she asked. It sounded like Zoe.

"Sorry!" called Track.

A moment later, three figures appeared on the other side of the gate. Mei, Bartholomew, and Zoe.

Mei turned around and motioned to someone. "Five hours, Sophie. Don't forget."

"Yes, ma'am," she answered.

John watched as the three scientists stepped through the portal, waving at them and smiling. As they ascended the ramp, he raised his arms. "Welcome to the party."

"Is there any cake?" asked Zoe.

"I think Short has some frosted crackers in her pack, if that counts."

She scrunched her nose. "Sounds great."

"So, you're already having issues, huh?" asked Bart. "No surprise. This is what you get for not bringing me along."

Mei looked up at him. "Don't start with that again. You know I need you back at camp."

"It's like she's loaning you out," said Zoe.

Bart scowled. "I'll loan *you* out."

She rolled her eyes. "Sure you will."

"Focus, you two," ordered Mei. "John, where's Brooks? She should be here to hand over her notes to Bart."

"Don't bother," said Bart. "Just give me some space and a few hours. I'll get there faster on my own."

"Brooks has been working all day on it," said John.

"She's not an engineer, is she?" asked Bart.

"No, but——"

"Then she's worthless to me." He looked around. "Is there a repeater nearby? Let's start there."

John waved Mickey over. "Show Bart here where the signal repeater is."

"Yes, boss. Anything else?"

"When he's done, escort him to the surface."

"You got it," said Mickey.

Bart started to follow him to the back of the room. "Don't let me catch you hovering."

John turned back to Mei. "Where to?"

"Zoe's here to check on the flippies while I collect some soil samples," explained Mei.

"Mortimer's battery died so I'm swapping it," said Zoe, holding up a small box.

"Track can escort you around," said John, nodding at the soldier.

"Is that the guy who threw this ball at us?" she asked, opening her palm to show the toy.

"The same," he said.

Zoe turned to Track. He sat at the base of the ramp staring at the floor. "Hey, you. Guy."

He blinked, looking up. "Huh?"

She tossed the ball at him. "Catch!"

Track made an unsuccessful grab at it, and the ball bounced into the corner. "Thanks!" he said, running after it.

"Guess I'll see you guys when I'm done," said Zoe.

"Looks like the kids are taken care of. You ready to head out?" John asked Mei.

"Sure. Did you manage to capture another animal for me?"

"Not yet, but we're working on it. There's a pond in the woods with some kind of snake thing in it."

"You never mentioned that in the last report," she said.

"Too busy worrying about the com system. We also found a tree."

"Huh?"

"Not just any tree," he pointed out. "A red one!"

"Oh, my," she said, placing her hand on her chest, feigning excitement.

"That's right. I've got a whole list of things you can gawk at."

"My, my," she said, wrapping her hand around his arm. "You sure do know how to show a girl a good time."

JOHN LED MEI to the eastern edge of camp. "It's a walk to get there," he told her when speaking of the red tree. "Twenty minutes or so."

She scoffed. "Easy."

John laughed, and together they headed east. Along the way, they passed through a small forest where his team had come the day before. Some of the trees had been marked with white lines to show the correct path.

The woods came out into wide and open plains, cerulean grass beneath their feet. The crimson tree lay further still, standing tall with outstretched limbs, towering over them like a red lighthouse in a blue sea.

Mei stopped when she saw it, her eyes widening.

"Pretty, isn't it?" asked John.

"It's beautiful," she muttered.

A set of hills rose in the distance, blocking the horizon. "What's over there?" asked Mei.

"We don't know," he admitted. "Could be more of the same. Could be something new."

They sat together at the base of the tree, a blanket of red and orange leaves beneath them, staring out into the blue fields. Mei leaned against his arm. "It makes you wonder what else is waiting for us out there."

They stayed there a long time.

JOHN SAT in the kitchen with his hands in his lap, dangling

his little feet beneath his chair, waiting for his mother to finish making lunch. Soy burgers, she had promised him, but he'd have to stay quiet if he wanted some. He tried his best to keep from fidgeting, but it was tough. He had so much energy.

His mother stood next to the stove, cutting open a box of frozen patties. One at a time, she dropped the burgers on the countertop with a light thud. John wished he was bigger. He wanted to help. Maybe if he did, the food would get there faster. He wouldn't be little forever, though. One day he'd be big and tall, just like his brother Trevor.

John had never met his brother, but Mother showed him pictures all the time. "He's so smart," she would say. "He always gets the highest grades in class. Trevor's on the fast track to the Science Division. Just think, Johnathan. You'll have a brother who's a scientist! He's coming home next year, too, so you'll get to meet him. Isn't that nice?"

John liked to think so. Having a brother seemed like fun. Maybe Trevor could tell him some cool stories. It really didn't matter, so long as he was nice.

His mother flipped the soy burger box around and began reading. "Let's see now," she said to herself, studying the directions. She turned around to look at Johnathan, revealing a large, swollen belly. "Ten minutes and they'll be ready, okay?" She smiled.

He grinned as wide as he could. "Okay!"

His mother placed her hand on her hip. "Whew," she said, exasperated. "Your little sister is killing me."

John laughed. "She wants burgers, too!"

His mother rubbed her stomach. "And watermelon, if my cravings are right."

"Gross," said John, scrunching up his face.

A buzzer rang through the apartment, startling them. His mother went to the box on the wall and tapped it. "Hello," she said.

"Samantha?" asked a voice on the other end. "It's Raine."

"Hey! How is everything?"

"Oh, you know how it is. Go here, go there. I'm always on the run," she said, laughing.

John ignored the conversation. Grown-up talk was so boring. Even worse, it meant he'd have to wait longer to get his hands on one of those burgers.

"Well, I'd like to get lunch with you, Raine, but I have to wait for Mr. Huxley to come by tomorrow."

"Is it evaluation time already?" asked the lady on the phone.

Mother looked at John and frowned. "Yes, I'm afraid it is. My little man is growing up."

"Hard to believe," said Raine. "My son's got his eval next week. Doesn't seem like it's been four years, does it? Only three more to go until our boys are gone. Off to bigger and better things."

Mother's eyes dipped. "Oh, of course. I suppose so."

John squirmed in his seat. "Mommy, I'm hungry."

"One second, honey," she answered. "Raine, I have to go. Johnny's getting—"

"I heard," said Raine, giggling. "Hey, I'll see you after the evals, hm? We'll definitely catch up. I have so much to tell you. I've heard some crazy rumors lately that you would *not* believe."

"Sounds good, hon. You take care." She disconnected the call. "Sorry, Johnny. We'll eat in just a second."

John clapped his hands. "Yay!"

She placed the food in the oven, setting the timer for ten minutes. "Alright, there. Now we sit back and wait. Sound good?"

He nodded. "Sounds good!"

She grabbed another chair and placed it next to him, then sat down. "It's hard to believe you'll have a new sister in three more weeks," she told him. "When Trevor gets here, we'll have all three under one roof."

"Trevor!" he exclaimed.

She smiled at him, brushing the side of his hair, then looked again at the box on the wall. John watched as her smile fell into a frown. "Bigger and better," she muttered.

"Mommy?" he asked, tugging on her dress. "What was the lady talking about?"

"Huh? Oh." She paused. "Don't worry about that stuff, alright? It's just grown up nonsense."

He nodded, but didn't understand.

She wrapped her arm around him and pulled him

closer. "You know I love you, right, Johnny?" she asked, suddenly.

He nodded. "Yeah, Mommy. Course I do."

She squeezed him tight, then kissed the top of his head, pressing her cheek into his hair. It tickled, and he laughed. "You remember that, Johnathan," she whispered. She began to tremble. "No matter what else happens, always remember I love you."

JOHN OPENED his eyes to a bright afternoon light. Vast, blue plains stretched before him, and a red-leafed tree stood overhead. He licked his lips and yawned.

He felt movement on his chest. "Something wrong?" asked Mei, shifting to look at him. Her eyes were heavy, same as his. How long had they slept here together?

"I had a dream," he said, softly.

"What about?" she asked.

He thought back to it, trying to remember the details, but already they were fading. "I was a kid, I think."

"Oh? Was it a memory?"

"Yeah," he said, and his eyes drifted to the ground. "I think my mom was in it."

John felt Mei's hand squeeze his fingers. He turned to look at her, only to see her smiling at him. "Let's go check out those hills," she said. "What do you say?"

"Sure. You think we'll find anything?" he asked.

She gave him a playful shrug. "Only one way to find out, right?"

They walked through the valley, away from the red-leafed tree. The hillside slope wasn't nearly as steep as it had seemed, and John found he could easily get his footing. His boots were made for this, grabbing and clinging to the hardened earth, and together he and Mei pulled themselves to the top in no time. As the horizon came into view, John heard a faint rumbling somewhere far into the distance.

"What is that?" John scanned the new countryside with his eyes. More of the valley lay ahead, with a blanket of trees beyond it. Further still, a couple of mountains pierced the sky, though they were encased in heavy clouds.

Mei tilted her head, listening, waiting. "I hear it!" she snapped, after a bit. "It's getting louder."

Indeed, the noise had grown slightly, and soon enough John could even feel the rumbling in his chest and legs. The ground carried the sound, vibrating ever so gently.

It seemed to come from the mountains beyond the clouds, as far as he could tell, so that was where he watched and waited, listening and focusing.

A sudden flash of light glimmered through the elevated fog, filling him with sudden apprehension. He waited, but there was nothing. Light from the suns, perhaps, reflecting off the clouds and snowy peaks.

But then he saw it, a great, silver bird sweeping through the white foam, parting the clouds like mist on the sea. A monstrous thing the size of a small building. An animal with—

No, he realized, looking with his hybrid eyes. It was a machine. A vehicle or drone.

It flew from the peaks, trailing clouds behind it, closing in toward the valley. A growing hum rose steadily as the craft drew nearer. John pushed himself to his feet, gawking at the soaring metal craft.

It flew overhead, filling the valley with the sound of thunder, heading off toward the camp site. John and Mei looked at each other, and without a word they started running. With a finger on his ear, John activated his com. "Brooks!" he yelled. "Brooks, come in!"

But there was only silence.

6

Ortego Outpost File Logs
Play Audio File 872
Recorded: February 11, 2351

MITCHELL: This is Sophia Mitchell. How can I help you?

HARPER: Hello, Sophia. This is Doctor Breslin Harper calling from Central. Is Curie around?

MITCHELL: Not at the moment, I'm afraid. Is there something I can do for you?

HARPER: That's too bad. I wanted to let her know my office has been authorized to handle your team's reports, at least in the near future until a better arrangement can be made.

MITCHELL: This is excellent news. I'll be certain to let her know when she returns.

HARPER: Can I ask where she's gone?

MITCHELL: *She and two of our engineers have joined Sergeant Finn's team on the other side of the gate. They are assisting in the repair of the communications system.*

HARPER: *I see. Well, in the meantime, would you be able to send me your files so my staff can begin their review?*

MITCHELL: *Certainly, ma'am. I can have those to you right away. Once Doctor Curie returns, I'll begin forwarding all future reports directly to you.*

HARPER: *Thank you, Sophia. If you need anything from me, you can contact me at this number. It's my direct line.*

MITCHELL: *That's very generous of you, ma'am. We definitely appreciate it. May I ask why you are requesting the backlog of reports? I could probably draft another document focusing on the highlights.*

HARPER: *I'd love any help you can give, but I still want to read through everything myself. As the board's liaison, I'll need to relay all of this information as effectively as possible to the board, which includes answering any questions they might have. I've got exactly eighteen days before the next meeting, which doesn't leave much time.*

MITCHELL: *You're presenting our findings?*

HARPER: *I suppose you could say that, yes. Your mission is still ongoing, so I'll only be summarizing the events up to now, bringing the other board members up to date. They like to pretend they're informed, you see, while accomplishing very little.*

MITCHELL: *Is that typical for the Science Division's board of directors?*

HARPER: *It's typical for politics in general, Miss Mitchell. Take it from someone who knows.*

End Audio File

Quarantine Zone
February 11, 2351

Lena Sol waited aboard the *Red Door*, filled with quiet reservations. Despite having absolutely no experience in the field to speak of, she now found herself in an environmental suit on her way to investigate a series of energy discharges somewhere in the quarantine zone. After seven years of active service as an analyst, now level-5, she had spent most of her time behind a desk. Her days were filled sifting through reports, filing data entries, and writing daily summaries for her supervisors.

In other words, not the most ideal candidate to be out in the field, especially when it came to investigating an energy spike from a two-hundred-year-old trans-dimensional wormhole experiment. What did she know about this sort of thing, other than what she'd read in a file? She wasn't qualified for this, was she? What could Master Gel be thinking?

Yet here she sat, waiting to arrive at a place that didn't appear on any modern maps. A location she'd only found because of an error in the Rosenthal satellite's systems—an oversight on the part of the designer. If only she'd never discovered it on her own, she'd still be sitting at her desk, going over the day's reports.

But she was here, nonetheless, and she shouldn't question it. Good citizens did what they were told, because it was the only way to keep everyone safe. It was how Everlasting had survived for so long, despite the inherent dangers beyond the outer shield—savage beasts, uncivilized and bloodthirsty natives, and of course the deadly atmosphere itself. The people had the Leadership to thank for its survival. They were the ones who kept them safe.

"How much longer before we arrive?" asked one of the scientists sitting nearby. Lena recalled the biographical summaries she'd previously memorized. This one was Emile Res, twenty-seven years old, level-6 physicist with some training in biology. Her previous work had involved matter displacement, yielding promising results, but nothing concrete as of yet. A real up-and-comer.

"A few more cycles," announced the pilot. "Shouldn't be long."

"The faster the better," said Emile, obvious impatience in her voice.

Lena Sol said nothing. The ship could take its time getting to its final destination for all she cared. She had never longed for field work, not in all her days in Analytics. *Damn you, Gel,* she thought, but then stopped herself, casting the negative thought from her mind. *Better not to think such things. Better to stay positive.*

No matter how miserable she might be, no matter how

poorly suited she was for this position, she had been placed here by her superiors to fulfill a purpose. Her personal feelings were unimportant, she reminded herself.

All was for the good of Everlasting.

"You, there," said Emile, staring at her. "Analyst Sol."

Lena blinked, glancing at the woman. "Pardon?"

"You're the analyst, correct?"

She nodded. "Yes. Lena Sol, level-9. I was chosen by—"

"Save the biography. Is this your first time in the field? I can't imagine you're used to this sort of thing."

"It is," said Lena.

"This is my fourth, personally, but I've never worked with someone from your division before. It's rather uncommon for an analyst to be out here, isn't it?"

It was a fair question, especially from someone like Emile Res who had worked largely in the Northern Islands, far from the city. She'd been stationed at the Love and Grace Laboratories for several years, working on classified research involving biological artifacts. That portion of the hemisphere was outside of Lena's jurisdiction, so she'd probably never know the details.

"Analysts don't usually participate," said one of the others. A man named Titus Ven, forty-seven years old, archeologist level-12. He was pudgy, with thick red hair and unshaven cheeks. "She's here because of the nature of our mission."

"Which part?" asked Emile.

"Hardly anyone goes into the quarantine zone, so having an analyst makes it easier to navigate. If the ship goes down and our equipment fails, her job will be getting us home. There's also the added benefit of having someone who can speak the local languages."

Emile's eyes lit up. "Oh, that's right. I forgot about the linguistics training. Tell me, Analyst, how many languages can you speak?"

Lena fidgeted in her seat. "I couldn't say offhand."

"Come on, don't be modest," said Emile. "I've heard stories about how some of you can speak dozens of them, at least."

"That's accurate, although it ranges, depending on the level of training and memory implant therapy. Master Analyst Gel, for example, can speak over three hundred different languages and seven hundred distinct dialects."

"Incredible," said Emile, gawking a little. "But are there really so many languages in the world?"

"Not quite," she admitted. "Many of them haven't been used in centuries, since Extinction Day."

"If no one speaks them, why do you learn?" asked Emile.

"Most languages may sound different, but they actually share many common traits, including syntax, making them rather simple to decipher once you understand what to look for. As Everlasting has expanded its reach across the globe, we have continued to encounter various tribes, each of which speaks a different language or dialect. Some of these are new to us, but because of our translation technology, we can communicate with them much more quickly than one might expect."

"I suppose if you've received the training and genetic enhancements, it probably comes naturally, like any other job," said Emile.

Not quite, thought Lena, but she didn't bother correcting her. It was true that many occupations required some level of enhancement, whether genetic or artificial. However, this was not the case for all of them. There were very few enhanced waste management personnel, for example, despite the essential nature of the service. In fact, much of Everlasting's architecture relied on the work of several hundred unskilled laborers who never had the opportunity for enhancement. What Emile had actually meant was that Lena's enhancements were similar in nature to other advanced occupations, such as those found in the various scientific, research, and mechanical fields. Everlasting mandated that such individuals receive mental enhancements and advanced training, ensuring peak efficiency and professional inclination toward one's assigned occupation. Every analyst was an exceptional analyst, for example, and they all took great joy in being one.

The *Red Door* shuddered. "Coming up on the destination," said the pilot.

"Finally," said Emile, leaning forward. "I can't wait to stretch my legs."

"Hold on. I'm detecting multiple bio-signatures in the area," said the pilot.

"Natives?" asked Titus.

"Unconfirmed," said the pilot.

"Send the image to our screens. Let's see them."

Lena activated her visor, and the image of the cabin quickly disappeared, replaced by the area outside. It was the landing zone, which she recognized from the Rosenthal scans, along with several unknown figures standing and running around. These individuals didn't resemble any of the local tribes—none that were familiar, anyway. Their clothing suggested they were foreign, perhaps hailing from a faraway region. Had they come this way to trade with one of the nearby settlements? Where their ears should be pointed, they were instead round. Where their noses should be flat, they were rather large. How strange it was to find a people like this in such a well-charted area. On the same continent as Everlasting, no less. The city's satellites had spent decades observing and mapping the various peoples of this landmass, so to find such a unique one here was very unusual. Were she not sitting aboard an aircraft presently, she might be inclined to run a database search to check for any populations with similar physical traits in order to determine their origin point. For now, she could only speculate.

Lena knew of tribes in the distant north with extreme body modifications, some of which had presumably never been observed. Everlasting had very little success monitoring them, given how they chose to live—building cities into the sides of mountains, burrowing beneath the stone, rarely surfacing except for trading. The primary resource seemed to be precious stones and metals, which they offered to traveling merchants in exchange for other resources. The analysts often had debates about what these cave people must be like, sometimes coming up with outlandish theories on the nature of their isolation, but there was never any proof. The cave dwellers surfaced only once every few months, and only for a few hours, revealing little. Such was the case for many other civilizations around the globe, though the analysts were intent on closing the gap of knowledge as quickly as possible. The more they learned and understood about the various tribes, the safer and more secure the great city of Everlasting would become.

Lena wondered if these people could be from such a region, somehow lost to the city's scans. There were no harbors close by, but it would only take six or seven days to walk to the nearest coast. The Rosenthal satellite hadn't detected anything out of the ordinary, last she checked, but she'd just spent the last nine days away from her post preparing for this mission. Perhaps her office knew all about them by now, but had neglected to include this information in the daily summaries they'd been sending her at the top of each day. No, Master Gel would never allow for such an oversight. If the information had escaped her, the fault must be her own. She'd have to go over the scans again when she had the time.

The *Red Door* began to decelerate, though she could hardly feel it. The floor beneath Lena's seat hummed, and a soft snap quickly followed, a sign the landing gear had been deployed. As the ship touched down, the natives outside began to scatter, disappearing behind the cliffs and into the woods. "Stay seated while we release the suppressor," said one of the pilots.

Lena felt her stomach turn. She hated the thought of the nerve suppressor, otherwise known as compound AX-12009-B3. It was a fast-acting toxin used to paralyze most organisms within two hundred meters. Once activated, the affected fauna remained in a state of paralysis, fully awake but unable to move. The toxin was extremely effective in any situation requiring the use of non-deadly force.

It was initially conceived as an aid for long-term biological stasis, back before the technique had been perfected. Unfortunately, since the subject remained awake after coming into contact with the toxin, the compound was discarded and believed to be a failure. It wasn't until several decades later that the Leadership decided to repurpose it, this time as a weapon.

Everlasting was part of a larger country in those days, long before the gas settled and transformed the landscape, killing or mutating billions. As time went on, and the world fell apart, the toxin was repurposed once again to deal with civil unrest and crowd management. In an age when riots happened on a daily basis, hundreds could be paralyzed in moments, all without risking any essential lives. It was the most effective means of crowd management the government had at its disposal, and many believed its implementation signaled the dawn of the modern age of peace in the city.

Right now, AX-12009-B3 was being used against these unknown natives. If the ship located any more beyond the dispersal zone, the pilot would release a small drone to deliver the toxin remotely. He would do this as many times as it took in order to secure the area.

Lena sat in her suit, staring at the display on her wrist, watching as over a dozen natives collapsed onto the ground. Several twitched as they fell into the dirt, flailing wildly before settling into a frozen state of immobility.

She already wanted to leave.

THE HATCH to the *Red Door* opened, and out walked Lena Sol, safe inside her environmental suit. With the local population incapacitated, she had little cause to fear her surroundings.

The bodies littered the ground like ornaments, as if placed by some unseen hand. *They must think I'm a demon,* she thought. *Some superstitious nightmare, sent to them from fairy tales and old religions.*

But Lena didn't like the idea of being someone's

monster. She only wanted to go home, sit in her little pod and proceed with her work, analyzing images and filtering data.

"Look at this," called Emile, pointing to one of the bodies. "They appear to have weapons. It's some kind of rifle."

"How do you know?" asked the pilot.

"Barrel. Trigger. What else could it be? And look at their padded uniforms."

"So what?" the pilot said. "Plenty of natives have armor and weapons."

Emile crouched beside the frozen body. "That's true, but I've never seen any like this. There's also the patchwork on the clothing. Look at the lettering. It's more advanced than what you'd normally see."

Titus disembarked from the ship a moment later, stopping at Emile's side and taking note of her findings. "Take some screens. Bag one of the weapons. As much as I'd like to examine them further, we're here for more important things."

"Of course," Emile responded. She raised her wrist above the body and snapped several pictures. "I can analyze these later when we're back in the city."

"Analyst Sol," called Titus. "Are you ready to proceed inside the facility?"

Lena nodded. She'd memorized the entirety of the underground tunnels, so she knew exactly where to go in order to find the designated areas. "Yes, sir."

"Good," said Titus. "We'll head to the gate room first, then we'll see about investigating the power station."

"As you wish," said Lena, and she quickly followed after him.

The mouth of the cave opened into a large stairwell, leading deep into the earth. From here, it was a straight shot through the first major tunnel, with only a few detours to the path before reaching the final room. The hardest part would simply be the distance and the time required to make the walk. The whole investigation would take them a few hours, at the very least.

The pilot would, of course, need to reapply the AX-12009-B3 multiple times before the end of the day while the rest of them worked, but it couldn't be helped.

"Hold a moment," said Emile as they neared the end of the stairs. She blinked three times, activating her implant, and her eyes dilated. "Scans are showing a few lifeforms further in."

"How many?" asked Titus.

"Four, it seems. Split into groups of two."

"We'll have to deal with them in close quarters. Ready your AX pistols."

Lena swallowed, reaching for the holster on her side. She'd never used a weapon outside of training before. Thankfully, the AX pistols were non-lethal, filled with the same compound they'd used on the surface only a few moments ago. "Maybe we should use the drone," she blurted out.

"We could," said Titus. "However, the ship only has one, and the drone is currently monitoring several targets in the nearby woods. If we take the drone further in, the others could regain mobility and attack the ship."

Lena frowned. "I understand."

"Stay close to each other and use your sensors. Remember, your suit has level-three plating on it. Even if they attack and manage to hit one of us, the damage should be minimal. You won't be in any real danger."

"Yes, sir," said Lena. "You're right, of course." She knew full well about the armor in her suit, but it didn't bring much comfort. A person could spend all the time in the world preparing for something, spend every moment calculating, looking at all the possible angles, but at the end of the day there could never be any true certainty. No definitive solution. For the world was complex, filled with too many variables. At the end of the day, nothing was ever one hundred percent.

"We'll go to the control room first, but let's see if we can activate the lighting system in here," said Titus.

Lena gave a swift nod, then activated her display. A series of holographic images appeared before her, representing menus. Before the mission, Master Gel had given her access to the system directory of this facility. Unfortunately, this required her to be present in order to actually do anything, including something as simple as turning on the lights.

Lena found the directory soon, then motioned with her

hand to activate the file. She found the switch and grasped her fingers, and suddenly the lights came on, filling the hall.

"Much better," said Titus, with a smile. "Good work, Analyst."

"Thank you, sir," said Lena.

Emile stared distantly for a moment, reading her map. "It appears the four I mentioned earlier are moving now. The lights must have frightened them."

"Keep your maps active and watch them," ordered Titus. "Let's get going."

JOHN RAN AS FAST as his legs could carry him. The ship—if that's what it truly was—had flown directly toward his team's camp. Because of their malfunctioning radios, John had no way of finding out just what the hell was going on. To make matters worse, the forest was too dense to see through, even with his enhanced eyes.

"John, wait," said Mei, trailing behind him. The words were hardly a whisper, but he heard them clearly. He stopped, letting her catch up to him. They were both fast sprinters, but Mei was small and her short legs worked against her.

John didn't mind the delay. No matter the situation, it was better to stay together.

Before long, they came to the edge of the forest, the

field finally in view. John stood next to one of the trees, holding tight against the bark so as not to be seen. In the distance, a short walk from the cave, the flying vessel stood unmoving and alone.

John stared at the machine. Mei touched his shoulder, startling him. "Look," she whispered, motioning to the field. John's eyes followed her finger, quickly discovering the bodies. None of them were moving.

His eyes widened at the sight of them, and his heart raced. He started to go, but Mei's hand held him back. "John, wait," she pleaded. "You don't know what that thing is. You'll be hurt, too."

He was breathing heavy now, his eyes dashing between the nearest body and the ship. Which of his friends was it? Judging by the size, it could be Brooks. Maybe Hughes. He couldn't see their face from this angle, so it was hard to say. What was he supposed to do?

"Look," said Mei, pointing to the other end of the field.

Several leaves fluttered through one of the distant trees, and suddenly a small metallic object appeared, speeding and whirling between the branches. "What's that?" he asked.

"Some kind of drone, maybe," said Mei.

"Must be looking for more of us," muttered John.

"What do we do?" she asked.

He scanned the field again, looking for any signs of movement. Something to point a weapon at besides a giant hulking piece of metal. Had there been any passengers aboard this thing, or was it simply another, albeit much larger, drone? "We need to get inside the cave," he said.

"But John, we've got no idea what we're even dealing with. We could be walking right into—"

A soft hum filled the space above them. Their eyes slowly rose toward the tree tops. The little drone was now hovering several feet in the air between the branches. John remained perfectly still. "Get to the tunnel," he whispered.

"It's just sitting there," said Mei, swallowing. "Maybe we can—"

The drone tilted toward her.

"Get ready," said John, raising his rifle to get its attention.

The drone retargeted, focusing on John, but before it could react a second time, he squeezed the trigger tight. John unleashed a barrage of rounds from the barrel, battering the floating machine's tiny body, knocking it to the ground where it lay, obviously out of commission. The sound of them hitting the little machine filled the area. Whatever secrecy they'd hoped to keep was now entirely lost.

"Okay, then," said Mei, looking at him. "Caves?"

"Caves," he repeated.

Together, they burst through the tree line and into the field. John leapt over one of the fallen bodies, which he recognized as Short. Her eyes were open, but she was completely still. He felt the sudden urge to stop, but shook it off.

A loud snap echoed from behind them, in the direction of the giant machine. John glanced back right as he entered the stairwell, managing a glimpse of the craft's hull as it cracked open. Before he could see anything else, he was inside, leaping down the stairs several at a time.

Mei followed with shorter strides. "The lights are on," she observed, still running.

John reached the bottom first, then scanned the area. "No one's here," he said before turning his weapon toward the cave entrance at the head of the stairs. He kept the target reticle on the opening in case anyone decided to follow them, letting Mei descend the rest of the way. When she finally caught up to him, he backed away. Together, they proceeded into the largest of the tunnels, toward the final room—the only one worth visiting in this barren, empty place.

LENA WATCHED as Titus incapacitated the two natives in the control room. It only took two shots from the AX pistol, which used a lock-on targeting program to ensure complete accuracy, and then it was done. Two soft thuds as they collapsed onto the floor.

"I suppose we should get to work," said Emile, taking a

seat at one of the nearby consoles. "Analyst, would you mind?"

"One moment, please," said Lena. She activated her neural link and called the interface to life, quickly locating the necessary sub-directory. Several of the computer terminals blinked to life, including the one Emile occupied. A hard-light display now sat atop each of the desks.

Hard-light, unlike neural holograms, did not require an implant to use. Hard-light was an outdated technology by today's standards, used primarily in construction projects. Its implementation in computer systems was simply too cumbersome to be useful anymore. Not to mention the lack of security and personal accountability. The modern neural interface was far more convenient and had since become the primary choice for computer interaction in Everlasting, though hard-light certainly had a nostalgic charm to it.

"Excellent," said Emile. She proceeded to type in a command, activating a screen. Lena and Titus watched as she navigated through a complex directory system. It took longer than Lena expected. "Ah, here we are. It seems the experiment was activated recently." She paused, brow furrowed in curiosity. "Today, in fact."

"What?" asked Titus. "Are you sure you're not mistaken?"

"If these logs are to be believed, then I'm afraid not," she said.

Titus looked back at the two men in the corner of the room. "Could these people have accidentally—"

"Activated the ring?" finished Emile. "I don't see how. They would need access to the network, and the logs show no authorized users in…it looks like two centuries."

"Then how?"

"They may have used an exterior device," said Lena.

"Are you suggesting they bypassed our systems?" asked Emile. "I don't know of anyone capable of such a thing outside of Everlasting."

A lull of silence filled the room.

"Maybe the system is mistaken," said Titus. "I know the logs say otherwise, but computers aren't perfect, and two centuries is a long time."

Emile nodded slowly. "Yes, perhaps you're right."

Lena said nothing. She'd spent the last decade observing this region of the continent. It was the whole reason she was here. In all that time, however, she'd never observed any tribe developing or using anything close to modern technology. For the most part, their methods were primitive and simple. Wooden ships and caravans, swords and short-range guns, outdated forms of medicine. In all the great, wide world, Everlasting stood alone, unrivaled in its social and technological achievements. Nothing even came close.

"Still, we have orders to download the logs and copy the database," said Emile.

"How long do you need?" asked Titus.

"It shouldn't take much time," she answered.

Titus turned to Lena. "As soon as she's done, we're

heading to the power station. After we shut the systems down, our mission will be concluded. However, I'd like to take some screens of the facility, as well as our guests."

"Do you believe they're involved with the ring's activation?" asked Lena.

"We can't rule out the possibility, no matter how unlikely we might believe it to be."

"Yes, sir," she said. "At the very least, I do not believe them to be indigenous to this area. Master Gel will find this most interesting."

"Perhaps you'll receive a commendation, then, Analyst," said Titus.

Lena feigned a smile. She had little interest in commendations or rewards. She only wanted to return to her desk back in Everlasting. The information she collected on this new tribe could help secure Master Gel's admiration, which could only help her.

An icon blinked in the corner of her implant display, indicating movement. There was someone nearby. Could it be the other two natives from before? Lena zoomed out on the map, searching. She quickly found the others, still on the other side of the facility. They hadn't moved at all. Lena turned to the entrance, not sure of what to do.

"What is it, Analyst?" asked Titus.

Lena kept her eyes on the doorway. "There are two life-forms moving in this direction. They are different from the two we observed earlier."

"Where did they come from?" asked Emile.

"I don't know," said Lena.

Titus raised his pistol. "We'll handle them the same as the rest. There's no need for concern."

Lena thumbed the side of her suit. The dots were moving on her display, drawing closer by the moment. She took a step back, toward Emile. *It will be okay*, she quietly assured herself, reaching for her gun. *Only a little longer and then I can go back home.*

Back to Everlasting.

JOHN AND MEI stopped a short way from the gate room, slipping into a nearby hall. They had no idea what was ahead, so they would do well to be prepared.

"Why are we stopping?" asked Mei.

John leaned next to the edge of the doorway, peering into the hall. Despite the control room being fifty yards from his position, he managed to spot a few individuals inside. Each of them seemed to be holding a weapon of some kind. A gun, by the look of it. They were also wearing some sort of full-body suit. Armor, perhaps.

"John, answer me," insisted Mei, gripping his wrist.

"Sorry," he said, sliding back into the corridor. "I need you to do me a favor."

"Huh? What are you talking about?"

He held her by the shoulder. "Stay here for a minute. I'll be back in a few."

She scoffed. "If you think I'm letting you go in there without me, you must be out of your—"

"Where's your weapon, Mei?" he asked, motioning to her side. "You don't have one. You're not wearing any gear. Even with your reflexes, you could still get injured. I can't risk worrying about that. I can't risk letting you get hurt."

"But what if something happens to you?" she asked, desperately.

"Hey, come on. I've done this a hundred times now," he said with a grin. "I'll be in and out in no time."

"But what if—"

He leaned in and kissed her, then beamed a playful smile.

Without another word, he backed away from her, then turned into the hall and sprinted through the corridor. She'd be angry with him later, but at least this way she was safe.

As he reached the control room, he saw the figures on the other side of the archway, their weapons in hand, moving toward him, staring. The nearest one—taller than the others—seemed to take aim at him.

John rushed forward, keeping to the side of the hall, and unlatched one of his flash grenades. With a quick flick of his wrist, he tossed it ahead of him. The grenade bounced through the doorway, landing beneath the first alien, who only stood there.

John collided with the side wall, falling into the left corner near the gate room's entryway. As he did, he shielded his eyes and ears with his arms, and a bright light erupted from within the control room, followed by several screams.

"*Bfoc bor shoc!*" cried one of the aliens.

John took a deep breath, raising his gun to his chest. He closed his eyes and focused. "Okay," he whispered, and a sudden calmness fell over him, and the air grew still and quiet. "Time to get to work."

He twisted around the edge of the wall, exploding into the room like thunder. The foremost stranger stood there, gawking, with his gun still in his hand. John slid beneath the alien's line of sight and took aim. With a single squeeze of his trigger, he fired his rifle, hitting the alien's pistol and knocking it away. He continued to slide, then pressed his hand into the floor, pushing up and springing into the disarmed enemy.

They collided, falling backward, and John wrapped his arms around the stranger's body to keep him from moving. As they tumbled, John caught a glimpse of the eyes inside the visor. The eyes of a man, he realized.

"*Bfoc qa bi qa!*" shouted one of the others.

"*Thaac ec! Thaac ec!*" cried the second.

John tossed the man to his side, then readied his weapon, taking aim at the others.

Seeing this, they dropped their handheld guns and raised their arms. "*Boec! Boec!*"

John got to his feet, rushing to the weapons on the floor, and kicked them into the corner of the room. "Step back!"

he ordered, but neither moved. Clearly, they didn't seem to understand. "Over there," he said, motioning with his rifle, pointing to the wall.

The two suited aliens shuffled clumsily to the edge of the room, keeping their hands up.

John turned to the third one, who was now on his knees several feet away. "You too."

The man seemed to understand, and proceeded to join the others. The three of them waited together, mumbling amongst themselves.

"Mei! Can you come in here for a second?" yelled John. He kept his rifle aimed at the invaders.

A few seconds later, Mei jogged into the room, pausing to gawk at the strange people in the funny suits now huddled in the corner. "Oh, good," she said upon seeing them. "They look nice and scared. How hard did you hit them?"

"Not hard enough," said John. "But the day's not over yet."

LENA SOL WAS TERRIFIED. Standing between Emile and Titus, she had been disarmed and subdued, and now stood helplessly at the mercy of these wild people. To make matters worse, they appeared to speak a foreign language which Lena didn't recognize—surprising, given her background. Wherever these people were from, it was far removed from Everlasting's observable reach. If only she could concentrate and listen—pay attention to the way they spoke—she might be able to piece together meanings, but it was no use. She couldn't stop shaking. She couldn't let go of her fear.

Tears began to fill her eyes, and suddenly her lips were trembling. There was a lump in her throat, almost choking her, and a warm flush in her cheeks. She felt like a cornered animal. *Maybe the pilot will come and find us soon,* she thought, trying to reassure herself. *Maybe he will send the drone.*

The smaller of the two wild people said something that sounded like a question, then stared at Lena.

"I don't understand," said Lena, shaking her head.

"You're supposed to be an expert with languages," snapped Emile. "Talk to them!"

"I can't," returned Lena, frantically. She tried to breathe, but was finding it difficult.

"Use the software, then," said Titus, who kept his eyes on the larger of the two.

The translation program. Of course. Lena had forgotten all about it. The software had been developed in order to decode almost any language on the planet, though there were certainly exceptions, depending on the complexity. Most of the time, the translator simply pulled from a digital dictionary, which stored and catalogued over ten thousand languages and dialects, streamlining the process. However, when a completely new language was encountered and required translation, the program would extrapolate based on sentence structure and phonetics, constructing the most likely translation it could with the data available. This did not always provide the best results, but the basic meaning was usually understood. In time, as more information was provided, the software would adapt and extrapolate further until the bulk of the language was deciphered. It wasn't perfect, but it helped.

Lena used her implant to activate the translator program. She'd let it run in the background while the foreigners talked. With any luck, it wouldn't take long for it to provide her with something she could use to communicate with these people.

"Titus, you should call the ship. Have them send the drone down here to incapacitate these savages," muttered Emile.

"I already did. The drone was destroyed."

"What about the pilot? Tell him to come down here."

"Protocol says he can't leave the ship. He'll leave us behind before that happens."

Emile grimaced. "He'd abandon us to these people?"

The smaller savage yelled, interrupting them.

"I think she wants us to stop talking," muttered Emile.

The larger one raised his weapon, then said something to his friend. She nodded, and proceeded to attend to the paralyzed foreigners in the corner.

Several words appeared across Lena's visor as the translation software attempted to do its job.

...they don't...maybe if...alive I think...

Not bad, thought Lena. *Not perfect, but not bad.* Now, if only she could get a full sentence out of it.

…good…maybe the others are…about these people…

Progress, but it would take a while before she could establish two-way communication. The translator had to receive and analyze enough words before it could do the reverse process, too.

…didn't think there were any…so much for being alone…aliens…

Lena paused as the last word scrolled by. Had the translator made a mistake? Not every word had the exact same meaning in every language, so "alien" might simply mean something like "foreigner" or "the other." Perhaps it was the case here. Regardless, the process had begun. With any luck, she might be able to open a line of communication before things got any worse.

…almost time for the call from…any second now, actually…

Lena felt a soft rumble in the wall behind her. She flinched, suddenly, and withdrew her hands from the stone.

Titus looked at each of the women, then at the strangers. "What is happening?" he asked.

The smaller of them motioned toward the large, elevated ring, and spoke. Lena waited for the translation to come through.

…better not try anything. It's only a friend of mine.

A dark cloud appeared within the ring, swirling like a dust cloud before coming to a stop moments later. When it did, the fog inside it cleared, revealing an image on the other side. Several artificial lights came into view. What in the world was happening? Did these people just activate the portal without using the computer systems, or had it activated on its own?

No, wait a moment, thought Lena. *The small one mentioned a friend. Could there be someone on the other end? Is that where they came from?*

A sudden realization swept over Lena Sol, and she felt her cheeks go cold. These people—they must be from the other side of that gate. They must be from another place altogether.

"What in the world is happening?" asked Emile. She sounded both afraid and in awe.

"They're from the other side of the gate," exclaimed Lena.

"That's not possible," said Emile.

"Look at the lights!" Lena insisted. "They're not natural. Look at them!"

The two strangers glanced back at her, and the smaller one said something. Her visor deciphered the words, this time much more efficiently.

What was that about the lights?

Lena paused. Had this person actually understood her? Lena looked at Titus and Emile, who were both watching nervously. "Yes, the lights," she decided to say.

The translator echoed her, but in a foreign language. A look of understanding fell across the small one's face. Her suit must have transmitted the last thing she said, translating it automatically. No wonder. A response came soon after.

Who are you?

"My name is Lena Sol," she explained. "And I've come from Everlasting."

7

Ortego Outpost File Logs
Play Audio File 888
Recorded: February 11, 2351

MITCHELL: *So, am I to understand you've encountered sentient alien life?*

CURIE: *That's correct.*

MITCHELL: *And they attacked and paralyzed everyone with a nerve toxin?*

CURIE: *Also correct.*

MITCHELL: *But you're all fine now?*

CURIE: *We took care of it.*

MITCHELL: *Boy. The things I miss by staying home.*

CURIE: *It's not nearly as fun as it sounds, Sophie. Believe me.*

MITCHELL: *You're one of the first people to encounter sentient, alien life.*

CURIE: *And it's a headache.*

MITCHELL: *Still, congratulations are in order, I believe. Shall I inform Central?*

CURIE: *Not yet. We're still assessing the situation. John has them here at gunpoint. Half our team is still incapacitated. Let's at least figure out what's going on before we file a report.*

MITCHELL: *I suppose now would be a poor time to tell you that Dr. Harper called.*

CURIE: *Again? What did she want?*

MITCHELL: *Our logs. She's organizing some sort of presentation for the board of directors.*

CURIE: *I see. Well, thanks for letting me know. I'll have to deal with it later.*

MITCHELL: *Completely understandable, ma'am. If she calls again, I'll let her know you're occupied.*

CURIE: *To say the least.*

End Audio File

Somewhere in Kant
February 11, 2351

Terry sat on the side of Hux's ship, dangling his feet over the edge, watching the water swell and break. The boat had traveled into the distant sea, staying far enough from the coast that the land was no longer visible.

How big was the world? How vast were the seas? In all the days since he'd traveled to this planet, when a hole in space had tossed him across the stars, he had only seen a small portion of it. A sliver of possibilities.

"Feeling nostalgic?" asked a voice.

Terry turned to see Hux towering over him, a jovial smile spread across his face. "I was just thinking."

Hux propped down beside him. "A dangerous practice, I'm told."

Terry laughed. "Maybe it is."

"What thoughts are in your head, my friend? Good things, I hope."

"I was wondering what else was out there. What other kinds of people."

"Ah." Hux nodded. "You've got the mind of a sailor, asking such things. Not many think about what lies beyond the sunset. Even fewer decide to go and see."

"I used to think I'd traveled pretty far, but sitting here and watching the ocean…now, it seems like nothing."

"Even the greatest of wavemasters have not seen the ends of the world, Little Traveler. It is too big for only two eyes."

"But you still do it," he said.

"That we do." Hux grinned again.

The day edged by with ease as Hux's boat sailed on. The ship came closer to the land in the late afternoon, and Terry watched the coast with some curiosity. Though nothing came of it, he did not feel his time was wasted, and realized there was pleasure to be had in simple observation. It seemed that after years of running, fighting, and surviving, he was finally able to relax. Despite the pressing goal before him and the dangers ahead, something about the open waters brought a calmness to him, a sense of mindfulness.

Perhaps when all was said and done, he would more seriously consider Hux's proposition to join the crew and travel the world. *I think I could get used to this*, he thought as he took a breath of salted air. *I think I'd like it very much.*

Bravo Gate Point
February 11, 2351

"You mean to say you aren't from this planet?" asked the woman in the suit, whose name was Lena Sol.

"Are you sure you should be telling her this?" asked John, still with his rifle aimed at the intruders.

Mei glanced back at him. "Don't worry. I'm leaving out specifics." She looked at the alien woman again. "You said you came here to investigate this portal. Does this facility belong to you?"

The woman hesitated to answer.

"What's wrong?" asked Mei.

Lena turned to the largest of the three, then spoke in a foreign language. The man answered, and she gave a quick nod in response. "Yes, this shelter is under our supervision," Lena finally said.

"Is he the one in charge?" asked Mei.

"That is correct."

"Can he communicate with me, too?"

"One moment, please," she said.

John watched as the three aliens talked amongst themselves. After a few minutes, the woman continued. "I am transferring your language to their translation software. It will only take a moment."

"Translation software?" asked Mei, cocking her brow.

"Hello," said the larger alien. "Hello, can you understand me?"

"I do," responded Mei.

"Very good," said the man. "My name is Titus Ven. These two are Lena Sol and Emile Res. We—"

"Why'd you attack our people?" John interrupted.

Titus stiffened. "We mistook you for the local people. It was a simple mistake. I apologize."

John scoffed. "Pretty sure Track and Mickey might disagree about it being simple. You paralyzed them."

Mei gave him a look that suggested he stop talking. "Titus, help us understand. What are you doing here?"

"I'm afraid I am not authorized to reveal such information. I will say, however, that we did not expect to encounter you here. In fact, I would very much like to know who you are and where you came from."

Mei motioned to the portal ring. "You saw that open, right?"

"I did," said Titus.

"Then you know where we came from."

"Where does it lead?" he asked.

"That part I can't tell you," said Mei. "Unless, of course, you want to reexamine your previous statement about what you're doing here."

Titus didn't answer.

"How about you start by telling me more about Everlasting? Your colleague mentioned it before," said Mei.

"Yes, Everlasting," nodded Titus. "It is our home."

"Is it a peaceful country?" asked Mei.

"Of course," said Titus, as though anything to the contrary were simply unthinkable.

"Good," said Mei. "Because we're peaceful, too. Do you understand?"

Titus nodded.

"Okay, so how about you help us get our friends back on their feet? Is there a way to do that?" asked Mei.

"Friends?" asked Titus.

"You mean them?" asked Lena, pointing to Track and Mickey, still in the corner.

"Right," responded Mei.

"They'll recover shortly. The toxin does not last very

long," explained Lena. "They should be on their feet again before much longer."

"The sooner the better," said John.

Lena held her hands together, fidgeting a little. "If it helps, there are two others somewhere in the facility. We saw them as we arrived."

"Others?" asked Mei.

"Two of them, yes," said Emile. "They were near the power station."

"That's probably Zoe," said Mei.

John tapped his radio. "Anyone reading me? Hello?"

A garbled mess of static answered.

"Looks like we're still getting interference."

"Interference," muttered Mei. She looked at the aliens. "Is your ship blocking our radio? We've been experiencing feedback over the last few days."

"Possibly. I don't really know," said Titus.

"Actually, that's likely due to our scans," said Emile. "As the ship has grown closer, we've gradually increased the frequency of them. You might have been experiencing some feedback because of that. They've been known to interfere with primitive forms of communication."

"Primitive?" asked Mei.

"I'm sorry. I didn't mean to imply—"

"It's fine," she said. "Let's just figure out how to fix it. Call your ship and have them stop the scans. My friend here will lower his weapon. Does that work?"

"Yes, thank you," said Titus.

John grabbed one of the pistols on the floor and examined it. "We're holding on to these, though. At least until we figure things out."

———

A FEW HOURS after their first encounter with the aliens, John and Mei managed to get a fair amount of information together. To begin with, these three strangers apparently came from a place called Everlasting, a city somewhere to the north. It was also its own country, completely isolated from the rest of the world.

Second, and even more surprising, the suits they wore were more than just armor. They were environmental suits. "We didn't know what to expect when we arrived," explained Emile. "This region previously experienced severe radioactivity, making it inhospitable. Our scans showed the radiation had fallen to negligible levels, but we could not assess the status of the tunnels themselves."

"Well, as you can see, it's clear," said Mei. "Why not take the helmet off?"

"Perhaps later," said Titus. "For now, we would prefer to keep them on."

The rest of the Blacks came out of their paralysis within the hour, just as Lena had suggested they would. Mickey and Track were the last to come back. It was a gradual recovery, with Mickey slurring his words in an attempt to compose himself, but eventually they all returned to normal.

John convened the team on the surface, right outside the entrance. He wanted to assess any damages and receive a full report of what had happened before he and Mei arrived. The story was fairly straightforward. Everyone had been working, same as usual, when the ship arrived. The toxin had hit them all within a few seconds, and all they saw from that point on was an extremely close-up view of the ground.

John stared at the ship, which Lena and Titus had referred to as "the *Red Door.*" It was an odd thing to call something, and John wondered about the significance and meaning behind the name, if there even was one. Nonetheless, he remained skeptical and on edge about these new visitors, reluctant to place his trust in someone who would so hastily attack another party.

At his insistence, Brooks and Meridy had taken to following Mei around as she walked and talked to the aliens. Mei seemed to understand the importance of it, so she didn't argue. He was thankful for it. The last thing he wanted was to leave her alone, but his team needed tending to, and a plan of action would have to be made, should the aliens prove hostile. "I want Hughes in the loft," he told them. "Keep your eyes on the aircraft. If you see another drone come out of its ass, you shoot it. Understood?"

"You got it," said Hughes. "I'll rip its wings off."

Titus had said the pilot couldn't leave his post inside the ship. It was his duty to stay put, no matter the situation, unless he received an order directly from Everlasting. The thought of a stranger sitting and waiting inside that machine gave John pause, but he played along. He trusted Mei to smooth this mess over and get things situated. In the meantime, he'd do his job and prepare for the worst-case scenario. His team wouldn't be caught off guard a second time. Not if he could help it.

Still, with any luck, there wouldn't be a problem. The last thing any of them needed was to start some kind of intergalactic incident. This was the first sentient alien species humanity had ever encountered, so they had to get it right.

God, thought John, staring at the alien ship. *How the hell did I manage to get myself into this?*

⁂

Somewhere on Kant
February 11, 2351

TERRY WALKED along the deck of the *Waveguard*, watching Hux and the crew drop anchor. They had decided on a spot near the coast of what appeared to be an island, still far from the mainland. The crystal white beaches stretched on, so at first Terry assumed this to be part of a greater landmass, but Hux had insisted it was only one in a string of islands. The Happy Rocks, he had called them, named for a nursery rhyme.

Ludo stretched his arm, cracking his neck and shoulder. "What are we doing here?" he asked. "I see no villages."

Hux let out a roar of laughter. "Rest easy, my friends. We've only come to retrieve a package, then we'll continue on our way."

"What sort of package?" asked Terry.

"A trade between two traders," Hux said, ambiguously. He went to the side of the boat, leaping onto the railing overlooking the water. "I'll return soon and we can leave."

"Are you swimming to the beach from here?" asked Terry.

Hux laughed again. "Not quite," he said, then jumped into the water, diving into the darkness below and disappearing.

Terry watched with curiosity, waiting for the wavemaster to return. A few minutes passed, however, and he began to worry. "Where is he? Shouldn't he be back by now?"

"He must be very deep," said Ludo, as though he wasn't concerned.

"He'll drown if he doesn't hurry," said Terry.

Ludo looked at him. "What do you mean? Hux is a wavemaster."

"So?" asked Terry. "What's that got to do with drowning?"

Ludo raised an eye. "Wavemasters don't drown, Terry."

"What?" he asked.

"Has Hux not explained this to you?"

Terry shook his head.

"Ah, well I apologize. I thought you knew. Wavemasters are expert swimmers and divers. They can stay beneath the water for hours."

"Seriously?" asked Terry. "Do they have gills or something?"

Ludo laughed. "No, my friend. Wavemasters are trained from the time they are children. In the same way that you and I have learned to fly, the wavemasters have mastered their bodies and learned to swim. It is in their chakka, and so they belong in the sea."

Terry watched and waited for Hux to return. After several minutes, when his attention had begun to fade, he noticed a bubble rise and pop from deep below the water. Several more followed soon. A figure moved below, and for a moment Terry could have sworn it was a large fish. The way it moved, gracefully and quickly and naturally.

Hux emerged, splashing water onto the side of the boat. He waved at the crew, and they cheered, lowering a rope ladder to lift him up. As he reached the deck, Hux swung his legs around, bringing a flood of saltwater with him.

Beneath his arm, Hux carried a small wooden box. Strands of seaweed had gotten stuck in the cracks, and Terry wondered how far below the surface the treasure had been waiting.

"I'll be in my quarters," announced the captain of the *Waveguard*. He motioned to Terry and Ludo. "Join me shortly, friends. I need to change out of these clothes first."

When Hux was out of sight, Terry looked at Ludo. "What do you think is in the box?"

"Perhaps some form of contraband," said Ludo.

"Contraband?" asked Terry. "You think he's smuggling illegal materials?"

"Wavemasters do not believe in laws," said Ludo. "If they did, we might not be aboard this ship."

Indeed, Hux had allowed the two of them to hide aboard his boat, defying the law in the process. He'd barely given it a second thought, in fact, taking them largely at their word. Anyone else might have turned them away, but not Hux. Not this wavemaster.

So, maybe he was more than a simple sailor. Maybe he was a smuggler, too. Did it really matter? Terry would choose to believe in his new friend, because it was preferable to the alternative. Everyone deserved the benefit of the doubt.

TERRY AND LUDO joined Hux in his cabin before long, gladly accepting his invitation. The wavemaster, now with a fresh change of clothes, took his seat and stretched out his legs and arms. He poured himself a drink immediately, and offered one to each of them. Both declined. Hux laughed, taking a sip from his fat wooden cup.

The box from the sea sat on the table beside him, and he smacked the top of it with a loud thud. "Has my crew told you what this is yet?" he asked, grinning. "I hope not."

"Not a word," said Terry.

Hux smacked the box again. "Good! Look here, friends." He reached a hand in his pocket and retrieved a metal key. It was shiny and fine, as though it had recently been polished. He twirled the key between his fingers, and then jammed it into the keyhole. As it turned, Terry heard a series of hard clicks. They continued for longer than he expected.

Hux cracked the box open, pulling back the top. He felt inside the chest with both his hands. "Here we are," he said, a little awe in his voice, lifting up the object. A metallic orb, by the look of it, smooth and seemingly untouched.

"What is that?" asked Ludo.

"They call them the God Eyes," said Hux.

"What are they for?" asked Terry.

"I wish I knew," said Hux, chuckling. "All I know is they're worth a hefty sum of money. Enough to keep my ship afloat for years and years to come."

"People pay money for that?" asked Terry. "Is it some kind of stone?"

Hux shook his head. "This is from Everlasting."

Both Ludo and Terry leaned in.

"The rumors say there are only twelve of these left in

all the great wide world, but I've only seen two, counting this one." Hux twisted the orb in his hands, revealing as much of it as possible.

"This really came from Everlasting?" asked Terry.

"So goes the tale," said Hux.

"Why would anyone give a fortune away for something like this? You don't even know what it does," said Terry.

"My buyer believes this to hold great power. He pays me whatever I ask for any Everlasting artifacts, so I've contacted several merchants and explorers and told them to keep their eyes open for such things."

"So much work for such a small thing," said Ludo.

"Indeed," agreed Hux. "Truth be told, I don't believe it to be anything more than a simple ornament, but some men would move mountains for an ounce of opportunity. A shred of prospect. They are hungry, driven by an over-whelming desire to collect and consume. To have every-thing. They build whole empires, but even then, it is never enough. The need for more is always there, scratching at the back of their mind. I've traveled much of the globe, and believe me when I tell you there are always powerful people seeking powerful things. There is always greed."

"If you don't believe in this thing, why did you go looking for it?" asked Terry.

Hux grinned. "I don't have to believe in fairytales in order to profit off of them."

"You don't think Everlasting is real?" asked Terry.

"I do," Hux corrected. "I've seen the city's towers

myself, riding my ship off the rocky cliffs of the eastern shore. What I doubt are rumors. Rumors by men who have never had to go and look with their own eyes. You will find there are two types of people in this world, Little Traveler: those who sit and wait, and those who go and see. The man in the golden chair will be fatter and safer, more ready to believe what he is told, but the one who leaves will find and know the truth, and he will come back changed. I would rather search the world for my own truth than be told what to believe by another."

Terry stared at the orb, not knowing what to say. Hux seemed to notice, and held the object out to him, offering it. "I couldn't," said Terry, shaking his head.

"Hold it," said Hux. "See with your own eyes. Touch with your hands. Experience this moment. Life is too short to look away."

"What if I break it?" asked Terry. "I might drop it. Aren't you worried?"

"The fact you asked the question tells me you won't," said Hux. "I believe you'll treat this as though it were a babe. Am I right?"

Terry nodded.

"I thought so."

Bravo Gate Point
February 11, 2351

A FEW HOURS of dialogue with the aliens had proven very useful, albeit a little frustrating. For starters, they refused to provide any detailed information about their home—the mysterious city of Everlasting. However, now that everyone was playing nice, Titus seemed open to the idea of introducing John and the others to his superiors.

Diplomatic relations were beginning to look like a real possibility. Sometime or another. John wasn't entirely sure. Titus kept reiterating how his team would have to return to Everlasting soon. This deadline could not be avoided—a strange notion, since encountering another sentient species seemed like it should be enough to warrant some sort of extended stay.

John just chalked it up to a cultural thing. Maybe their society prided itself on protocol. Maybe they had prior experience with aliens and had specific guidelines for dealing with them. He had no idea.

After going to the ship to radio his people about the situation, Titus returned and expressed a desire to leave behind one of his team members. "Lena Sol will stay here until we return. She is experienced with linguistics. Please help her learn your language."

"You expect us to teach her English by the time you get back?" asked John.

"It shouldn't take long," Lena said.

"As long as Sergeant Finn doesn't mind," said Mei.

"She'll have to stay in certain areas," said John, examining the woman. She was small, even in her environment suit. Not very intimidating, but he knew well enough not to judge a person based on their size. "You get it, right?"

"I'm afraid Sergeant Finn is correct," said Mei.

"An understandable precaution. Your terms should be acceptable. She only needs to learn the language," said Titus. "It won't take long."

John stared at Lena curiously. How could learning an entire language not take long? Maybe their sense of time was different. It was one thing for a machine—her translation software—to figure out a way to communicate in a short amount of time. Machines could do that sort of thing. Not people, though. Not even close.

Titus and Emile boarded the aircraft, leaving Lena behind. John watched them leave with some interest, mostly to gauge the maneuverability of their transport. It lifted into the air with little resistance, hovering with an unusually quiet engine, and then quickly accelerated forward, speeding into the distant horizon, back to the mountains.

When it was finally out of sight, John looked at Mei. "Well, this is interesting."

"I should think so," she said.

"Guess we'll have to let Central know about it."

"I'll make a call. They might want to send an actual ambassador, but we'll see. I might have a way to keep them away from this."

"You've got that kind of pull now?" he asked.

"I'm not sure *what* I've got just yet," said Mei. "But I'll keep you informed."

8

Ortego Outpost File Logs
Play Audio File 908
Recorded: February 11, 2351

CURIE: *Sophie, I need you to contact the office of Breslin Harper. I'm sending you a report and I need you to forward it to her.*

MITCHELL: *Of course, ma'am. Shall I add anything to it? A note, perhaps?*

CURIE: *Tell her I'll be contacting her as soon as I return through the gate.*

MITCHELL: *When will that be?*

CURIE: *In a few days. I have some things to do first.*

MITCHELL: *Understood. I'll make the necessary arrangements. Are you enjoying your trip? How are the aliens?*

CURIE: *Mysterious. Annoying. They don't like questions, I've* *noticed. I spent over an hour trying to get information out of them about this Everlasting place, but it was mostly fruitless. The ship left a few hours ago and headed home. There's only one of them now. A girl named Lena Sol.*

MITCHELL: *For what purpose? An ambassador?*

CURIE: *I'm still not sure. Titus mentioned something about her specializing in linguistics. It seems they want her to learn as much from us as possible.*

MITCHELL: *Do you suspect she'll try to spy on you?*

CURIE: *Maybe. John and I have agreed to keep her isolated to a single building. She's not to leave unless accompanied by a soldier.*

MITCHELL: *You're so trusting, ma'am.*

CURIE: *When someone refuses to tell you anything about themselves, it's hard to put any faith in them. For all we know, these people could be xenophobic cannibals.*

MITCHELL: *Technologically advanced alien cannibals. I believe I saw that in an old television show once.*

CURIE: *A show?*

MITCHELL: Zeta Bounty Hunters X. *It was an old pulp science fiction program. I'm sure you wouldn't like it.*

CURIE: *No, I probably wouldn't. John might, though. You should talk to him. I never knew you were into that sort of thing.*

MITCHELL: *We all have our vices, ma'am. Mine just happens to be hastily made, low-budget entertainment.*

CURIE: *And here I thought you were boring.*

End Audio File

Somewhere in Kant
February 12, 2351

"Ready yourselves, men," roared Hux as the waves beat against the side of the ship, knocking them about. A storm had struck, and its wrath was fierce and powerful.

Terry sat with Ludo in the belly of the boat, gripping the side of his bed as the whole world shook around him. Rain poured outside, filling the room with noise. He hated sitting still while others worked. It made him feel so helpless. "We should go see if they need help," he shouted, trying to speak over the downpour.

"Stay and wait," said Ludo. "We would only hinder them."

"But they might be able to use our help," said Terry, standing up.

The boat shook, and he wavered. When the storm had first appeared early this morning, neither of the suns had risen yet. The crew only had an hour to prepare for it, so they hoisted another set of sails, which they called storm sails, and attempted to outrun the chaos behind them. When they could run no further, Hux ordered the ship to stop and heave to, facing the wind and readying it for a full-on collision.

Terry quickly put his hand on the wall to steady himself. "This is crazy!"

"These storms are notoriously violent," Ludo remarked. He was strangely calm, given the circumstances.

"It makes me wish we'd walked there," said Terry.

"You should sit before the force of these waves knocks you down."

Terry nodded and took his seat again. "The storm's been going for hours. How long until it's over?"

"I do not know. I've never been in one, but the sailors say they can last days."

Days? Terry didn't know if he could make it that long. All the banging around was already too much for him.

"Easy!" yelled Hux. "Keep the cargo down! Don't let the wind grab anything!"

"They need to get inside before it gets any worse," said Terry.

"Hux said they would as soon as possible," said Ludo. "Try to relax, my friend."

Lightning cackled from outside. "Careful there! Don't you dare go falling overboard!" shouted Hux.

"Dammit, they need help," snapped Terry, getting up and going to the door. The ship rattled and he nearly fell.

"Please, you must stay here," Ludo pleaded.

But Terry wouldn't hear it. He left the room and traveled quickly down the hall toward the deck. He gripped the handle and pushed, but was shocked at the weight of it. Could it be the strength of the wind? He would find out soon.

Terry focused and breathed, and with a mighty surge,

pushed open the door. It cracked slowly, but almost immediately left his hand as the wind took hold of it, slamming it against the side of the wall. A shower of rain blew into him, stinging his face.

Looking out across the deck, he could see the crew drenched in rain and working. Nearly all of them were holding onto something, using their free hand to ready the ship and its cargo. Hux was among them, holding a rope in place. He shouted an order to a crewman by the name of Sederin, telling him to hurry up.

Sederin was new, having only recently been recruited back in Capeside. He had some prior experience on the water, but nothing more than a few voyages to the neighboring harbors. As far as Terry was aware, this might very well have been his first encounter with a storm. Sederin gave a signal in response to Hux's order, raising his hand to acknowledge the command. In doing so, however, he lost his grip. The wind tugged at him, and he slipped on the deck, which was covered in several inches of water. Sederin slid towards the stern, tumbling into a nearby crate. The impact was enough to snap the rope lashing the cargo to the deck, and the motion of the deck immediately began tossing crates about. The boxes plowed into him, pushing him further back, and finally over the edge of the deck. His scream was abruptly cut off as he was swallowed by the heaving waves.

"Man overboard!" shouted one of the crew.

"Throw the lifeline!" ordered Hux. "Lock the cargo down and get inside!"

"We can't just leave him!"

Hux ran to the edge of the deck. "Don't worry," he yelled. "I'll get him back!" Hux dove headfirst into the roaring sea, plummeting into the waves. Terry watched from the cabin door, waiting for the rest of the crew to do something. They only continued their work, though, acting as their captain had ordered.

A few minutes later, as Terry quieted his mind and listened, he heard what sounded like sobbing in the distance, along with a series of gasps. "Hold onto me," Hux commanded.

The other man attempted to answer, but could only give a whimpering slur in response.

Terry watched as a single arm came over the edge of the railing, followed by another. The wavemaster, drenched from the sea and carrying his crewman, brought himself onto the deck with incredible ease. Sederin's arms were wrapped around Hux's neck, keeping him in place. Hux carried him further toward the cabin, calling on the crew to take the man inside. Two of them brought Sederin to the cabin door, passing Terry and taking him to a bed.

Hux approached, a victorious look on his face. "Ah, Little Traveler!" he cackled. "What brings you to the storm?"

"I came to see if you needed any help," he answered.

"I appreciate the thought, but there's no need to worry."

"But someone almost died," said Terry.

"You mean that?" he asked, pointing to where Sederin had fallen in. "It wouldn't be a storm if someone didn't fall!" He let out a hearty laugh. "This is how the sea turns children into men, Little Traveler." Lightning cracked the sky, and thunder bellowed so loud it hurt. Hux grinned and beat his chest. "These are the days I live for!"

Bravo Gate Point
February 12, 2351

LENA SOL SAT in the CHU with her hands in her lap, listening intently to the strangers talk amongst themselves. She kept the translator program active, letting it display their speech in the corner of her visor as she attempted to memorize and decipher as much of their language as she possibly could. So far, her new vocabulary had expanded to nearly a hundred words. Not bad considering it had only been about half a day, a portion of which she'd slept through. With any luck, she'd have enough of the language by the end of the day to go home.

"Don't you ever take that suit off?" asked Mason Hughes.

Lena looked up at him from her seat. He stood there, a

curious look on his face, towering over her. "My suit?" she asked.

"You can breathe the air, can't you? You've had that thing on since you got here."

"It is easier," she responded.

"Easier how?" he asked.

She turned the translator's voice on, knowing she wouldn't be fully able to express her thoughts if she continued without it. "I have to wear a device on my mouth. It's very uncomfortable. The suit also protects from any radiation or hazardous disease. Please, take no offense, but you could be carrying a deadly pathogen. Until Titus returns with a medical expert, it is safer for me to remain in this suit." She bowed her head. "I mean no offense."

"None taken," he said, casually. "Just wanted to make sure you were comfortable."

"I am. Thank you."

"Doesn't it make it hard to eat or, you know, use the bathroom?" asked Alicia Short, another soldier.

"There are several nutrient bags attached to the back of the suit. On my command, the suit will rotate them and feed the contents through a straw and into my helmet," explained Lena. "If I manage the bags properly, they can last for over two dozen days."

Short looked at Hughes. "Yummy."

"Do we even want to ask about going to the bathroom?" asked Hughes.

"The suit also takes care of—"

"Alright, alright," interrupted Short. "I get it."

Hughes laughed. "So, moving on, what's it like on this planet? Is it pretty violent? What's your city like?"

"What do you mean?" asked Lena.

"I think you gotta get more specific," said Short. "She doesn't have a clue what Central's like, or even Earth. She's got nothing to compare it to."

Hughes nodded. "I get you. Well, Lena, do you live in a big place?"

"Everlasting is quite large. It has over sixty thousand residents," explained Lena. "In fact, the city is growing every year. We recently expanded the reach of the dome-guard to incorporate more landmass."

"Domeguard?" asked Short. "The hell is that?"

Lena hesitated, remembering how Titus had told her not to give them any information pertaining to the city's defenses. She shouldn't have said anything. What if her admission got back to Master Gel? She could be reprimanded. Maybe even sent to one of the facilities. A nervous flutter ran over her chest. "I apologize," she said. "I misspoke."

The door opened and Johnathan Finn entered. "How's it going in here? You two teaching her how to butcher our language?"

"You know it, sir," said Short.

"This sort of job seems better suited for a diplomat or a scientist, don't you think, boss?" asked Hughes.

"Yeah, probably," answered Finn. "But that'll have to

wait until Central sends us one. In the meantime, you two are stuck with the job."

"What about Curie's team?" asked Short.

"Left a few hours ago. Mei has to go get the person you were just asking for, or at least put in the request. She says she knows someone who can help."

Short glanced back at Lena, smiling. "Well, this one's a quick study. She's already talking in full sentences. Not sure we'll need anyone by then."

Finn closed the CHU door. He walked over to the table in the center and sat on it, facing Lena. "Is that so?"

"Show him what you got," said Short. "I'm telling you, sir. She's unreal."

Lena deactivated her translator. "Thank you, but I still have far to go. It will take me some time before I am fully conversational."

Sergeant Finn raised his brow. "Wow, you guys weren't kidding. You already know how to talk like this? It's only been a day."

"Thirteen hours, approximately," said Lena, a little proudly.

"It takes most people years to learn another language," said Hughes. "She's been at it for less than a day and she's already almost there. How nuts is that?"

"Yeah, nuts," said Finn, staring at her. "Lena, do you know when your friends are coming back? Doctor Curie went home to let our people know what's going on, but it would help if we had something more to give them."

"They should arrive within a few days. Perhaps more. It depends on what the Leadership decides."

"A little vague," said Finn.

"I apologize," said Lena. She didn't know what else to say. Everlasting had little experience dealing with technologically advanced civilizations. Certainly, these people were not on the same level as Everlasting, but they were far above the primitive tribes inhabiting this continent. There were very few protocols in place to deal with such a scenario, particularly when it came to alien lifeforms from another universe. Another reality.

Perhaps there had been, though, back when this facility had first been constructed and the portal was activated. Maybe Master Gel had access to such a document and could use it to decide what actions to take next. Such protocols were very important in Everlasting. The entire society relied on them. Order was crucial to the longevity of the city and its people. Without such practices, civilization would cease to exist. Master Gel and the rest of the Leadership had taught them as much.

"We'll just have to hold down until they get here," said Finn. "Hopefully Mei can—"

A loud roar came from outside, followed by a series of gunshots. "The hell was that?" asked Hughes.

"Better find out," said Finn, gripping his weapon. "Hughes, you're with me. Short, stay here with our guest."

Short grunted. "Alright, boss."

"Sorry, but someone's gotta babysit."

"I get it," she said.

Finn ran outside, along with Hughes. Short closed the CHU door once they were clear. "This sucks," she said.

"Sucks?" asked Lena, hearing the word for the first time.

"It means it's unfortunate," explained Short.

"The incident outside?" asked Lena.

"No," she answered, shaking her head. "It sucks I'm missing all the action."

As soon as John left the CHU, he could see motion in the woods. Several of the trees were moving, almost dancing, like weeds in the wind, except these were sturdy trees, and the wind was almost nonexistent. Something was inside the forest. Something big.

Gunfire echoed, a spray of bullets from a weapon John recognized—the same sort he carried by his side. His team was under attack. "Hurry, Hughes," he snapped, bolting through the field.

"Right behind you," said the sniper, who was readying his own weapon, bulky as it might be.

The two of them ran through the tree line toward the chaos and gunfire. They found the source of it quickly, as three soldiers had gathered around a massive beast, a snarling animal with thick legs and a large snout, with daggers for teeth.

Brooks held her rifle steady and yelled, "Let him have it!"

The other three opened fire, unleashing a swarm of heat. The animal staggered, but regained itself, seemingly uninjured. It turned toward them and snarled, heaving and growling, dripping spit and slime. "The hide's too thick," said Hatch. "Aim for the mouth and eyes!"

Before they could follow through, the animal charged, aiming itself at Brooks and Meridy. The two dodged to the side, landing several meters away, and the animal continued into a tree, ripping it from the ground. It roared a mighty cry, so loud it shook John's chest.

He could feel the adrenaline building in his body, giving way to instinct. He felt his heart calm and his muscles relax. The world around him slowed, and he heard the heavy breathing of the animal before him, grunting. The beast had its back to him, so he'd have to get around it. "Get ready to fire," he told Hughes. "I'll set you up."

"Right," said the sniper.

John bolted forward, passing to the side of the animal, firing his gun into its ribs in an attempt to get its attention.

The animal screamed at him, charging in his direction. John took a few steps back, squaring himself between two trees. As the beast pounded forward, John kicked himself off the bark and over the head of the creature, firing his weapon into his skull. Most of the bullets deflected, but a few managed to graze the animal's mouth. John landed on its spine and ran onto the ground, rolling free. He fired into its back, letting it know to turn around. "When you see its face, hit it!" he yelled.

Hughes and the other Blacks took aim and waited.

The hulking creature shook its head erratically, roaring for revenge, and soon enough it turned to find its enemy waiting patiently to its back.

The entire squad let out a storm of bullets, filling the beast with pain. Its eyes tore apart as heated metal grazed its flesh. In a fit of panic, the creature roared. It ran head-first in the direction of the camp, kicking its back legs like a raging bull.

John and the others hurried, keeping pace as best they could. But the animal was fast and wild, too afraid to stop and fight. "It's heading for the CHUs!" cried Hughes as they chased after it.

"Get out of there, Short!" John screamed so loud his voice cracked. "Short, get out of the building!"

A second later, the mammoth beast plowed straight into the structure, toppling part of the structure to the ground. It stumbled, rolling onto its side.

A woman screamed. "What the shit!"

"Short!" John yelled again. He unsheathed his knife, preparing for a close range fight. No bullets here where people could get hit. John leapt into the air, landing on the creature's back. He gripped the top of its head, readying the knife.

The animal took quick notice of him and started bucking.

John held firm, plunging the blade into the beast's eye socket and twisting.

With a wail, the animal stumbled and fell, kicking, tossing John to the ground. He rolled to his side, scrambling away, trying to avoid getting trampled. Blood gushed from the animal's skull, pooling into the broken CHU and the ground around it. It gargled as the blood filled its throat, and then all at once it went quiet and still.

Hughes ran to John's side, a look of wonder in his eyes. "Are you okay?" he asked, breathing heavily.

John nodded, slightly dazed. "I...yeah, yeah, I'm good."

"Well, I think you got him," said Hughes. "I'd say he's good and dead."

* * *

"I GOTTA SAY, Lena, your planet's getting on my nerves," said Johnathan Finn, who now wore a fresh set of clothes after the last one had been drenched in blood. "Seems like every other day, our camp is attacked by some crazy animal."

Lena had been moved to another CHU, following the destruction of the last. It was all very startling, to say the least.

She didn't fully understand the capabilities of the weapons these people carried, but she was certain they could handle themselves. If they were anything like the pistols she and her team had been assigned, then they must be powerful.

"Next time, can you boys give me some sort of heads-up? Talk about a surprise," said Short.

"I tried yelling," said John.

"Well you weren't loud enough, boss."

"Oh well. Just another monster," said John. "No big deal."

"A monster?" asked Lena.

John sat on the nearby table. "Sure. You know, deadly monsters with horrible breath that try to kill you. Haven't you ever seen one? We've had to kill at least a dozen by now."

She paused at the word *kill*. Was that the right translation? It couldn't be. Only savages and the uncivilized killed. "Please, say this again."

"Which part?" asked Short.

"Did you say you killed the animal?" she asked.

"That's right," said Hughes.

"Was it necessary? Do you not have the capability to paralyze them?"

"If you're talking about that stuff you used on my team when you first got here, the answer is no," said John.

"Then you have no means of peaceful resolution? No way to avoid violence?"

"We always try to avoid it," said John. "Sometimes you can't. Did you see how it plowed into the CHU? You were inside, right? What were we supposed to do? Let it trample you?"

"It is forbidden to kill in Everlasting. That is why we use the toxin," explained Lena.

"Sure, but like I said, we don't have that. Besides, you don't even bother to ask questions first before you dish that stuff out."

"Questions?"

"You came into our camp and took us down without so much as a hello. You didn't even try to reach out first."

"But the toxin is harmless. We would never—"

"I think our definition of the word harmless is different. We don't consider getting paralyzed a good thing."

"It's kinda bad, actually," said Hughes.

"Yeah, no good," agreed Short.

"Look, Lena, we do everything we can to avoid killing, but when it comes right down to it, you have to defend yourself," said John.

Lena gave a slight nod, but she still found the notion disturbing. It reminded her of the recent terrorist attack back home where Jinel Din, a fellow analyst, had been killed. Only extremists did such things. Only the uncivilized or the mentally ill.

The Leadership had always taught against murder, even in self-defense. If someone was found to deviate from this, they were promptly sent to either the reeducation facilities or the wellness centers. Everlasting took care of its people.

It was a safe place.

9

Ortego Outpost File Logs
Play Audio File 920
Recorded: February 12, 2351

CURIE: Have you had a chance to look over the files I sent you?

   HARPER: I only finished a few moments ago.

CURIE: And what did you conclude?

   HARPER: That you must be out of your mind.

CURIE: It's not the worst thing anyone's said about me.

   HARPER: This is incredible, Doctor Curie. Sentient life? I don't even know what to say.

   CURIE: Thank you, but I didn't do anything. We assumed whoever built that facility had long since disappeared. When they actually showed up, it was a surprise.

HARPER: *It said in your report they incapacitated your entire group. Is that right? Do you think they're dangerous?*

CURIE: *I don't think so, but we still know little about them. Their leader wasn't very forthcoming about their home. Or anything, really.*

HARPER: *This Everlasting…it's such an odd name for a city, almost as though it's missing another word. What sort of culture do you think they have?*

CURIE: *That's sort of why I'm calling. I need you to send an ambassador. Someone who represents Central. I assume you'll want a politician who knows how to speak with people. Maybe one of the board members in the Science Division.*

HARPER: *I see. I'll have to ask them. Do you have any suggestions?*

CURIE: *Not really.*

HARPER: *I'll ask around and see what I can do. I might have to get in touch with Colonel Ross as well. She'll probably want to send her own representative.*

CURIE: *Thank you for your help, Doctor Harper.*

HARPER: *Hey, you're the one who just discovered an alien race. I'm only helping you with the details.*

End Audio File

Somewhere in Kant
February 13, 2351

The ship pulled into the dock at Edgewater in the late morning. Terry helped unload a few barrels, though there wasn't much to be done.

The bulk of Hux's cargo would remain on the boat, headed straight for Tharosa. The spices and materials from Capeside and the other villages further south would sell for quite a bit upon his return. Tharosa was frozen for most of the year, locked beneath snow and ice, with very few native crops to call its own. The plants it had were deep inside its city caves, far underground. The cities were vast and sprawling with life, as busy as one could imagine, Hux had explained, with thousands of people living and working together. He'd spoken of it with such pride—strange, since Hux seemed more inclined to travel the seas than live in a city.

But then, every traveler needed a home to come back to.

When the barrels had been delivered to a merchant by the name of Plead, Terry returned to Hux's side, along with Ludo, and together the three shared a brief meal. "I have talked with Plead and he tells me he can show you the way to the border," said Hux, drinking down his glass of wine.

"Thank you, Hux," said Ludo. "There are too few men as kind as you, sir."

"No need for thanks. I would go with you myself, were I able to leave this ship. Deliveries must be made, though."

"It's more than enough," said Terry.

They finished their meal together, and Hux walked them to the dock. Plead stood there waiting, holding a cloth satchel. "Welcome to Edgewater!" exclaimed the merchant. "I'm Plead, your guide to the temple. It is good to meet you both!"

"Please, tell me of your route," said Ludo.

"Of course, dear sir," said Plead. "Please, allow me to show you a map."

Terry felt a hand on his shoulder. "Give me a moment, if you will," said Hux.

"Of course," said Terry.

Hux had a serious look on his face. "The place you're going...I trust you understand what it is."

"It's dangerous. I already know."

"Dangerous, yes," said Hux. His eyes grew distant, like he was remembering. "There is a great wall there, which stretches far and wide beyond measure. On the other side, there is a valley, stretching into the mountains. That is where they perform the ritual with the priestesses. It is where Ludo's wife will be, should you delay too long."

"What kind of hazards?" asked Terry.

"The Guardians," said Hux. "Legendary beasts. They say they protect the city of Everlasting and the gods who dwell there."

"Ludo mentioned them once. Are they real?" asked Terry.

Hux nodded. "I've seen them myself, but I don't know

what they truly are. In all my travels, I've yet to see any animal like them. They seem more like giants. Like men."

"Men? How?"

"Two legs. Two arms. A head with eyes to see. You'll know when you find them, but be wary. Do not venture into the valley unless you have to...unless there is no other choice. Do you understand?"

"I think so," said Terry.

Hux extended his arm, and Terry took it. "I am glad to have met you, Little Traveler from the unknown lands. I will see you again, once you've done what you need to. On that day, you should bring me good news."

"I will," said Terry, grasping Hux's arm. "Thank you for everything."

Bravo Gate Point
February 12, 2351

JOHN WAS SURPRISED at how quickly Lena Sol adapted to English. He'd always heard it was one of the more complex languages, but it seemed she had very little trouble with it. By the end of the first day, she was speaking basic sentences, but midway through the second she was already nearly fluent. It was truly remarkable, and that was coming from a man who'd seen some extraordinary things.

"There's always new surprises," Thistle used to tell him,

back in the early days. "Every single day, there's possibilities. That's why we can't let our guard down, kid. You never know what's around the corner."

John had listened and believed, without question. He could see the truth in what the old soldier said, and it stayed with him, even now. He thought about it often, and it kept him ready.

Always ready.

The morning suns dragged into the zenith, looming overhead and passing between a set of clouds, providing random fits of shade. The temperature on this planet was more or less the same as Earth, but it was hard to know how much it varied. Maybe if he stayed here long enough, there'd be snow. John had only ever read about blizzards, since the weather back home was generally lukewarm most of the year. He wondered if he'd find out.

The whole reason he came here in the first place was to locate Terry. So far, he'd found nothing. Maybe Lena could help him. Could Everlasting, with all of its advanced technology, track down a missing person? When he actually thought about it, John wasn't so sure.

On the one hand, Lena said the city had a satellite, which allowed them to scan large sections of the surface. They'd know there were people here before they arrived. On the other hand, they'd believed John and his team to be part of a local tribe. This, despite their armor and weapons, their physical differences. How useful would such technology be if it couldn't tell the two apart?

Oh well. He'd still talk to them and try, should the opportunity present itself. In the meantime, his team would continue to expand their search through the neighboring valleys and forests, exploring and scanning as much of the landscape as possible. With any luck, he wouldn't need to rely on these aliens for help at all.

"Boss, you got a sec?" called Short, standing near the CHUs.

John was currently on his way to the latrine, but stopped when he heard her. "Make it quick. I've got business."

"Yeah, yeah," she said. "Just wanted to let you know, Lena says her people are on their way. Should be here soon."

"Why didn't she tell us before now?" he asked.

"She told me as soon as they called her. At least, that's what she's saying."

"Alright, give me a few and I'll relieve you. When I do, I want you on the perch with Hughes. He needs his spotter in case things go south."

"I got you, boss."

John continued on his way, and Short returned to the CHU. The portal was scheduled to open once an hour now, so he'd send an update over to Mei as soon as he could. After the initial encounter with Lena's crew, a decision was made to shorten the time between openings. The portal was their only line of communication, and for now it could only be opened from the other side. Perhaps in time they'd find a way to activate it from this side, but not yet.

Hopefully, if Mei was successful, a delegate from Central would already be on their way. If not, then John might be all on his own. He'd be stuck as the first human representative to an alien species, a job which he was absolutely unqualified to do.

John checked the timestamp on his pad. Twenty more minutes before the next portal opening. That wasn't too long. He'd probably have plenty of time.

BROOKS' voice came over the radio. "We've got company!" she announced.

John came running out of the latrine, still holding his unbuttoned pants around his waist. "You gotta be kidding me," he said. "What kind of short notice—"

"Boss!" yelled Short, coming out of the CHU. "What're your orders?"

"Tell Lena her people are here," he said. "Ask her to come outside."

The aircraft landed in a matter of seconds, gently touching the ground. The CHU door opened and out walked Lena Sol with Short by her side. John joined them, and together they waited for the door of the ship to open. When it finally did a few moments later, a strange man appeared. "Hello," his suit said, translating his speech.

"Uh, hey," said John.

"My name is Master Gel," said the man. He held a case in his left hand, marked with strange symbols. He stepped off the ship and joined them on the ground. "I apologize for the delay. Leadership had to convene to provide authorization for our meeting."

"Alright," said John. He glanced at Lena, who stood quietly to his side. What would have happened if their superiors had decided against this meeting? Would they have left this woman here alone? "I sent for someone to come and talk to you. An ambassador. They haven't gotten here yet."

"Do you not speak for your city?" asked Gel.

"I do today, I guess," said John, half-smiling. He scratched his neck.

"I brought a medical scanner to examine you for contaminants. I hope you understand the necessity. We don't want to risk the spread of disease. You are from another world, after all."

"Sure, I get it," said John. "No needles, though."

"Rest assured, Sergeant Finn, our scans are extremely accurate. There is no need to penetrate your skin." Gel looked at Lena. "I hope our analyst was not unpleasant for you."

"She was fine," said John. "Already knows English and everything."

"That's good news," said Gel.

The scans proceeded soon afterward. Brooks volunteered to go first, followed by Short. John took the opportunity to step away and place a call through the portal, since the allocated time had come for it to open. Mei was already waiting for him.

"They're back already?" she asked upon hearing the news.

"Yeah, I only got a few minutes' notice. Guess that ambassador of yours needs to get here ASAP."

"I haven't heard back yet. I'm supposed to talk to Harper in a few hours. Think you can play nice with the aliens until then?"

"I'm no politician, but I'll do my best. Can't say I'll enjoy it."

"Thanks," said Mei. "Skip the next call, and I'll try to have something for you in two hours. With any luck, Harper will know who she's sending."

"Sounds good," he said.

"Stay safe over there," she answered.

He ended the call, then joined the others near the ship. When he arrived, Gel was putting the scanner back inside the case. "Already done?" asked John.

"Yes, thank you. Your people don't seem to be carrying any deadly illnesses, and whatever microorganisms you have are nothing for us to be concerned about. Though, before we allow you access to Everlasting, we will need to perform an examination on the rest of your team."

"What about germs?" asked Short. "Our immunities are different, right? Won't you get sick?"

"Everyone in Everlasting has received extensive gene therapy to prevent such illnesses. However, they are not definitive, which is why we had to perform the scans."

"So, you guys don't get sick?" asked Short.

"Illnesses have been known to happen, but such incidents are catalogued and used to prevent further outbreaks. Our medical teams work diligently to avoid contamination."

"Hold on a second," said John. "Did I mishear you, or did you just say something about entering Everlasting?"

"You heard correctly," said Gel.

"Are you inviting us to visit your home?"

"The Leadership has authorized me to escort you back to the city under certain conditions. Should our exchange go well today, you will be granted limited access and permitted to meet with some of the Leadership."

John wasn't sure what to say next. He didn't want to seem like he wasn't up to the task, but he was no ambassador or diplomat. He needed to wait for Mei to find someone.

"We have some questions to ask you, if you are willing, about your home and your people. Leadership has also given me permission to provide you with answers to a range of questions, should you decide to ask."

"I'll try to think of something," said John. He had no idea what to ask them. What the hell was he even doing in this situation in the first place?

"Would you mind if we spoke privately with our analyst? There are some things we must discuss."

"Go right ahead," said John. Whatever he could do to stall until Mei called him back. There was no way he was going to Everlasting without someone else to do all the talking.

Lena and her companions boarded the ship and closed the door.

"Wonder if she'll tell them about the wild animal almost killing her," said Short.

"Hope not," said John. "If they really look down on killing like she says, we might have a problem."

"You don't think they'll understand?"

"Who knows? We'll have to wait and see. If she's got any brains, she'll understand that we did what we had to do."

"Not sure brains are the problem, boss. Seems more like common sense."

John grunted. "Theirs or ours?"

LENA SAT aboard the *Red Door* and removed her helmet. It was good to have it off at last. She took a seat near the back of the aircraft with Master Gel. "How was your stay?" he asked her.

"It was not unpleasant," she answered.

"How is your grasp on their language?"

"I have memorized approximately six hundred words so far. Their language is more complex than some of the tribes', but not entirely foreign. It still operates on the same basic structure of many other languages in our database. The slang is rather jarring, though. They use it frequently."

"Excellent. I'm pleased to hear your progress. I was also told to ask you about their behavior. Did you see anything especially concerning about them? Anything I should report to the Leadership?"

Lena paused at the question. If she mentioned the animal attack, Master Gel would almost certainly not approve. Killing was forbidden in Everlasting, even when it came to animals. However, she did not believe these people to be intentionally hostile. They simply had no other choice. As Johnathan Finn had said, they had no toxin with which to incapacitate their enemies. Still, the thought of actually killing another living thing made her feel uneasy. That people should have to do such a thing in order to survive…it was unthinkable.

"Analyst?" asked Gel. "Was there something you wished to share?"

Lena turned over the various possibilities in her head, going through each of the discussion paths her answers might provide. The Rosenthal satellite could scan this entire region in great detail, so there was a chance the attack had been recorded. Given that she was the primary analyst for this sector, it stood to reason she had been replaced, albeit temporarily. No doubt, Master Gel had likely requested ongoing scans of this facility, especially given the arrival of an alien species. He would probably already know of the event, and so would the rest of the Leadership. In fact, such a scenario was far more likely than the alternative.

At the same time, Gel had still arrived, bringing promises of further discussions and dialogue between the two groups. The Leadership must have seen more value in maintaining the relationship than dismissing it over the death of a wild animal, no matter how forbidden such a practice might be.

So, they likely already knew, and probably didn't care. If her line of thought was accurate, she had no choice but to tell them the truth. "There was an attack on the facility by a wild animal, resulting in its death," she explained. "I did not witness the event, but I was nearby."

"We already know," said Gel, holding his hand up. "Leadership believes there was no alternative to the ordeal, based on what was observed. However, they have authorized a memory purification session for you, should you need it."

"Thank you," said Lena, but not meaning it. She had no interest in a memory purification session, despite the promise of a Sin-Din injection afterward. Twelve hours of ecstasy was hardly worth the cost of losing one's memories. "I appreciate the generous offer."

Somewhere in Kant
February 13, 2351

TERRY AND LUDO followed after Plead as he led them to his shop. Once inside, the bearded merchant shut the door behind them. "Give me a moment to get everything together for you," he said, heading to the rear pantry.

"What are you talking about?" asked Terry.

"Hux gave me a few sacks of coin in exchange for your accommodations. You can stay here tonight in the guest room upstairs, and I've got food for the journey. It will take me some time tonight to prepare everything, but don't worry. I'll have it all ready for you by the morning. We can leave as soon as you want."

"Hux gave you money for us?"

"He did," said Plead. "A generous amount, too, I should say. You'll tell him I helped you, yes? He's a good customer. Always brings me the best materials from Tharosa."

Plead disappeared into the back, leaving them alone in the shop. "Hux is a good man," said Ludo. "I should like to thank him when I see him next."

"Me too," said Terry.

"The border is not far from here. Less than a day, if I remember correctly."

"Do you think we'll run into any trouble?"

"There are no checkpoints between here and the temple," said Ludo. "But anything could happen."

Terry thought back to the attack on the farm. Gast

Maldeen had captured them and burned their house to the ground, and neither Terry nor Ludo had seen it coming. *I won't be caught off guard again*, he thought.

Plead reappeared after a few moments with a stack of bread and cheese in his arms. "I've brought a snack," he exclaimed, cheerfully. "Something to tide you until the bird is ready."

"Thank you so much," said Ludo, smiling.

"Think nothing of it. Any friends of Hux are welcome here!"

Terry took a piece of bread and several slices of cheese, wolfing them down with startling speed. As he did, he grew even hungrier. The pain in his stomach intensified, which surprised him. Had he really been so famished?

The meal itself was ready within the hour. Roasted matta, a type of bird, with sides of krinto and pallin, two delicacies exclusive to this city. The krinto was similar to mashed potatoes, but crispier and spicy, while the pallin had the texture of a bean with the taste of honey. Every dish was different and new, and Terry found he enjoyed them all. Was this what it was like to travel to different places around the world? Was this what Hux's life was like?

They finished eating, and Plead showed them to their room upstairs. "I'll wake you in the morning," he told them, and left them to themselves.

As he did on most days, Ludo took the time to meditate. He had missed a few sessions, but still found time whenever possible for the practice. It was a necessity, he would say. A part of one's life, the same as breathing or sleeping.

Terry joined him, taking a seat on the floor beside him.

Soon, he found himself inside his own mind, walking in the summer fields of Ludo's farm. The warm breeze blew hard against his cheeks. Birds fluttered overhead, and in the distance the soft flow of a river gushed through a forest.

Terry smiled and took a deep and pleasant breath. No matter where he walked in life, no matter what cities or continents he visited, he could always return to this scene.

Hux had spoken of his own home with such longing and reverence, despite his desire to travel. It was good to have a place to come back to, and while this farm no longer existed in the real world, at least it would not be lost to him, not as long as he had it here inside his mind.

Not as long as he had the memory.

10

Ortego Outpost File Logs
Play Audio File 932
Recorded: February 13, 2351

CURIE: Has the board come to a decision on the matter of who they want to send? We need someone as quickly as possible.

HARPER: I'm happy to say that we have.

CURIE: Wonderful. When can I expect them?

HARPER: Right now, I'd guess.

CURIE: You mean they're already on their way?

HARPER: Oh, not quite. I was referring to you, Doctor Curie.

CURIE: Me? What do you mean? I can't—

HARPER: Of course you can. You're more familiar with the situation than anyone else. You had to know we were considering you as a representative.

CURIE: *Not really. I'm no ambassador.*

HARPER: *Neither is anyone else in this city. Remember, we've been alone for two centuries, and it's not like anyone's sitting around training for the job. Nobody ever expected us to find another group of survivors, let alone an alien race. Considering you've already spent time with them, you're more prepared than anyone around here.*

CURIE: *I don't know how I feel about representing Central in any sort of negotiations. I'm not even a board member.*

HARPER: *You know as well as I do how useless the board is. Imagine if we sent one of those idiots there. They wouldn't know what to do.*

CURIE: *Aren't you a board member, too?*

HARPER: *And look where I am. Sitting behind this desk answering calls from a scientist in the field. No, Doctor Curie, you're the one for the job. There is no one else.*

End Audio File

Bravo Gate Point
February 13, 2351

John watched as the portal opened, Lena Sol and Gel standing beside him. They had asked to see the activation process in action. John couldn't see the harm.

The ring erupted into a dark void, swirling chaotically

as it transformed itself into a window. A second later, the cloud settled, and an image of the other side appeared.

Mei walked through, two bags in her hands.

Sophie stood behind her near the back of the room. John waved at her, and she returned it right as the event horizon collapsed.

"Sorry to keep you waiting," said Mei, stepping off the ramp.

"Mei, you remember our pals," said John.

"I remember Lena," said Mei.

"This is Master Analyst Gel," said Lena.

"Sergeant Finn tells me that you'll be representing your people in our talks," said Gel.

"It looks like it," she said, handing the bags to John. He took them, frowning.

"Whenever you're ready, I'd like to discuss our guidelines regarding outsiders entering Everlasting."

"Entering Everlasting?" she echoed.

"You are to join us in the High Room. The Leadership would like to meet with you. They're very interested to meet the visitors from another universe."

Mei blinked. "Huh?"

"I think your translator's busted," said John. "Sounded like you said another universe, unless that's what you guys call a planet."

"I don't think so," said Gel. "Analyst?"

"I believe the translation is correct," said Lena.

"This portal breaks the seal between realities. It is a

trans-dimensional gate. Were you unaware of this?" asked Gel.

"Wait a second. Are you saying we've been traveling back and forth between two universes?" asked Mei.

"Absolutely. Our predecessors built this facility specifically for that purpose," he responded. "They were exploring a method of transporting matter across vast distances. Things did not proceed as planned, however, and this bridge was made instead. A portal between realities."

"Wait," said John, trying to think. "You're saying we're not in the Milky Way anymore?"

Mei sighed. "That's a galaxy, John, not a universe."

"Oh," said John.

"Anyway," Mei continued, "if I'm understanding this correctly, this is simply another version of our world. Very different, but still the same."

"That's a difficult question to answer. No one from this side has ever seen your world, so comparisons are impossible. We would have to collect our own data for analysis."

"There's two suns, though," said John, tilting his head. "How can you have two suns and still be the same planet?"

"Theoretically, there are multiple universes, possibly infinite, each a little different from the last. In this reality, the solar system has two suns instead of only one. In another, it might not have any at all." Mei scratched her ear, tugging a strand of her hair. "For all we know, there could be a billion universes layered on top of one another, each with a different race, a different atmosphere."

"There you go again with your head in the clouds," said John.

"It's fascinating to think about. If what you're saying is true, Gel, the implications are staggering," said Mei.

"Indeed," he said. "Though, I must admit I am surprised to learn of your ignorance. We assumed you understood the capabilities of this machine, given how you were able to activate it from the other side."

Mei's eyes reflected a brief annoyance, but the look quickly disappeared. Had John not known it firsthand, he may have missed it entirely. She was good at concealing her feelings, especially when dealing with strangers. Central had chosen their ambassador wisely, whether or not they knew it. Mei had a higher tolerance for this sort of thing than anyone else he knew. "Well, thank you for clarifying the situation."

Gel nodded. "If you wish, we can leave immediately," said Gel without missing a beat.

"Of course. I just need to speak with Sergeant Finn for a few minutes to go over some things. It won't take very long."

"Understood. We'll be waiting on the aircraft whenever you're ready." He started to leave.

"Sir," said Lena.

He stopped. "What is it, Analyst?"

"The machine. Do you remember?"

"Ah, yes," he said. "I brought a technician to assist you

with the bridge. We believe we can open it from this side so that you no longer have to wait."

"Oh, that would be helpful. Thank you," said Mei.

"We are happy to assist," said Gel.

"You understand we'll need to supervise the process."

"Of course," he said.

They headed back to the surface. Gel and Lena joined their people aboard the ship, while John and Mei proceeded to the largest CHU. John collapsed into one of the chairs. "This sucks. I can't believe Central didn't send someone else to do the talks."

"You don't want me going?" asked Mei.

"I don't like the idea of you alone inside their city. We barely know those people," he said. "You'd better take a few of my crew with you, just to be safe."

She giggled. "I meant to talk to you about that. After I spoke with you last, Harper contacted me again. Apparently, the military wants their own representative to be there."

He straightened. "Oh?"

"It's funny. I was about to tell her to put your name in, but it seems Colonel Ross already did."

It made sense, he supposed. John was already here, and he had the most experience. Ross probably weighed her options and he was simply the most logical choice. "She just likes me. That's the reason."

"Sure she does," said Mei.

"I'm a likeable guy, you know. Everyone says so." He

leaned in and put his arm around her. "I lured you in, didn't I?"

She beamed a grin at him. "You're just persistent, that's all."

"Same difference."

"Think you'll be able to handle the responsibility you've just been given?"

"Probably not. I'm kind of reckless, ya know. Untamed, you might say."

"Whatever. I'll keep you in check."

"What about you? Think you can handle being an ambassador to an alien race of technologically advanced weirdos?"

"I've dealt with worse," said Mei.

"Sure, your old boss," said John.

"She was demoted and moved to Salamander outpost. Don't mess with me, buster. I'm dangerous."

John laughed, not because it was funny, but because it was true.

Somewhere in Kant
February 13, 2351

TERRY WAS glad to be on the road, though he liked the sea as well. His time with Hux had shown him something new, and for that he was thankful. There was so much variety to the world, he had found. The more he thought about it, the more he wondered what else there was to see.

After providing them with sacks of food and drink, along with a few extra sets of clothes and a clean bath, Plead took Terry and Ludo to his traveling cart, which he had parked a short walk from his shop. Plead often traveled between the nearby villages, carrying supplies and selling them to his many clients. Hux delivered a variety of materials to Plead, and the partnership had made him very wealthy over the years. It was for this reason, he explained, that he had agreed to assist with escorting Terry and Ludo to the Temple of the Eye. Plead did not go there often, but he knew the path well enough.

He did not foresee any delays, and Ludo was thankful to hear it.

Ahead of the cart were two domesticated animals, which Terry had only had the pleasure of seeing one other time, back in Capeside, and only in passing. Plead had called them haddins, similar in many respects to oxen but without the horns. Large, muscular, and with burgundy fur, the animals could pull fifteen hundred kilograms for two days without tiring. They were also fairly intelligent, and would stick to whatever path their master put before them. If trained properly, they could even memorize routes. Haddins, Plead had told them, were the perfect laborers.

Terry jumped into the back of the cart, along with Ludo, as Plead handed him some supplies. "We'll be at the temple by tomorrow," said Plead.

"That soon?" asked Terry.

"My cart doesn't stop. We can travel through the night. I'll sleep once we arrive."

"Thank you for doing this," Ludo told him. He'd expressed his gratitude to the man several times since yesterday.

Plead smiled and raised his hand. "Please, sir, you flatter me. I am happy to do it. I've been meaning to sell some of my incense to the priests and priestesses. This is the perfect opportunity to try to open a new route."

Ludo gave the merchant a happy nod and continued moving supplies. When they were finally done, Plead set the haddins to moving, and the cart began its trek across the eastern countryside.

As the hours passed, Ludo and Terry decided to meditate in order to prepare themselves. "We must clear the mind if we are to stay vigilant," said Ludo. "There will be opposition when we arrive, and things may not go smoothly."

"You think we'll get into a fight?" asked Terry.

"I would not presume to guess our fates, but I believe in being prepared. The temple guards are some of the most decorated in the region, given their station because of their valor and proven worth in combat," said the farmer. "We would do well to be as cautious as possible."

Terry believed his friend, as he often did about such things. He would not let down his guard when they arrived, not for a single moment. The lives of his friends were in the balance, and Terry would do whatever it took to keep them safe. This he swore to himself, sitting there in the back of the traveling cart, meditating, and reflecting.

THE JOURNEY to the temple lasted for over a day. The sun set and rose in the time it took to travel through the countryside, but when Terry opened his eyes to the morning light, he could hear voices in the distance. Dozens of them. Maybe more.

Ludo sat meditating on the other side of the cart, his eyes shut. He was entirely motionless. Probably far away somewhere, dreaming of another world.

Terry sighed and licked his lips. He was more than a little thirsty, having drunk most of his water the night before. What he wouldn't give for some Academy cafeteria orange juice right about now.

The cart continued to bump along the road, and the sounds of the temple grew louder. "Ludo," said Terry. "Hey, we're almost there."

The farmer stirred, but was slow to open his eyes. "Already?" he asked. "Has so much time gone by?"

"How long did you meditate?"

"Not meditating," muttered Ludo. "I was dreaming."

"Good things, I hope," said Terry.

Ludo smiled, although there was a touch of sadness to

it. "We were on the farm, all of us. You and I, Ysa and Talo. Even Grandmother…and everyone was happy."

"It sounds like a good dream," said Terry.

"We must make it come true," Ludo insisted. "Together, as chakka-kin, we will bring our family home again."

"We will," agreed Terry.

The cart came to a stop a short distance from the edge of the temple grounds. Plead dismounted and came to the rear, raising the flap. "We're here, or nearly. Are the two of you prepared? Shall I take us in?"

Terry waited for Ludo, letting him give the order.

The farmer replied immediately. "Let us go," he told the merchant. "We are ready."

Plead clapped his hands together with excitement. "Right! I'll take the cart to the rear of the temple with the other traders. There is a stretch of them there selling knockoff jewels and lackluster goods. Wait until they see what Plead has brought." He smirked and closed the flap.

As the cart proceeded, Terry listened with great interest to the voices from the temple grounds. He wondered who they were and why they had come. As Ludo had told him, the temple was a place of both worship and sacrifice, where priestesses came to pay tribute, often with their very lives.

How many Gast Maldeens were walking on these hallowed grounds? How many people with unbelievable power? Would he have to fight them all to save a farmer's wife? Would he and Ludo have to kill again?

As humanity itself had shown, true believers could be

dangerous. They did terrible things to each other, and in their minds it was always justified. Genocide wasn't so bad as long as the gods gave it their blessing.

All throughout mankind's history, death had followed faith. Here, it seemed, the tradition was still ongoing.

The cart came to a stop right as it entered the grounds. "Hello, good sir," said Plead. "It's a wonderful morning, isn't it? The Eye is on us today!"

"What business do you have here?" asked a man with a husky voice.

"I've got goods to sell. Fabrics for the temple, food, and spices. A variety of things from the southern harbors and across the sea. All the finest things!"

The man grunted. "You brought it all yourself?"

"Oh, certainly not! I have two apprentices in the back. Stronger than me, I can assure you."

The stranger walked to the rear of the cart, each footstep growing louder. Terry focused on the motions of his body, the clanking coins in his pocket, the wind against his tunic. By the time he reached the rear, Terry already had an image in his mind. "Hello, sir," said Ludo, opening the flap before the guard could do it. He stepped out into the dirt. "It is good to be here...in such a holy place."

The man nodded, turning to Terry. "You there. Step outside."

Terry did as he was told, saying nothing.

The guard observed him, a look of growing concern on

his face. "Is something wrong with you?" he asked, after a moment.

"This one is a foreigner," said Plead, almost dismissively. "Pay him no mind."

"A foreigner?" asked the guard.

"He is from Lexine," said Ludo.

"Where?" asked the man.

"From across the sea to the east," said Plead.

"What sort of place is it?"

"There are a lot of deserts. Not very civilized."

"He's so pale, though," said the guard.

"I came here when I was younger. I arrived in Capeside as a baby and never went back," said Terry, trying to hasten the conversation.

"I've heard of your country, I think," said the guard, nodding along.

"Shall we continue, sir? Oh, and please take one of these fruits. Ripe and delicious, believe me," said Plead.

"Yes, very well. Go ahead to where the other merchants are. Stay out of the way, and no selling during the Day of the Eye. That's tomorrow. Do you understand?"

"Yes, sir. Thank you very much for your patience," said Plead.

Terry and Ludo got back into the cart, leaving the guard with the husky voice to munch on his newly acquired piece of fruit. As Plead brought them around to the side of the temple, Terry caught a glimpse of something standing in the distance, blocking the horizon. It was a wall, and he was surprised at how far it seemed to stretch. Even with his hybrid eyes, he couldn't see its end. The wall was mostly obsidian black, though smaller pieces were white and gray. He couldn't tell what sort of material it was, though it rose at least a hundred meters into the sky. "Is that the border?" asked Terry, gawking.

"It is, indeed, and inside lies Everlasting," answered Ludo.

"Does it go all the way around the city?"

"So the stories go, but no one knows for certain. Some have tried to walk the whole of it, but most gave up and returned."

"Why? How hard could it be to follow it around?"

"There are mountains eventually, and even an ocean," explained Ludo. "But worse, still, there are the Guardians, who stop any who linger near the wall for too long."

The Guardians Terry thought, remembering what Hux had told him. Demons shaped like men. Deadly and dangerous. Giant killers looking to destroy.

Despite his own curiosity, he would stay far away from the border's walls. They had come to retrieve Ysa and bring her safely home. With any luck, they'd be gone this time tomorrow.

PART II

The only means of ridding man of crime
is ridding him of freedom.
— Yevgeny Zamyatin

Cage an eagle and it will bite at the wires,
be they of iron or of gold.
— Henrik Ibsen

11

Ortego Outpost File Logs
Play Audio File 965
Recorded: February 15, 2351

CURIE: *This is the last time I'll be able to speak with you for a while. Zoe and Bart will remain behind at the outpost. They'll return in a few days, once their work is finished.*

    MITCHELL: *When should I expect you back?*

    CURIE: *I don't know. Maybe a few days. I can't imagine we'll stay longer than that. In case we do, though, I need you to do something for me, Sophie.*

    MITCHELL: *Of course, ma'am. What is it?*

    CURIE: *If you haven't heard from me in five days, I need you to disable the portal.*

MITCHELL: *Disable it? Oh...I see. You're concerned we might get attacked, is that it?*

CURIE: *Right as always. I've seen their technology. The ship they came here in is highly advanced. The same goes for their armor and weapons. John managed to disarm a few of them, but Central only has so many Variant hybrids. Even if we had an army, it still might not be enough.*

MITCHELL: *I understand. Don't worry, ma'am. I'll do the job.*

CURIE: *I know you will, Sophie.*

MITCHELL: *In the case of such an event, what should I tell Harper and the rest of the board?*

CURIE: *The truth, I'd imagine. Tell them you were following orders. I don't mind taking the blame. I'll be too far away to give a damn.*

MITCHELL: *You'll excuse me if I remain optimistic about your return.*

CURIE: *Of course. I'm not planning to go off and die. I still have things to do.*

End Audio File

Bravo Gate Point
February 15, 2351

Mei ordered Zoe and Bart to stay behind to work in

conjunction with the technician from Everlasting. "Don't let him out of your sight. You limit his access and observe his actions as carefully as possible," she told them.

"You don't trust them?" asked Zoe. "What am I saying? Of course you don't."

"Nor should she," muttered Bart.

"We barely know these people. Just because they've offered to help, it doesn't mean they're our friends," said Mei.

"Got it. No trust," said Zoe.

"Record everything, if you can. Have him explain everything he does in detail as he does it. If you suspect he's doing something suspicious, pull him away."

"Brooks is in charge while I'm gone," continued John. "She'll post someone in the room with you while you work, just in case."

"I don't need any babysitting," Bart insisted.

"Not saying you do, but everyone needs backup."

"So, how do we get in touch with you if we need you?" asked Zoe.

Mei took out her pad, showing her the screen. "See this?" she asked. It was a picture of a small device resting on a crate.

"What is it?" asked Zoe.

"That's a communicator that Lena gave me. Gel brought it for the exact reason you're asking about."

"Why'd you take a picture of it?"

"In case it's bugged," she said. "Obviously."

Zoe laughed. "You sure are paranoid, ma'am."

"After what happened with Tremaine bugging our entire outpost, can you blame me? We can't let these people know everything. Not if there's a chance of them betraying our trust."

"Smart thinking, Doc," said Bart. "I like where your head is at."

"At any rate, we need to understand how this machine works. Should everything fall apart and these people prove hostile, we may have to shut the whole operation down. If so, I don't want any hiccups. Find out how this thing works. Learn as much as you can."

"We understand," said Zoe. "Don't worry, ma'am. We won't let you down."

Mei nodded. "I know you won't. You never do."

John escorted her back to the landing zone, signaling his team to break apart. Half would remain behind to guard the gate, while the rest would go along to Everlasting.

Short, Hughes, Track, and Mickey all piled into the aircraft, taking seats along a side adjacent to one another. John sat next to Mei. "Think this Everlasting place is worth the trip?" asked Short.

"I'll tell you one thing," said Track. "If it's underground, you can count me out. I'll stay inside the plane."

"I'm not sure this thing's a plane," said Hughes.

"Whatever it is, I ain't leaving it."

"The city is on the surface," said Lena, surprising them.

She'd apparently snuck into her seat without anyone realizing.

"How's that work if you can't breathe the gas?" asked Hughes.

"There's a protective shield in place. It has its own atmosphere."

"Neat," said Mickey.

The engines started, and a low hum erupted from the floors, vibrating their seats. John watched from behind a glass window as the *Red Door* lifted off the ground. Several of the remaining Blacks—Meridy, Brooks, and Hatch— waved. John hoped to be back as soon as possible, but his confidence in Brooks to handle things was firm. She'd led this team for several months while he was visiting Mei at the Ortego outpost. She could handle this, too.

The *Red Door* began to accelerate, leaving the camp and the other Blacks behind. John watched as they faded from view, overshadowed by the forest trees and, eventually, the mountain peaks. The ship soared high into the stratosphere, piercing clouds. When it emerged, the world seemed to transform. The land faded beneath them, revealing the clearest sky he'd seen in days.

He wondered how far Everlasting truly was from their camp, and what such a place might be. Would it be dangerous? He hoped not. The last thing they needed was another fight. With any luck, the aliens would have some kind of technology to help him locate Terry. It was the reason he had, after all, leapt through the rift in the first place.

It was the only thing that mattered.

The Temple of the Eye
February 15, 2351

THEY HAD BEEN at the temple for nearly a day. The first afternoon was spent unloading supplies and transforming the cart into a standalone shop. As Plead had said, they had to play the part before beginning their true mission. During the day, they'd sit around and sell their goods, talk to people and ask questions about the temple, walk around and get a feel for the layout. Once they knew where to go, they'd strike at night and rescue Ysa, then be packed and gone before the suns rose in the morning. No one would know until it was too late.

With any luck, they'd be out of here by tomorrow.

"Hand me that jug, would you?" asked Plead, motioning to the side of the cart.

"Oh, sorry," said Terry.

"Your mind somewhere else?" asked Plead. "It's best to stay here. Keep your head on the prize, you know?"

Terry handed over the jug, and Plead poured him a cup of water.

"Don't leave for a bit, yes? I'm going to talk to our friends at the meat cart. I'll see if I can get some information."

"Be careful," said Terry.

"Don't worry about me. I'm as subtle as they come," said Plead, leaving with a grin.

Terry wasn't so sure about that, given what he saw at the gate the day before. Plead was a good man, probably not used to wearing such a big lie. If he wasn't careful, the entire operation would be blown.

Ludo came around the side of the nearest building, carrying an armful of chopped wood. He'd gone into the forest with a few of the other apprentice merchants to retrieve some kindling for the community fire, which the band of travelers lit together every night. Ludo volunteered to do it himself, suggesting he might learn a thing or two from the other men. Maybe even catch a glimpse of something. Perhaps Ysa, if he should be so lucky. Maybe he would spot her leaving one of the tents, preparing for the upcoming ceremony.

But as he returned from the woods still wearing the same expression he'd left with, Terry knew his friend had been unsuccessful. Nothing had changed, and Ysa was still lost.

Ludo dropped the firewood off at the rear of the cart. Terry poured him a cup of water and handed it over. "Thirsty?" he asked.

"Thank you," said the farmer, accepting the gift.

"Plead took off for a few minutes, but he should be back in a bit. Did you learn anything new from the others while you guys were in the woods?"

"Nothing we did not already know, I'm afraid," said Ludo, gulping the water down. "They only talked briefly about the ritual. A bet was placed on how many of the priestesses would die this year. The average was three." The energy in his voice was entirely gone.

"Don't worry. We'll find Ysa before it comes to that," said Terry.

"Right," said Ludo. He climbed into the back of the cart. "I'm going to rest for an hour. Wake me if I sleep too long, would you?"

"Sure," said Terry.

It was concerning, seeing Ludo with such a dour look in his eyes. Perhaps the many restless nights had finally caught up with him.

Plead returned from the meat cart after a while with a slab of bloody flesh resting on a metal hook. It carried an awful smell, like something rotten. Terry couldn't help but plug his nose.

Plead laughed when he saw him. "Sorry about that," he said, taking the meat behind the cart. There were several small pikes in the ground, which he used to hang the meat. "They call this Pinstridge. It might not have the greatest scent, but the taste is incredible, and it's filling."

"If you say so."

Plead motioned for Terry to come closer, near the side of the cart where no one could see them. "I was talking to the owner of the other shop. I mentioned that I had only been here one other time, so I was unfamiliar with the layout of the temple. He was happy to help with information."

"We already know what most of the tents are for, though," said Terry.

"Right, but not all of them, and we still don't know where your friend is," said Plead, referring to Ysa.

"Did you find out?"

Plead grinned. "They're not here."

Inside the cart, Ludo stirred.

Terry kept his focus on Plead. "What do you mean?"

"Each of the priestesses are staying in another location. It's not too far from here, but we'll raise suspicion if we go right now. I suggest waiting for nightfall."

"Where are they?" asked Terry.

"Further east. The butcher called it the Sanctum. It's a cathedral, by the sound of it."

"We will go tonight," said Ludo, speaking at last.

Plead looked surprised. "I see our friend is awake."

Terry leaned in closer to the side of the cart. "Ludo, wouldn't it be better to wait for them to come to us? He just said they'll be here tomorrow."

"No, it must be tonight. If we wait too long, we may lose our chance to rescue Ysa," he said.

"He's right. This temple has guards stationed all around it," said Plead.

"You don't think the monastery will be the same?" asked Terry.

"Perhaps so, but when the priestesses arrive, they will

likely bring their guards with them. The odds of success would drop considerably," explained Plead.

"Alright, you've convinced me. How long after dark should we leave?"

"The two of you," began Plead, "will leave a few periods after Jino sets. I'll wait here and prepare the cart for departure." Jino was the name given for the second sun, with Luxa being the first. According to legend, there was once a great war in heaven between thousands of immortal gods. Jino was on one side of the conflict, while Luxa was on the other. They were both considered the greatest fighters in existence. It was said that if the two should meet on the battlefield, the fate of the war would be determined.

As it happened, this was exactly what happened, but instead of trying to cut each other's throats, the two gods found they were unable to raise their swords. They fell in love almost immediately—a common theme in Kant's ancient stories—and resolved to end the conflict once and for all. After a few days of intense debate, they finally managed to convince their leaders to lay down their arms and end the war. All because two warriors fell in love.

Afterwards, Jino and Luxa were gifted the responsibility of protecting Kant, blessing them with the gods' most favored world. Terry had always thought it was a nice story in an otherwise violent world.

"You're not coming with us?" asked Terry.

"Of course not. Don't be ridiculous. Do I look like a soldier or a high priest? I'd end up dying in a ditch somewhere if I went along with you," said Plead. "No, I'll stay here with my cart, if you don't mind."

"Ludo, does this work for you?" asked Terry.

"If it means finding and saving Ysa, then I will do what needs to be done," he answered.

Terry walked around to the rear and raised the flap, shining some light on his exhausted friend. "You need to get some rest beforehand. You understand, Ludo? I can't have you keeling over on me when we're in the middle of a fight."

"Don't worry," said Ludo, sitting up and closing his eyes, taking on a position of meditation. "I need only clear my mind. It may take a few moments, but I'll be ready when the time comes."

Terry nodded. "I'll come and get you later." He closed the flap, leaving the farmer to rest. If only they'd arrived a few days earlier, Ludo might still have enough energy in him to be useful. If he hadn't slept by the time the hour came, later tonight, Terry might very well have to leave him behind.

The Red Door
February 15, 2351

THE SHIP FLEW over the landscape of Kant with unparalleled speed. It was unlike anything John had ever witnessed.

Forests, rivers, and lakes came into view and then faded, all within the same minute of one another. The only things that lingered were the mountains in the west, which rose high into the violet sky, piercing clouds for several kilometers.

According to Lena, Everlasting was far to the north, near the edge of the continent. John expected such a trip to take hours, but was surprised to learn it would be much sooner.

After about forty-five minutes, the pilot announced they had entered Everlasting airspace. They would be there shortly.

"How far did we just travel?" asked Mickey.

"I'm sure they measure distance differently than we do," said Mei.

"Indeed. It would be difficult to answer without knowing your measurements," said Gel.

"Do you have a map?" asked Mei.

Gel nodded. "Lena, can you show them?"

"Yes, sir," she responded, and a holographic display appeared before them. It showed a large landmass, ripe with mountains, rivers, and lakes. There were several dots scattered across, with strange markings next to each. One of the dots lit up, blinking neon blue. Lena did all of this without moving. "This is where the facility is. Where we retrieved you."

Another dot began to blink, also blue, far to the north. "This is the *Red Door*."

A third dot followed, finally, a short distance from the second. It was much larger than the others. "And here is Everlasting."

"Are these mountains to scale?" asked Mei.

"They are," answered Lena.

"Incredible. We traveled…this has to be at least a thousand kilometers. Probably more. We did this in under a few hours?" asked Mei.

"The ship achieved suborbital status and then descended to where we are now, making for a faster flight than if we would have stayed at this elevation," said Lena.

"What's she talking about?" asked Mickey.

"The ship went really high up and then came back down," said Short.

"And that made us go faster?" asked Mickey.

"I've heard about this," said Mei, looking at John. "We used to have ships like this, before the Jolt. You could make it from Tokyo to New York in just a few hours."

"What's Tokyo?" asked Hughes.

"It doesn't matter. The point is those two places were really far from one another," said Mei. She glanced out the cabin window. "Only the military and billionaires had them, if I remember right. Taking a plane like that was expensive because of fuel costs. They used to tell people this type of transportation would eventually be affordable and easy, but it never actually happened."

"Because of the Jolt?" asked Hughes.

"Correct," she answered.

"Then you understand?" asked Lena.

"We do," said Mei. "Thank you for the explanation."

"You're very welcome," said Lena, and the hologram shattered, dissolving back into the air.

John leaned against the hull, staring out into the distance, and spotted an object. It was massive, filled with glistening towers and activity—vehicles flying from one place to the other. It was Everlasting, and he could already tell it was massive and sprawling with life. "Hey, check it out," he said, pressing his finger against the glass.

"I can barely see anything," said Hughes.

"You don't have the Sarge's eyes," said Track.

Mei leaned in beside John. "I see it," she whispered. "It's incredible."

There were so many buildings, John couldn't begin to count them. So many people walking on the ground between them, and those were the ones outside. "It's bigger than I thought it would be."

A sudden fear rose in his gut as he watched from behind the glass. A reminder of what could happen, should the talks fail. If Everlasting was so powerful, and its people this plentiful, then Central stood no chance at all. The threat would be undeniable.

Maybe I should let Mei do all the talking, he thought, right as the *Red Door* began its descent into the city.

JOHN HARDLY FELT it when the aircraft touched down on the landing platform. It was certainly a graceful machine, if nothing else.

The door opened almost immediately, and a blue light filled the cabin. "The hell is that?" he asked, shielding his eyes.

"The biometric scanner. It's automatic. Please ignore it," said Gel.

"Hard to ignore something so bright."

John stepped off the ship, but stopped when he saw where they'd landed. The ship had brought them into a loading bay of some kind, with curved walls resembling the inside of an egg. The landing platform sat in the center, connected to an elevated path into the facility. Lights flickered in the distance. He spotted a few other platforms at various points above and below this one, many with ships of their own.

Everyone piled out of the *Red Door*. "Whoa, check this place out," said Track.

Short cracked her neck and stretched out her arms. "Finally. Can't stand sitting that long."

"It was only a few hours," said Hughes.

"Quiet down," ordered John. "Eyes up and ears open while we're here. Everyone follow?"

"Yes, sir," said Short, suddenly serious.

Lena and Gel disembarked from the ship, following the others. "If you will come with us, please, we'll take you to your rooms. The Leadership has expressed you be given whatever you need during your stay with us," said Gel.

"We appreciate it, but when will we be meeting with them?" asked Mei.

"Tomorrow morning, I believe. For now, Lena Sol will show you to your rooms." He gave a slight bow. "Good day to you."

"Thank you," said Mei.

"Follow me, please," said Lena. She led them out of the landing bay and through a corridor. Everything was so clean and smooth, a far cry from what Central had to offer.

"Think the food here is good?" asked Hughes.

"Seems classy so far," said Short.

"Wonder if they know what chocolate is."

"I wouldn't count on it."

They came around a small corner and entered another room. It reminded John of the train stations back home, only smaller. Like those, this one had a tunnel running through it, with a loading platform at the center. Lena Sol approached the side of it, standing completely still and saying nothing.

A sound erupted from within the tunnel, like a piece of metal unlatching itself. "Did you hear that?" he asked, looking around.

"Yeah," said Mei. "Is it coming from the tunnel? Can you see anything—"

Before she could finish, a vehicle appeared from inside.

It was much smaller than the trains, more compact. The whole thing looked like a long, white box with curved edges.

It came to a stop right in front of Lena, and two doors slid open. "This is a transportation vehicle known as an ipp." She paused. "I believe the proper translation is egg."

John tried to see the resemblance to an actual egg, but couldn't. *Must be a cultural thing.*

"Inside, please," said Lena, inviting them in with a sweep of her hand.

"Guess we're going on another trip," said Hughes.

"Hopefully not a long one," said Short.

The inside was fairly minimalist, with a single row of seats lining each of the walls. As soon as the doors closed, however, the walls flickered and changed, transitioning into what seemed to be glass. It was like it was no longer there. "The hell just happened?" asked Hughes.

"Did the walls disappear?" asked Track.

The vehicle started moving, passing into the tunnel, accelerating quickly and quietly. John couldn't help but feel like he was riding through the barrel of a gun.

As the tunnel curved, a flicker of light caught his eye from further down the line.

The vehicle exited the covering and a blanket of sunlight swept over them. They were outside now, driving on a slightly elevated track several yards above a pool of water. Several ships flew overhead, cruising between skyscrapers.

To their right, a second vehicle identical to their own passed by them, heading in the opposite direction. It appeared to be filled to capacity with people, many of whom were smiling and talking.

The light faded as they entered another building. Like the one before, the tunnel was long and winding. John felt the momentum begin to shift as the vehicle slowed, finally stopping at another station. The walls turned white again, losing their transparency, and the doors slid open.

"We've arrived," said Lena, stepping onto the platform. "Your rooms are down the hall. Please follow me."

"Do these things run through your entire city?" asked Mei.

"Yes. Public transportation is a vital part of our infrastructure," said Lena.

"Sounds familiar," said Hughes.

"We have a similar system where we're from," said Mei.

"Fascinating. I wasn't certain if you had the capability for such technology. It's good that you take care of your citizens," said Lena.

Their rooms were right next to each other at the end of a long hallway, far from anything else. Lena touched the side of each of the three doors, opening them. "Here you are. Please come in and I'll show you where everything is. The food dispenser is located over here. The beds are on the other side. If you need anything specific or have any questions, you can contact me directly by touching this tile." She motioned to a carved block on the wall, which illuminated whenever she brought her hand near it. "I'll receive a notification immediately."

"How do we come and go from the rooms?" asked Mei.

"The doors are synced to your biometrics. No one else can enter."

"How does it already have our signature on file?"

"Remember the scanner in the landing bay?"

Mei looked slightly annoyed, but seemed to let it go. "Alright."

"Can we wander around?" asked Track.

"Yeah, I wanna check this place out," said Mickey.

"You've been given access to most of the building. If there's an area that is off limits, the doors will simply not respond to your biometric signature."

"If you leave, you go in pairs," said John.

"Gotta love the buddy system," said Hughes.

"If you'll excuse me, I must return to Master Gel. There is much to do in preparation for tomorrow," said Lena. She left, heading back the way they came.

John waited until she was out of sight before turning to his team. "Okay, everyone check your rooms. If you see anything weird, tell me."

"Looks like they only gave us three. Does that mean we gotta share?" asked Short.

"We'll double up. Mei and I will take this one. You four figure it out."

"Buddy system," repeated Track.

"I'll stay with Short," said Mickey, almost too excited.

"Too late. I'm with Hughes." Short touched the door to open it, then went inside.

"Sorry," said Hughes, shrugging. He followed behind her.

"Damn," said Track.

"What do you expect?" asked Mickey. "She's his spotter. They go everywhere together. Don't fool yourself."

"Looks like you two are stuck together," said John, motioning at the third room.

"Oh, well. What else is new?" asked Track.

Mei tapped her door. "Here's hoping they know what a shower is."

"I feel the same way about dinner," answered John. "I haven't eaten since breakfast."

12

Central Command File Logs
Play Audio File 112, 193
Recorded: February 15, 2351

HARPER: Hello, Colonel. Thank you for taking my call.

ROSS: No problem, Doctor. It's good to hear from you again. Has the board finally wised up and promoted you to chairman?

HARPER: No, ma'am. We've yet to make a decision on a replacement for Tremaine yet, but I've been given authorization to handle these responsibilities.

ROSS: So, you get all of the work, but none of the benefits? I've certainly been there.

HARPER: If I'm being honest, I don't much want the job. I like working from behind the scenes. Makes it easier. Less red tape and fewer problems.

ROSS: *You're not wrong, Doctor. Have you heard back from our intrepid explorers yet? Please tell me you're calling with good news.*

HARPER: *I'm afraid not, but I don't expect to hear from them for a few days more, at least. They're visiting the alien city at the moment, which keeps them out of communication range.*

ROSS: *I still can't believe that's even happening. It's both exciting and terrifying.*

HARPER: *I agree, which is why I'm calling. I wanted to start coordinating with you on how we should proceed.*

ROSS: *Is the current plan insufficient?*

HARPER: *I believe it's sound. Blowing up the portal in case of emergency should be adequate in the short term, but I thought we'd want an alternative…just in case. If the aliens prove hostile and somehow find a way to stop us from destroying their gate…or, let's say, we succeed, only for them to rebuild it, we'll inevitably need another option.*

ROSS: *What are you suggesting?*

HARPER: *A contingency plan. A way to defend ourselves in the unlikely event that everything fails and we're faced with an invasion.*

ROSS: *Based on the information you've already sent me, I can't imagine our military would be enough to withstand an attack from such an advanced civilization. A single aircraft was able to take out one of our best squads. That toxin of theirs is something else.*

HARPER: *Yes, although we did have one of the hybrids there. I heard Finn took control of the situation rather quickly.*

ROSS: *He did, but we only have so many of those children, and they're hardly an army.*

HARPER: *Did you have something else in mind? A weapon, perhaps?*

ROSS: *I've been considering the sort of situation you're describing. What would happen if another portal opened and an army of thousands landed on our planet? How could we combat such a force?*

HARPER: *As I understand it, you have a handful of bombs. We could arm a few, have them waiting at the Ortego facility in case they decide to open another rift.*

ROSS: *Are you so certain they would come through at the same place? What if they enter from fifty kilometers away? What if it's on another continent? For that matter, what happens when it isn't just a single gate, but a dozen? A hundred portals open in the sky and out pops a flying armada. There's no way to predict how it might unfold.*

HARPER: *Damn, I suppose I don't think like a military commander, do I? What would you do in a situation like that?*

ROSS: *There isn't much we could do, except run and hide. Go back into our little hole in the ground and lock the doors.*

HARPER: *Are you saying you don't plan on fighting back?*

ROSS: *Oh, on the contrary. I'd use every weapon at my disposal against them. Remember El Rico Air Force Base?*

HARPER: *Sure. That's where the military evacuated from when Variant was released.*

ROSS: *We sent the Blacks there last year to retrieve some medical tech. In doing so, they managed to find the arsenal. We're trying to repair a handful of those weapons as we speak.*

HARPER: *I had no idea you were doing any of this. God, our departments don't communicate nearly as often as they should. What did you even pull from there?*

ROSS: *A few stockpiles of long-range ballistic missiles, but those are largely useless without any working silos…and we don't have time to build them. We did find some bombs, though, and plenty of useless ammunition.*

HARPER: *Useless ammunition?*

ROSS: *Leave some bullets in an uncontrolled environment for a few hundred years and watch what happens. You'll find they're mostly unusable.*

HARPER: *It doesn't sound like we have enough.*

ROSS: *We don't. That's why we'll have to hope those kids succeed with the talks. If they can't, then I trust Finn to finish the job and blow the gate.*

HARPER: *You recommended him, so I have to imagine he knows what he's doing. It's the same reason I put Curie's name forward to the board.*

ROSS: *Here's hoping we made the right call with those two. If things go south, I doubt we'll get a second chance.*

End Audio File

The Temple of the Eye
February 15, 2351

The moon was absent tonight, shielded by a blanket of far-reaching clouds. A fire blazed within the temple yard, surrounded by a group of traveling merchants, and the scent of roasted meat floated through the air.

A short walk from the fence, two men moved silently beneath the trees, minding their footing, trying not to draw attention.

Terry and Ludo had left the camp a short while ago, slipping out while the other merchants were occupied. Plead had managed to make a fuss over the butcher's cut of the meat, providing an adequate distraction.

Ludo had slept through most of the afternoon, exhausted from days of traveling. Terry nearly went on without him, but the farmer would not be so easily abandoned. He stirred from his sleep an hour before sunset, ready for the task.

Now they crept together, moving like thieves in the night. The neighboring monastery wasn't far, only an hour's walk. Before they had reached the halfway mark, Terry could already spot the other camp's fire, a dying light in the distance.

"Let's go," he whispered. "Almost there."

There were a handful of guards posted around the monastery, but nothing they wouldn't be able to handle. Terry focused and listened, trying to estimate their numbers. Two on the north side, four to the south, one inside the building. Seven altogether. Easy enough.

The two to the north would go down easier, so Terry would start there. The others had gathered around the fire on the other side of the camp. It would be best to save them for last. "We can sweep the whole yard if we're quick."

"We must avoid bloodshed," said Ludo. "Let us infiltrate silently. We can rescue Ysa without anyone taking notice. This is a holy place, and violence here would anger the Eye."

"Are you sure?" asked Terry.

"I would rather not spill blood on holy ground unless it is necessary," said Ludo.

"Okay, but if it comes to it, we may not have a choice."

"If the need arises, I will do what must be done to protect Ysa. Do not worry."

"Alright. I'll follow your lead."

The monastery was comprised of several small buildings surrounding a rather large one at the center. Each of the little ones were shaped like domes, the same design Terry had first found when he arrived on this planet, while the main structure had a more complex design, showcasing several floors and rooms. Many of the walls and floors were cracked, with gaping holes from centuries of decay. The eastern wall of the main building had a gap so large it could have doubled as a door. Clearly, years of neglect had taken its toll on this place. Why had no one bothered to maintain it?

Ludo ran to the side of one of the domes, motioning for Terry to join him. Once there, they made their way toward the center building, minding the guards, and entered through one of the open walls.

It was filthy inside, with rubble and broken debris scattered all across the floor. The door was missing from its hinges, replaced instead with a large cloth. Ludo swept it aside and entered into the hall, which was noticeably less cluttered. He continued, with Terry behind him, pressing on toward the innermost section. Like the previous room, most of the others were in shambles. Vines grew over much of the walls, and flowers bloomed through cracks in the floors. Only a handful remained in working order, containing beds and chests. No doubt these were the guards' quarters.

Terry touched Ludo by the shoulder, then motioned at the farthest room. He could hear deep breathing coming from there. Someone was sleeping.

Ludo seemed to understand. He moved slower now, passing by the room. Terry took a moment to peek inside, and as he had expected, two men were in their beds, their faces buried in their pillows.

When they had gone far enough away from the guards, Ludo stopped before another curtain at the end of the hall. "The priestesses are here," he whispered.

"How do you know?" asked Terry.

"I have been here before, a long time ago," he answered, and then proceeded through the curtain.

Inside, the monastery finally opened up, doubling the height of the previous rooms. Statues lined the walls, each with a different face. As Terry scanned them, he realized they were all women, dressed in similar robes, and each with a bald head. Patterns of varying sizes had been carved into their scalps, each with its own unique pattern. Beneath each of them lay a handful of candles and a bowl of flowers, filling the room with a naturally fresh smell, unlike the rest of the otherwise damp building.

At the far end sat another statue, this one much larger than the rest. A city resting on a cloud, with a beautifully carved eye above it all. "There, behind Everlasting," motioned Ludo.

Terry touched one of the city's towers. It was hard not to be impressed by the detail. Dozens of buildings, many with windows, filled the bulk of the pillar, while layers of patterns took up most of the base. Terry could only guess what the scribblings meant.

Ludo ran behind the pillar to a set of stairs, calling for Terry to hurry. "The purification chamber is below," he said, taking the first step.

Terry clutched the side of the stone. "Ludo, what did you mean when you said you'd been here before?"

"I served here, many years ago, back before I left the Order."

Terry followed after him. "You said you ran away with Ysa. Did you meet her here? Is that what happened?"

"No, we met in Three Waters, several years before. I was assigned to protect her, and I did for a long time."

"So, how did you end up here?"

"She was chosen for the ceremony, so they brought her here to prepare. As her protector, I was tasked to follow."

"Why didn't you say anything about this place before?"

"The priestesses did not stay here for very long. They used to spend most of their time at the temple, performing blessings and rituals for the visitors, which lasted for many days, right before the ceremony. I assumed nothing had changed."

"Did you run away from here together?" asked Terry.

Ludo stopped and turned to him. "You must understand, I could not let her die. I wouldn't be able to live without her."

Terry didn't say anything.

"The priestesses are sent to the other side of the wall where many are killed. I told her if she went, I would follow. Along with Talo, Ysa is my life. We both feared our sins would return to us someday…and now, here I stand again."

"You didn't do anything wrong," said Terry, looking him in the eye. "We'll get Ysa out of here, just like you did the last time."

"Thank you, my friend, but make no mistake. I do not doubt my actions. Not for a moment. I would sin a thousand times to be with Ysa. She gives my wings strength." He faced the curtain at the base of the stairs. "I would fight the gods for her."

IN THE FOLLOWING ROOM, two men sat together near a wall,

several feet from the entrance. They immediately noticed the two would-be rescuers. "Who are you?" one barked, reaching for his knife.

Ludo leapt toward the man, barely giving him time to respond. He slammed into his side, pushing him against the wall, holding him by the neck.

Terry spotted the armed soldier, then went for his gun, grabbing it by the barrel. In a single, fluid motion, he pushed the rifle so it was aimed at the stranger's temple. "Let it go!"

The man relinquished the gun, and Terry backed away. The soldier raised his hands.

Ludo kneed the second one in the stomach, knocking the wind from him.

"What should we do?" asked Terry.

"Keep them there until I can get Ysa."

"Don't touch the priestess!" one of the men insisted.

"You'd better stand still," said Terry. "My hand could slip and this gun could go off. You don't want to chance that." It was a lie, but he would never admit it. Terry had no wish to kill anyone, not unless he had no other choice. Besides, the sound of a rifle would only bring more trouble.

Ludo motioned at the adjoining room. "Bring them this way. The cages are here."

Terry nodded to the soldiers. "You heard him. Start walking."

They did as he said, slowly.

They entered through the curtain and into a much

larger area. Inside, several barred cells lined the walls. It was like a tiny jail.

"Ysa?" called Ludo, scanning the room.

Terry spotted a woman in the corner, sitting completely still with her eyes closed, most likely meditating. "Over there," said Terry.

One of the guards took this as an opportunity to try his luck, turning and reaching for the weapon. Terry elbowed the man in the jaw, knocking him to the floor in one quick motion. The guard spit blood on the other soldier's shoe.

"I told you not to try anything," said Terry.

"We're sorry," said one of them. "Please, here." With a shaking hand, the guard grabbed his keys and dropped them.

"N-no," muttered the man with the bloodied face, still trying to breathe.

"Quiet!" said the other. "Let them take her. She's a traitor."

"Shut your mouth," said Terry, grabbing him by the wrist. He gave him the keys and pointed at the nearest cell. "Open it."

Once the door was open, Terry pushed him in. "You two, inside," he said. He slammed the metal door behind them, sealing them in. "Say anything and I'll shoot."

Once he had it locked, Terry helped Ludo open Ysa's cell. The farmer ran to his wife's side, touching her face. She didn't move, not at first. Only sat there, no doubt deep in her meditation.

Ludo kissed her cheek, and tears filled his eyes. He wrapped his mighty arms around her, holding her close. "My love," he whispered. "I've come to take you home again."

She cracked her eyes, as though from a long slumber. "Ludo…?"

He buried his face in her neck. "I've found you!"

She blinked a few times, apparently startled, but soon relaxed. She placed her arm on his back and rubbed him gently. "It is alright now," she told him.

"I'm sorry it took me so long."

"Do not say such things," she said, stroking his face. "You should never be sorry. Not you. Never my Ludo."

"My Ysa!" he exclaimed.

He kissed her bald head, and she smiled.

Ysa also had several cuts across her thighs and stomach, apparently made using a sacred vessel—the same sort of weapon Ludo had killed Gast Maldeen with in the prison. "Why did they cut you?" asked Terry, staring at the marks.

"To clip my wings. The blade prevents me from flying," said Ysa.

"So, you can't use your abilities?"

"It is barbaric!" snapped Ludo.

She touched her husband's face. "I will soar again. Worry not, my love."

"Where are the other priestesses?" asked Terry.

"The night before the great ritual, another ceremony is performed. This one is to ask the Eye for protection and guidance," said Ysa.

"There is a single idol not far from here. A statue of one of the guardians. They will have gone there," said Ludo.

"They didn't bring you with them?" asked Terry.

"They know I would attempt to escape."

"If that's the case, what makes them think you won't just leave when tomorrow comes?"

"The final ritual requires us to go beyond the wall. Once there, we cannot come back until it is complete."

"They force you to stay there?"

"The gate is sealed from this side. They lock us in."

"Like animals," muttered Terry.

"We need to go before the others return," suggested Ludo. "Facing the priestesses would not be wise."

"Let's return to Plead. He'll be able to hide Ysa until we leave."

The three of them ran out of the basement as quickly as they could, climbing the stairs and ascending into the upper monastery. The guards were still asleep, thankfully, so they could avoid further unnecessary confrontations. In the yard, the active patrols remained at their posts, but something was wrong. Terry could hear voices in the distance, slowly drawing near.

"They are returning," whispered Ludo. "Quickly, to the forest."

The trio ran to the fence, squeezing through the planks. They entered the tree line and hid behind a few of the thicker trunks. Across the yard, where the fire blazed, a group of ornately dressed individuals were walking toward the monastery. The guards bowed as they passed, backing away. "Tomorrow is the day of glory," decreed one of the priestesses.

"We shall bask in the presence of the guardians, sisters. What a remarkable day!" cried another.

"Except Ysa. She doesn't have the blessing. The guardians will feast on her heathen flesh."

"Without her wings, she is nothing. Even if she had the blessing, it would do her no good."

The light of the flame flickered off their bald heads, revealing a range of tattoos, each with a unique pattern. They reminded Terry of the statues he saw in the monastery.

The women entered one of the smaller structures surrounding the main building. Was Ysa the only one forced to stay in the monastery's basement? He had to assume as much, given her status as a traitor. No doubt the others received far better treatment.

"Quick," whispered Ludo. "They will hear the guards' cries soon. We must leave this place."

"Right," said Terry.

They ran into the woods together, under the cover of

darkness, leaving the monastery behind. With any luck, they'd reach the other camp in a few hours. Plead would be there waiting, hopefully prepared to go. They could find Talo and return to the farm. Rebuild and regrow.

It's almost over, thought Terry. *We'll finally be able to go home.*

THEY MANAGED to get Ysa inside Plead's cart a few hours before sunrise. She wasn't eager to sit inside another box, but given her injuries, it was the only option. She had to stay out of sight.

Terry had suggested to Plead that they depart as soon as they could, but the merchant refused. "Leaving before daylight is unusual. When it is discovered that there's a priestess missing, we're bound to have pursuers."

"If we sit here too long, they might find her," said Terry.

"Have a little faith," said Plead. "Besides, I've already promised the butcher that I would have breakfast with him. I can't go breaking promises at times like this. The best thing we can do is act normal and follow our routine. Several other merchants are departing this morning, so we will do the same."

Ludo joined Ysa in the cart, bringing her a blanket and some water, while Terry and Plead remained outside.

The two suns rose soon enough, breaking light over the eastern woods and filling the temple grounds. Terry sat against one of the cart wheels, flicking a piece of blue grass, watching Plead eating breakfast with the other merchants.

When everything had been concluded, the other carts began preparing for departure. Plead returned with a few bowls. "Eat quickly. Give this to your friends."

"Thank you," said Terry. He distributed the food and then assisted Plead with feeding the haddins their morning grains.

Plead took his place at the front of the cart, reins in his hands. "Sit here with me, Terry," he said, tapping the seat. "Let your friends stay to themselves. I could use someone to talk to, anyway."

"Sure thing," said Terry, climbing aboard.

The caravan began moving a few minutes later, staying to a single line. The guards allowed them to leave without a request to search anything. *They must not know about the escape yet,* thought Terry.

Plead kept the cart between the others, following the road to the north. "We'll stay with them until we reach the fork. The caravan will continue west, but our path will keep us north and curve around to the east."

"Why not just go back the way we came?" asked Terry.

"We aren't returning home. I'm to take you elsewhere."

"What are you talking about?"

"Hux gave me specific instructions. There is a place to the northeast…a cabin with some supplies and furnishings near a dock. You shall wait there for Hux's ship to return for you. From there, he will escort you to Capeside."

"He never mentioned this to me," said Terry.

"In case you turned him down, I should wager," said Plead.

"How long until he comes back for us?"

"A few weeks. Not nearly as long as usual. He's going to drop off some merchandise to a client and then he'll return."

Terry didn't know what to say. Hux had proven quite the ally in their travels. A generous man, to be certain. "I need to thank him."

"Yes, you do. Can you imagine trying to return to Capeside through the many military checkpoints with an injured priestess from the Temple of the Eye with you? You'd have an army at your back."

Terry couldn't argue. Without her abilities, Ysa couldn't do much in a fight. If they ran into another priest or priestess before getting home, they'd have a serious problem on their hands.

Plead's cart eventually pulled off the main path, turning north. He waved farewell to his new caravan friends, including the butcher. They returned the farewell and disappeared into the next valley. As the new road curved north, the border wall came into view.

It stood like an dark scar, reaching beyond the horizon, splitting the world in two.

13

Ortego Outpost File Logs
Play Audio File 1012
Recorded: February 16, 2351

MITCHELL: *Zoe, have you received any news? Did Doctor Curie arrive safely in Everlasting?*

MASTERS: *I'm fine, thank you, Sophie. So good of you to ask.*

MITCHELL: *I assumed as much, given that you answered my call. Have you heard from Doctor Curie?*

MASTERS: *I haven't, no, but I'm guessing she's a little occupied.*

HIGGS: *Is that Sophie? Tell her to send us some food.*

MASTERS: *Get out of here, Bart. I'm busy!*

HIGGS: *Sophie, did my potatoes come in yet?*

MASTERS: *I'm talking to her about actual business and you're yapping about food? Get out of here, Bart!*

HIGGS: *Not until I get some answers. This is serious.*

MASTERS: *Ugh, Sophie, do you have his stupid potatoes?*

MITCHELL: *Yes, they arrived yesterday.*

HIGGS: *Can you send them through? Do you need me to come get them?*

MITCHELL: *I'm afraid neither will be necessary. They're already gone.*

HIGGS: *What? How the hell are they gone? Did they get infected? Don't tell me there was a crack in the box.*

MITCHELL: *Doctor Tabata cooked us a stew last night. It was quite tasty. You would have enjoyed it.*

HIGGS: *What?! You ate them? Why would you do that?*

MITCHELL: *I'm sorry. I expected we'd have time to order more before you returned. It was delicious, though.*

MASTERS: *Don't apologize, Sophie. He deserves it!*

HIGGS: *I can't believe this! Just wait until I get back.*

MASTERS: *Oh, yeah, like you'll do anything, you big baby.*

HIGGS: *I hope the stew was worth it, Sophie, because it's going to be the last meal you ever get. Do you hear me?*

MITCHELL: *I do…and I have no regrets.*

End Audio File

The Border

February 16, 2351

The road near the wall was thin and full of stones and roots. Hardly anyone traveled this path, and it showed. How long since the last carriage pressed its wheels to this dirt? Weeks? Months? For all they knew, the path ahead had been blocked by fallen trees or a flood.

Doesn't matter, thought Terry as he rode alongside Plead. *I'll get out and push if I have to. We'll make it.*

The wall towered over them, they were so close to it now. Were it not for Plead telling him to stay in the carriage, Terry would have gone to examine it. For hours, he watched the metal structure as they rode along the rocky path. How long had such a thing stood here, guarding the forbidden kingdom on the other side? He could scarcely guess.

Terry had Plead stop the cart a few times throughout the day in order to check on Ysa. She was still under the influence of the knife. Still powerless and unable to fly. Ludo had no idea how long her affliction might last, given the number of cuts on her body. He suspected a few days, but the doubt in his voice was obvious.

Gray clouds filled the skies to the north, and were moving toward them. "We'll need to find a good place to stop," said Plead. "Don't want the wheels getting stuck in the mud."

When the first drops hit, Terry pointed out a small clearing in the nearby trees, suggesting they stop there. By the time they brought the carriage to rest, the strength of the storm had come upon them.

Terry and Plead climbed in the back of the cart with Ludo and Ysa. Combined with their supplies, it was a tight fit. "Can't we toss some of this to make some room?" asked Terry.

"Not unless you want to starve when we arrive," said Plead.

"What do you mean?" he asked.

"We'll need all this to help us last until Hux comes. Did you think I brought it all to sell?"

"What if the people at the temple had actually tried to buy some of it?" asked Terry.

Plead laughed. "There's a reason I rarely travel there. You saw how they are. Holy men are not in the habit of spending money. The other merchants go because it's on the way to Delionos, and they stop again on the return journey, but no one stays for long."

"What's Delionos?"

"A city to the west. There's a string of towns between my home and there, and the caravans stop at all of them, including the temple."

"Is it on the coast, too?"

"Oh, no, certainly not. Delionos sits atop a river—the fattest river there is, actually—called the Plume. Beyond that, there's only mountains."

"The world is so big," remarked Terry, surprised to hear of even more cities.

"Bigger than any of us could hope to guess," said Plead.

Terry stared at the falling rain outside the cart, letting it relax him. His eyes drifted through the trees, watching little birds fluttering from branch to branch, trying to hide, and chirping. Beyond them, the wall stretched on, its dark gray stone now drenched, shining the sky's reflection. He remembered the underground city he'd found before, unlike anything else he'd seen since his arrival in this world. He recalled the computer room with its massive ring at the center, surrounded by terminals and equipment. Advanced technology beyond the primitive capabilities of the native people here. Did the same people who built this wall also construct the other place? Had they built other wonders throughout the rest of the world as well? Was a place called Everlasting truly waiting beyond the protection of the wall? Were those people even still alive...or were they gone and lost to time?

If anyone could have answered Terry's questions, it was, he wagered, the people of Everlasting. How disappointing, then, that they were nowhere to be found.

JOHN STOOD in the hall outside his temporary quarters, waiting for the rest of his team. They'd received a call from Lena informing them of her arrival. She would be here soon to escort them to another part of the city in order to meet with the Leadership. With any luck, he and Mei would be able to convince them to open some sort of trade deal between Everlasting and Central. At the very least, he hoped to leave here today on good terms.

Short emerged from her room, popping her head out, geared and ready. "Hey, boss."

"Hey," he returned.

"You and the lady have a good night?" she asked.

"As much as you can in a weird, alien megacity," said John. "What about you? How was staying with Hughes?"

"It was fine," she said, breaking eye contact.

"Just fine?"

The door opened, and Hughes stepped out. "Did I hear my name?"

Short pushed him back inside. "No one's talking about you." She shut the door in his face.

"Not what it sounded like from in here!" said Hughes with a muffled voice.

John grinned. "Interesting."

"What's interesting?" asked Mei. She'd snuck up beside him, with hair still damp from the shower.

"Hughes and Short," said John.

"Hey, don't go making assumptions. Just because we stayed in the same room don't mean nothing," said Short.

"Oh, I see," said Mei.

"Hey now, don't go saying it like that. I told you, nothing's going on," she insisted.

"The more you deny it, the more likely it seems," said

Mei, tapping her chin.

"It's true," said John, nodding thoughtfully.

Short's eyes dashed back and forth between the two. "I just, um," she said, flustered. "Hughes, hurry up in there!" She opened the door and ran into the room.

John snickered.

"You're so mean to your people," said Mei, laughing.

"They like it," he said.

"Do you think she knows we could hear them last night?"

"I think they forget how good our ears are sometimes."

"Four walls between us and it still wasn't enough," she said, shuddering. "I could've done without all that."

"If you say so," he said, winking.

She punched him in the arm. "Pervert."

Several minutes later, John's team had fully assembled, ready to go.

Lena Sol arrived to greet them. She was holding a bag in her right hand. "Hello," she said.

"What's in the sack?" asked Track.

"Don't mind him," said John.

"I've brought a few gifts," said Lena. She took out a weird orange orb and handed it to him. "Try a piece."

"Is this food?" asked John, cautiously taking a sniff.

"Oh, yes. It's a fruit, and very difficult to find. We discovered them on the other side of the planet several decades ago. They can only be grown in temperate climates on volcanic soil, high above sea level. We have a greenhouse specially designed only for these. You'll find nothing else like them."

"That's a lot of work just to grow a piece of fruit," said Mei. "What do you call them?"

"Jesotni," explained Lena. "*Miracle.*"

"How do we know we can eat this? It could be poisonous to us," said Mei. Before now, the team had used their personal rations to sustain themselves.

"Our scans confirmed your biology is surprisingly similar to ours. I also had our botanists examine the fruit's genetic markers to ensure compatibility. Rest assured, no harm will come to you. The only uncertainty is your level of enjoyment. The taste may be slightly different."

The fruit felt soft in John's hand. He considered returning it, but dismissed the idea. If they wanted him dead, they could use the toxin and be done with it in a matter of seconds. No need to send a timid girl like Lena to deliver a piece of fruit they might not even eat. With a slight shrug, John quickly took a bite, breaking the skin with a hard snap. Red juice gushed out of it and slid down his fingers. A flood of tastes filled his mouth. It was so sweet, almost like candy. It reminded him of butterscotch, only better, purer. He took another bite, and somehow it was even more delicious than the first.

"Man, this is good!" Track exclaimed, inhaling the food.

"Slow down," Mei told him.

"Oh, I'm so happy you like it," said Lena.

Mei still had the fruit in her hand. She nudged John's leg with her own. "How is it?"

"*Really* good," he said, very seriously.

She stared at the orange ball in her hand, a skeptical look on her face. After a long moment of consideration, she gave in and took a bite.

John watched as her expression shifted from reservation to one of pure delight. She took several more bites before finally swallowing.

"I guess you like it, huh?" asked John.

"I can have a crate of them prepared for your return journey, if you like," said Lena.

"What do you guys think?" asked John, glancing at the others.

"It'd be rude to say no, right?" said Hughes.

"Very well. One moment, please." Lena's eyes dilated as she stood quite still, staring at nothing in particular. A second later, she blinked. "There we are. All finished."

"I'll never get used to that," said Hughes.

"Wish I had me one of those implants," said Short. "She can do all kinds of stuff with it."

"No thanks. I don't need no tech in my skull," said Track.

"They are quite convenient, and the procedure is completely painless. If Leadership allows, perhaps we can arrange for you to receive one," said Lena.

"Let's worry about the talks first," said Mei. "One step at a time."

JOHN STEPPED out of the egg and onto the boarding platform. As Lena had explained, this was the Grand Foyer, a central hub of the different offices. "To the left you will find the Department of Agriculture, the Department of Labor, the Office of Civic Duty, the Office of the Interior, and the Department of Transit. To the right you will find several others, including the Office of Compliance, the Department of Civil Protection, and the Department of Pacification. There are many others in this building, scattered through the various floors, but our destination lies ahead in the Department of Leadership."

"So many departments," said Track.

"And offices," added Mickey.

"Think they've got any branches?"

"Nah," said Mickey. "Divisions, maybe. A couple of sections."

"Oh, boy," exclaimed Track.

"Will you two shut up?" said Short.

Lena led them to a set of double sliding doors. "This platform will take us to the appropriate floor."

Everyone piled into the elevator, though it was little more than a box. There were no controls on the wall, nor any indication to let them know what floor they were on. Lena stared with the same blank expression she had when using her implant. A second later, the box began to move.

It arrived in less than a minute, its doors sliding silently open. The new floor looked remarkably similar to the first, minimalist design and all. The only difference, as far as John could tell, was there were no branching paths to speak of. Instead, only one option lay before them: a single door on the other side of the room. "Right this way," said Lena, motioning with her hand in a courteous gesture.

The door was elegant in design—charcoal black with gold trim, standing out amongst the room's plain, white design. It opened as they approached, and everyone stepped through.

On the other side, a solitary figure awaited them. He had the sort of relaxed look one might find on an old grandparent. Tender brown eyes and a kind smile invited them. "Welcome, explorers," he said with a slightly husky voice.

"Master Trin," greeted Lena, touching her chest.

Trin did the same. "Hello, Lena. I heard you were given the honor of escorting our new friends. I'm happy to see you in good health."

"Thank you, Master Trin," she said, looking happy.

"Who are you?" asked Track.

Mei glared at him. "Don't be rude."

"Morning, sir," said John, getting right to it. "It's good to be here."

"Ah, yes, you must be Johnathan Finn," said the old man.

John was surprised to hear his name, but he knew he shouldn't be, given the situation. Everyone in upper management probably had a dossier on every single one of them. "That's me. Nice to meet you."

"You're certainly larger than I expected," said Trin, looking up at him. "Are there many in your home as tall as you?"

"A few," he answered.

"How wonderful, and you all seem like such nice people." He smiled.

"Thanks," said John.

"Master Trin, is Master Gel with the Leadership?" asked Lena.

"He is. The entire Leadership is already seated and waiting. Shall I escort you inside?"

"Yes, please," said Lena.

John and Mei exchanged glances. She took a deep breath.

Fingers crossed, he thought.

THE BLACKS STOOD before a dozen individuals clad in white garments, each sitting comfortably behind an over-sized and surprisingly long desk. "Welcome to the Hall of Leadership," said Master Trin, touching his chest. He proceeded to take his seat alongside the others.

John looked around for Lena, but she was far behind them, still at the edge of the entryway. She stood quietly to herself, arms in front, almost like she didn't belong here.

Mei glanced up at him. "Ready?" she mouthed.

He tilted his head as if to say, *Sure. Why the hell not?*

Mei cleared her throat and stepped forward. "Thank you for inviting us to meet with you today," she began. "We're honored to be here."

A short silence filled the room as the leaders watched from behind their great desk. John could see in each of their eyes the same blank expression he'd witnessed on Lena's face many times before. They had to be using their implants. Were they managing their translation software? Perhaps they were going over the files they had on John and his team, or maybe they were talking to each other, somehow, trying to decide what to do next. Could the implants allow for that level of raw communication?

A man with a short, gray beard and charcoal eyes sat at the center of the table. He seemed to look them over, one at a time. His composure was steady, unwavering, and his presence commanding. John had known commanders in his time. He had known leaders. The man before him, here in this strange, empty place—he was the backbone of this council. He was the central pillar. The rest of them didn't matter.

John stared at him with heavy curiosity.

"The Leadership welcomes you," came a voice, breaking the silence. It was Master Gel, sitting at the opposite end to Trin. He let out his hand. "We invite you to tell us as much as you are willing about your home world. We understand you might not wish to disclose certain details, and we accept this, but nonetheless remain very curious."

John leaned over to Mei. "I think this is your cue."

She stiffened. "I suddenly hate this."

"You nervous?"

"Aren't you?"

"Is there a problem?" asked Master Gel.

"No, we're okay," answered Mei. She took a deep breath. "I'm not sure where to begin. There's a lot to cover."

"How about you start by telling us about your home and what brought you to ours? Tell us whatever you think is appropriate."

"Alright, from the beginning," she muttered, looking one more time to John. "Two hundred years ago, a group of scientists unwittingly opened a bridge to another world, killing nearly every living thing on the planet."

THE LEADERSHIP SEEMED VERY PLEASED with the answers Mei gave about the nature of Earth. Every question posed was immediately followed by a series of follow-ups, asking for more and more detail. Mei was very precise with her answers, providing enough to satisfy them, but leaving out anything that could be considered sensitive or pertinent to the security of Central and its outposts.

Since they had only been in Everlasting for a day, there

was hardly enough time to gauge whether these people could actually be trusted. Even if John and Mei did believe them, they couldn't risk the safety of humanity just to satisfy curiosity. When the Leadership asked about Central, Mei only revealed surface-level information. When they persisted with further questions, she would respectfully decline to answer. Master Gel seemed to understand and would often change the topic of interest rather quickly.

John listened intently to the back and forth. Some of the questions were expected, though a few surprised him. "Your weapons are very curious," said Trin. "I have been told that they can kill."

Mei looked at John. He nodded, letting her know he'd handle this one. "That's right," he said, stepping forward. "We use them for defense."

"Defense against what?" asked Trin.

"Animals, mostly. It's dangerous back home." He paused. "Actually, it's dangerous here, too."

"Why do you not simply develop a non-lethal alternative?" asked Trin.

"You mean like the toxin you used on my guys?" asked John.

Trin said nothing.

"We don't have anything like that, unfortunately."

"Our customs forbid the use of deadly force, you understand," said Trin.

John nodded.

"Everlasting has taken a more sophisticated approach to

dealing with conflict. We understand your level of technology is less…refined…than our own when it comes to personal defense, but we need your assurances that you will do everything you can to avoid such acts while visiting this planet in the future. To clarify, we simply request you not kill any lifeforms, be they sentient or otherwise, in or outside of Everlasting."

"Exceptions can be made, naturally," Trin interjected. "We know that without the toxin you cannot always avoid fatalities."

John was surprised at the lack of an emotional reaction. Lena had been quite upset at the notion of killing anything, even in self-defense, so why weren't these people more appalled? Why weren't they squirming in their seats at the very idea of it? They had expressed their concerns and made some objections, but it all felt so mechanical. For a group of people who considered all forms of killing unthinkable, they were surprisingly forgiving. "Thank you for understanding," said John. "If we can avoid killing, we will."

"Very good," said Gel. "With that matter closed, we would like to pose a question to you regarding your biology. Would such a topic be appropriate?"

"Depending on the question," said Mei.

"As you may have guessed, the people of Everlasting cannot breathe the corrupted atmosphere outside our borders. I believe you call it Variant, correct? It is why Titus Ven and his team were wearing environmental suits when you encountered them. Should the atmosphere come into contact with them, they would most certainly die."

"I thought Variant was from this planet," said John.

Each of the Leadership froze, briefly. The man at the center of the table moved, but only barely, tilting his head slightly to the side.

John watched him with growing interest. "Something wrong?"

The man twisted his lower lip, flicking his nose like he was about to sneeze. A second later, the blank stare on all their faces receded. Master Gel smiled. "The atmosphere of this planet was not always as it is. A few centuries ago, the gas as you know it was released into our world, altering the entire ecosystem."

"Where did it come from?" asked Mei.

"There is some debate on the matter, but our records suggest it originated from within the ground," explained Gel.

"The ground?" asked Mei.

He nodded. "At the time, a competing nation was attempting to show their strength by drilling the largest hole ever made. A rather meaningless endeavor, obviously, but it had unintended consequences. XM-13, the contagion you call Variant, was released soon afterwards."

"Did the drill hit something?"

"We think so, yes. A pocket of gas, long hidden away and stored underground, completely isolated from the rest of the world. It is now believed that the drill breached a layer of ancient stone, allowing the trapped gas to escape. Everything you see on this planet is a result of that occurrence."

"Why wasn't Everlasting affected?" asked John.

Master Trin smiled. "The domeguard, of course."

Gel nodded. "The threat of biological weapons was strong in the old world. Our ancestors focused their energy and resources on protection. The domeguard was intended to be used all across the continent, back when this city was but one of many. When XM-13 struck, however, only Everlasting was prepared."

"Fascinating," muttered Mei.

"Now that we have answered a few of your questions, I hope you will do the same."

"Certainly," she responded.

"Our next question is related to this very topic, in fact," continued Gel. "We have noticed that some of you do not require breathing devices while immersed in the gas. Would you please explain the details of why this is?"

"You want to know why a few of us can breathe Variant?" asked John.

"Very much so," answered Gel. "Our scientists have expressed some curiosity over the matter. Upon your arrival, our scans showed a distinct genetic difference between those of you with breathing apparatuses and those without. Is this accurate?"

"I'm not sure I'm authorized to—" He stopped, unsure of what to do.

"You're right," Mei interjected, taking over for him. "It's genetic. Our people have been working on a solution to the gas for almost two hundred years. We are the fruit of that labor."

"Would you be willing to show us your research?"

"That research is no longer in circulation. It's been sealed by our superiors."

"For what purpose?" asked Gel.

"I'm not authorized to detail that information," said Mei. "I apologize, but—"

"Who *is* authorized?" asked Gel.

"Other people," she said, flatly.

Track leaned in to Mickey's ear. "I thought these guys were pretty advanced. What's the deal?"

"Maybe they don't know as much as they say," answered Mickey.

John cleared his throat, quieting them. They both stiffened and shut up.

The Leadership's eyes froze again in unison. They didn't move for several seconds. John was about to say something—to ask whether or not there was something wrong with them—when Gel finally opened his mouth to speak again. "We would appreciate the inquiry. How quickly can you contact your superiors, Doctor Curie?"

"Provided I leave soon, I could contact them within the day."

"We will arrange for one of our ships to escort you back immediately. It will wait for you as long as you require. Tell your government we are willing to make an offer on the information, should they be interested."

"What kind of offer?" asked Mei.

Master Gel leaned forward. "Our own research on the gas, to begin with, along with supplies and resources. We're also open to further negotiations should this offer prove insufficient."

I'll deliver your request immediately," said Mei.

"Very well. My analyst will show you to the aircraft. It's already waiting."

Lena scurried up beside them. "If you'll follow me, please."

The Blacks began to leave, following Lena toward the exit, but John kept his place. He flicked his thumb, staring at the Leadership. These people had such advanced technology, but for some reason they seemed to come up lacking in this particular field. If ever there was a time to request their assistance in finding Terry, this was it. "Excuse me," said John, looking directly at the silver-haired man at the center of the table. "I have something you could do."

All the eyes in the room were suddenly on him.

"You've probably heard we're looking for our friend. He came through the portal a few years ago," said John. "His name is Terry, and he's lost somewhere on this planet."

"We have been informed of this, yes," answered Gel.

"I want assurances that you'll help me find him."

"Assurances?" asked Trin.

John nodded. "A promise to do everything you can, to

use all your technology to help us." He looked at the man in the center of the table, who returned the stare. He had the eyes of a contemplative man. "Please."

"We will have to discuss this request," said Gel. "It is not something we can so easily—"

He stopped, a blank expression suddenly on him, along with the rest of the Leadership—all except the man with the silver hair, who let out a long, soft sigh and licked his lips. As he did, the rest of them returned, no longer statues.

"Is something wrong?" asked John.

Gel sat down, and each of the Leadership members turned to look at the man in the middle. The stranger leaned forward. "We hear your concern, Sergeant Finn of Earth." His voice was deep and rough. "Rest assured, Everlasting will assist in your search."

"Thank you, sir," said John. "Can I ask your name?"

"I am Kai, Master of Public Safety."

The title surprised John. He'd expected something with a bit more significance.

"Master Gel will oversee the search. Consult with him on this matter in the future," said Kai.

"Thanks," said John. "I appreciate it."

"It is the least we can do for our new allies," said Master Kai. "Rest assured, we will do everything in our power to find your missing friend."

14

Ortego Outpost File Logs
Play Audio File 1035
Recorded: February 17, 2351

HARPER: *Let me see if I understand what you're saying. These people...the Leadership...they're asking for all of our research as it pertains to the Variant gas? More specifically, everything from the Amber Project, itself. Is that correct?*

CURIE: *It is, and they're willing to hand over their own research in exchange for it.*

HARPER: *I assume you explained the classified nature of it.*

CURIE: *It was the first thing I mentioned.*

HARPER: *Putting aside the fact that the research itself is highly unethical and morally reprehensible, what in the world could they possibly need it for?*

CURIE: *They have the same vulnerability to Variant that we do, unfortunately. I should have guessed as much, based on their environmental suits, but the team we first encountered implied they were for protection against disease and radiation, not Variant.*

HARPER: *Didn't you say these people were scientifically advanced? I was under the impression their technology was far above ours. Were you mistaken?*

CURIE: *That's the interesting part. From what I've been able to gather, they gave up on solving the Variant problem with genetic therapy some time ago. Their scientists concluded it was impossible to stop the gas from invading the cell membrane. They've been looking for a breakthrough ever since, mostly in other fields that they believed were more viable.*

HARPER: *Other fields?*

CURIE: *Everlasting invested in dozens of other fields of inquiry. Environmental suits, strengthening the shield, medicine, implants, communications, transportation, and so on. They have outposts all over the planet, each with a different purpose. They seem to have cast a wide net, believing the solution would eventually present itself.*

HARPER: *I see, so when genetics seemed like it might not yield adequate results, they had no qualms with abandoning it and looking elsewhere.*

CURIE: *Precisely.*

HARPER: *Sounds familiar. Before Archer made his infamous discovery, our people believed the same thing. Of course, his ideas were outrageous for the time. No one took him seriously. Not until he found Bishop.*

CURIE: *It also doesn't help that Archer discovered his solution by changing his ethics. Dozens of women were nearly killed in the early trials, while countless fetuses had to be aborted and discarded. What's more, several of my own classmates never made it out of the gas chamber alive. He did it all without a second thought, because he believed the ends would justify the means. Maybe these people just don't think that way.*

HARPER: *Perhaps it never occurred to them to even explore it. It sounds like they felt safe behind their shield, patient to look for their own solutions. We put all our money on genetics because time was running out. Desperation was our motivator, and a powerful one it proved to be.*

CURIE: *You're right about that. Their shield hasn't had a breach in eighty years, according to Lena. Maybe if death was knocking at the door, they would've kept trying.*

HARPER: *I guess that makes us lucky, then, since our grim reaper came early and pushed us into giving Archer his way.*

CURIE: *It's just a shame it had to happen this way.*

HARPER: *Maybe so, but you're here, aren't you? Despite every-thing the old man did, all the lives he ruined, something good came from it in the end. The children of that project have been a vital asset to this city. To humanity.*

CURIE: *Is that your way of saying we should give them the research? Because it could help them?*

HARPER: *No, not exactly. They don't need to know all of our dirty secrets. We can start with some light reading and go from there. If they play nice, maybe we'll do more. What else did they offer in exchange for all this?*

CURIE: Supplies, research, authorization to use the portal and establish an outpost.

HARPER: Anything else?

CURIE: Sergeant Finn made a personal request, which I supported. He asked them to help us look for Terry.

HARPER: The Matron's missing son? What did they say?

CURIE: They agreed. Lena says the chances of locating him are minimal, but it's a start.

HARPER: If that's true, then I'd say it's reason enough to help them, don't you?

CURIE: You won't hear me disagreeing.

HARPER: Then let's make this work.

CURIE: Do you think the board will approve it?

HARPER: If I've learned anything about politics, it's that you can do anything if you phrase it correctly. Don't worry, Doctor Curie. You leave the old men in dusty jackets to me.

End Audio File

The Border
February 17, 2351

Despite the rough country road, Terry managed to sleep through the night. He once again used the meditation practices to push real-life distractions out of his mind, ignoring them. Ludo had said it was dangerous to fall

asleep during meditation—while visiting the mind palace—
but there didn't seem to be much harm in it. During these
moments, nothing could stir him, but when he finally
awoke from his long rest, he felt reinvigorated.

As soon as he opened his eyes, Terry caught the first
glimpse of a dome building, hidden between hundreds of
blue forest trees. "Are we here?" he asked, pointing into the
woods.

"You've got some good eyes on you," remarked Plead.

Finally, thought Terry, leaning back. With any luck,
Hux's ship would arrive before much longer and take them
home. Ysa and Ludo could be with their son again, and
things could go back to normal. *After the farm gets rebuilt*, he
reminded himself.

Terry still wasn't sure what he would do once that was
finished, though. Would he stick around and live the quiet
farmer's life with his friends or would he take Hux up on
his offer to travel the world? In truth, he'd be happy with
either scenario. Maybe I'll do both, he thought, watching
the trees as the cart passed through the forest. I'll join Hux
and then come back. Live the quiet life.

He pictured himself on the deck of the ship, staring out
into the sea, observing a new land. Then he imagined
himself by the river, lounging under the suns. He could
have them both in time, and what a life it would be.

Plead's cart came through the tree line at the edge of
the woods and into a field. The house lay at the peak of a
small hill overlooking the beach. Based on the size of the

home, Terry wagered they'd have more than enough room. For all its simplicity, it was a nice spot of land. Were it not for the wall to the north, standing less than a quarter kilometer away, he might have suggested they stay.

Terry helped unload the supplies, placing everything into the centermost room of the house. Ludo immediately ran to the kitchen and began sorting through dishes and utensils. He was excited to be in a relaxed setting, it seemed, a familiar smile across his gentle face.

Ysa was still weak, so she went to one of the rooms to rest. She'd slept for most of the trip and would likely continue to do so until her strength returned.

Plead had told them Hux would arrive in a few weeks. Would Ysa be back to normal by then? Terry hoped so. Traveling was dangerous, so it would do them well to have everyone in full health, especially someone like Ysa who could help fight.

After all the supplies had been unloaded and the animals fed, Plead grabbed a few poles from one of the closets. "Shall we catch some fish?" he asked.

"Right now?" asked Terry.

"There's no better time. The dock is always swarming with churin. Not very fat, but delicious. You'll see."

"Do you fish a lot?" Terry took one of the poles.

"Only when I'm here, but I know a great deal about fish. I'm an expert!" He laughed.

Terry followed the merchant to the dock at the bottom of the hill. The waves heaved back and forth along the beach, reminding him of his time with Hux. He smiled instantly.

Plead stuck some bait on the end of the line, then dropped the hook into the water. He sat with his legs dangling off the edge and took a deep breath. "After so much time on the road, there's nothing like the sea, is there?"

"It's nice," answered Terry, staring out into the water. He followed the horizon, spotting several tiny isles in the distance. His eyes stopped when he saw the border wall. He hadn't noticed before, but it continued from the land and went far into the ocean, eventually curving north after several kilometers. *Wonders never cease.*

By the time the suns had set, Plead had caught three fish. Ludo was very pleased with them, and cooked enough to satisfy everyone. Ysa joined them for a few hours around the central fire pit where her husband served a pleasing meal. For a few hours, things felt familiar again, the way they ought to be.

Before it was time for bed, Plead asked Terry to hold on a minute. "I want to give you something," he said, motioning toward one of the storage rooms. "Hold on, would you?"

Terry agreed, and waited for the merchant to return. When he did, he had an object in his arms, wrapped in an old cloth. "What's that?"

Plead grinned. "Ever hear of the Carthinians?"

Terry said he hadn't.

"The Carthinians used to rule the lands across the sea before they were banished. You've heard of Lexine, right? There was a civil war there, maybe a hundred years ago. The Carthinians ended up scattered, but most took shelter in Tharosa."

"That's great, but what does it have to do with the thing in your hand?"

"The Carthinians were expert craftsmen in the old days, particularly when it came to weapons. They made the finest swords on the planet, you follow? They found a way to take ancient metals and repurpose them. Most folks today, like those priests in the Temple of the Eye—they think the swords are holy. They call them vessels."

"You mean the ones you can kill a priest with?"

"Sure, that. The Carthinians made them. Only a few weaponsmiths are left who still know the craft, but if you've got the supplies and the money, you can find them in Tharosa. I know a lot about these things, you know." Plead smiled proudly.

"I always wondered where those things came from," said Terry.

"Those blades can cut through just about anything, but they're also hard to find. That's why I keep this one here in the cabin. It's worth a small fortune." He removed the cloth, revealing a black piece of metal, glimmering in the afternoon light. "Impressive, isn't it?"

"Wow," remarked Terry.

Plead flipped it over a few times, letting him get a good

look. "Here," he finally said, rewrapping it in cloth. "For you."

"What's that?" asked Terry.

"The sword. I want you to hold on to it."

Terry blinked at the blade, shaking his head. "I can't! Plead, it's too valuable. Look at it."

"It's also useful...and I'm not a warrior. Not like the rest of you."

"But what if—"

"Will you take it? I'm not giving it to you as a gift. You're a fighter and this is a weapon. Use it to protect me." He gave a devilish smile. "We all have our strengths, don't we? Yours is looking out for me."

"When you put it like that, I guess it's true," said Terry.

Plead handed him the sword. "I'll get you the sheath so you can carry it without dulling the blade."

"I don't know what to say," Terry muttered, looking down at the priceless weapon in his arms.

As the night came, and everyone went to bed, Terry lay awake, staring into the darkness of his temporary room. For once, he'd chosen to keep himself awake, listening intently to the sounds of the neighboring forest and its activity. As much as he enjoyed this place, it was new. He had to ensure nothing was out there.

He concentrated, pulling in the sounds of the woods and the field and the ocean. He listened to the waves crashing softly against the shore, the insects buzzing on the leaves, the heavy breathing of the haddins outside, still hooked to the cart. The world was alive, even in the middle of the night, but it was nothing new to him.

But that was when he heard it. A different voice from the other creatures, singing out of tune. It came from far away, something buried in the distance.

Zhaa, zhaa, zhaa, it gently cried. *Zhaa, zhaa, kaa.*

Terry filtered more until he had it, clear and present as the rest. A sound unlike any other, like a child crying...or perhaps an engine whirling.

Zhaa, zhaa, zhaa, he heard it say. *Zhaa, zhaa, kaa.*

He didn't get out of bed or go outside, but instead waited...and listened, clutching the sword Plead had given him. Terry did this for hours until the sound began to fade. Until the light at the edge of the horizon appeared. Until the night had come and gone, and the sound finally faded, replaced by morning birds.

The Border
February 19, 2351

TERRY AND LUDO walked through the forest near their temporary home, their hunting equipment in hand. Plead had noticed a cheche grazing early this morning, telling the others upon his return. Ludo expressed some interest in attaining some fresh meat, as they'd had nothing but grains and fish for the last several days. Terry agreed to accompany him, eager to get some exercise.

Ludo found the tracks exactly where Plead had suggested, then proceeded to follow them north near the wall.

Terry carried a large knapsack full of rope and knives, along with the sword Plead had given him. He'd wrapped the hilt to his hip, allowing access to the blade at any time, should he require it. He wasn't very adept at using the weapon, but he'd figure it out. Probably. Maybe if he started practicing, he could get a better grasp on the fundamentals.

They followed the trail for nearly three hours, tracking the cheche as steadily as possible. It took them west for nearly half a kilometer, but eventually they found their prey.

The cheche stood beside an old tree, rubbing its neck against the bark, presumably scratching an itch. It did this for several seconds, sticking out its long tongue between each stroke.

Terry debated whether to use his new sword or the knives in his pack, but opted for the larger weapon. He needed to get some practice in with it.

Ludo took out a few of his own throwing knives and readied himself behind one of the trees. The cheche looked distracted, so he gave Terry the signal to attack.

Terry rushed toward the animal, readying the weapon in his hands. He wasn't entirely sure how to hold it, but decided the optimal position was over his shoulder. Not that it mattered. Swing and hit. That's all it took, right?

Lunging at the cheche, Terry brought down the sword with a heavy swing. The weight of the unfamiliar blade had surprising momentum, and the handle was wrenched out of his hand and flew in the direction of the beast, hitting the tree and falling to the ground. The cheche exploded into a dash, spooked by the commotion.

A small knife cut through the air a few feet beside Terry, piercing the animal's rear leg and forcing it to the dirt. It rolled in a pile of mud and twigs, letting out a sharp cry. Ludo released another wave of daggers, hitting it in the neck and side. He ran to it, quickly grabbing it by the neck and ending its struggle with one final puncture. The noise stopped instantly, and blood leaked freely from its wounds.

Terry regarded the sword at his feet with some embarrassment. He'd made himself look like a bumbling idiot.

Ludo picked up the weapon and wiped the mud on his boot. "You should have used the daggers," said Ludo. "They're much better for hunting. No one hunts with swords."

"I was trying to get better."

"I can teach you." He handed the sword back to Terry, a forgiving look in his eyes.

"You know how to use it?"

"The temple guards are trained for years on many weapons. This design is very similar to the one I used to carry. I will show you how." Ludo put his hand on Terry's shoulder. "Come, my friend. We have done well today. Let's return so I can prepare the meat." He beat his chest, chuckling. "Wait until you taste what I have planned for dinner. You'll love it. I know it!"

Since they were so far from the house, they decided to field-dress the cheche on the spot, removing its organs and draining most of the blood in order to better preserve the meat. Once they had it clean enough to move, Ludo wrapped the legs and mounted the beast on his back, securing it in place.

They made it home within the hour, and Ludo got to work in the kitchen. Terry helped him further clean and skin the meat, then assisted with the cooking, all despite Ludo's protests.

The dinner was delicious, though it was hardly surprising. Ludo's skills in the kitchen were unparalleled. Afterwards, Terry returned to the field, taking his new sword with him.

Ludo followed, calling for him to wait.

"I'm going to practice," explained Terry.

"Let me show you first," said the farmer. He asked for the weapon, so Terry relinquished it. "Come with me."

Ludo led him to a standing tree in the nearby field. It had many branches of varying sizes. "Hold the blade like this," he said, showing him. "Firm fingers. Next, do you see the curve of the edge?"

Terry nodded.

"This is not for piercing," explained Ludo. "Some

swords are long and thin. Others are fat and wide. This one is curved and sharp on its whole edge. You must slice with it." He motioned for Terry to stand back, then raised the weapon to his side, keeping the sharper edge away from him. "Stand like this, and then move in close."

"Don't you want to stay away from whoever's attacking?"

"With a sword like this, you must get close. Most blades are built to pierce from a distance, but once you get through, they're left defenseless. This is how you win."

Ludo leaned in and cut the tree, slicing one of its branches clean off, almost effortlessly. It fell to the ground with a soft thud. He stepped back, looked at Terry, and then lunged forward again, slicing at the tree. It left a clean, but deep, marking on the bark. Ludo handed the weapon to Terry, who took it somewhat hesitantly. "You make it look easy."

"Anything is easy with enough practice," said the farmer, smiling. "Every talent is merely repetition, performing the same action ten thousand times until it is perfect…until it is divine. With enough strikes of this sword, anyone can become a master, but there is always a beginning. There is always the first strike." Ludo moved aside, letting Terry replace him.

Terry gripped the hilt of the sword, mimicking the position Ludo had shown him. He raised his hand to his chest, and with a single, fluid swipe, stepped forward.

15

Ortego Outpost File Logs
Play Audio File 1115
Recorded: February 25, 2351

HARPER: *It took some doing, but I was able to convince them.*

CURIE: *So, you'll be sending us the files? How much of it did they authorize?*

HARPER: *The board decided against full disclosure, but you knew that already. It should still be enough to help them get started. From what you've told me about the state of their progress, what little we give them should prove invaluable.*

CURIE: *Did you manage to get any of the Amber Project files?*

HARPER: *Only a few. Nothing about the experiments involving the Chamber. The board doesn't want to give them a way of creating their own batch of super soldiers. No offense.*

CURIE: *None taken. I'm a scientist.*

HARPER: *Right. Sorry.*

CURIE: *It's okay. I understand what you're saying. Another set of hybrids could be problematic.*

HARPER: *To prevent that, the board has agreed to disclose some of our other research. Specifically, the stuff we're doing now to modify living humans without creating hybrids. We don't have anything conclusive yet, but we're close to solving it.*

CURIE: *Doesn't that require hybrid cells to work?*

HARPER: *It did in the beginning, but we've since managed to synthesize something artificial to do the same job. It omits the section of your DNA that grants you your abilities, which consequently lowers the mortality rate, and it can be used on existing humans instead of embryos. Still doesn't solve the breathing problem, but we're working on it.*

CURIE: *Is that the injection I keep hearing about?*

HARPER: *Right. You take it once a week and it allows you to breathe Variant. It's also in testing, like the rest. We'll see what happens.*

CURIE: *Thanks for doing this, Doctor Harper. I'll look over the files and get them to Everlasting as soon as possible. I'm sure this will go a long way toward getting us what we need.*

HARPER: *I hope so, but do be careful, won't you? The last thing I want to do is brief the board on something happening to you or, worse, an impending invasion. Imagine the paperwork involved in that nightmare. I'm not sure I could handle it.*

End Audio File

Tower of the Cartographers, Everlasting
February 25, 2351

Lena sat in Master Gel's office, reporting as requested. She had no idea what she was doing there, but wagered it had something to do with Doctor Curie's recent contributions to the city's genetic research project.

Master Gel cleared his throat. "Thank you for coming today," he told her. "I wanted to discuss something very important with you, but it will require some background information, which you are not currently authorized to receive."

She opened her mouth to speak, but he raised his hand to quiet her.

"Don't worry," he said. "I've updated your clearance. You have nothing to worry about."

"Thank you, sir."

He nodded. "Before I get on with it, I must explain something critical to you. It will not be easy to hear. Should you find it overwhelming, simply let me know and we will have you brought to the Department of Pacification for memory therapy treatment immediately. Do you understand?"

"Yes," she said, but no matter how she felt, she'd never allow herself to go to such a place.

"Something is happening in Everlasting, Analyst Sol.

Something very dangerous," said Master Gel, calmly staring at her from across the desk.

The statement caught her off guard. What was this about, exactly?

Master Gel called up an image with the help of his implant. A holographic screen appeared above them, hovering like a cloud. "This is the square outside the Second Scientific Research Center. Most of the citizens here work in that department. Keep your eyes on them, and look for anything you consider out of the ordinary. Tell me what you see."

The video played. There were people walking back and forth. Some were sitting together on benches, casually talking. An average setting with average citizens. Nothing out of the ordinary, except—

Except for the man in the back, standing alone under the overhang. His mouth was covered by a breathing mask, which implied there was a leak in the city shield...but none of the other people had their masks on, so what was going on? He also wore an unusually thick coat, despite the apparent warm weather. All the other visitors had thin clothes on, with no sign of discomfort. Did this stranger have some kind of disorder? An illness, perhaps? "Who is that man?" Lena finally asked.

"Ah, so you noticed," said Gel. "Keep your eye on him."

The video played, and the oddly dressed man just stood there. He watched his fellow citizens continue their routines, all the while doing nothing. After nearly two full minutes of this, Lena started to ask what was going on, when suddenly the man stepped forward. What happened next left her speechless.

The masked individual opened his jacket and took out a canister. He began to yell, but there wasn't any audio. Odd, she noted, given how each of the monitoring stations used specialized sound amplifiers to record audio up to hundreds of deci-units away.

The people panicked immediately, taking off in every direction and emptying the scene. It would not take long for the Department of Civil Protection to respond with full force, releasing the toxin and disabling the suspect. No doubt the man knew this.

As soon as the area was clear, the man turned and threw the canister at the building, igniting the scene in a white flash. Master Gel stopped the recording.

Lena stared at the screen. "What happened?" she asked, quickly.

"The suspect was killed in the explosion," explained Master Gel.

"Who...why did he do that?" Lena had never seen anything like it. Why would he show her such a horrible thing?

"Do you recall the discussion we had the day before you left for the quarantine zone? I called you into this very office and told you of the death of Jinel Din."

"Yes, sir. I could never forget something so tragic."

"At the time, I was not at liberty to disclose the truth about this matter, due to your lack of security credentials. You had yet to prove your nature, Analyst Sol, but that has since changed. What I am about to tell you is not to leave this office. Is that understood?"

"Yes, sir."

"As you know, the city of Everlasting has long stood as the single greatest bastion for scientific curiosity throughout the world. Because of this, we are left with the greatest of responsibilities: the preservation of all that we have…and all that came before." Master Gel's eye twitched, and the video feed reversed, freezing just before the blast. It quickly zoomed in and focused on the individual as he raised the canister. "But there are some who do not agree."

Lena stared at the man on the screen. Who in their right mind would do such a thing? Who would go against their city? "People say there's an organization behind the attacks. Is it true, sir?"

Gel waved his hand dismissively. "False rumors, I can assure you. The cause is much less sinister." The holographic display changed instantly. An image of a brain came into view, replacing the man in the square. It had several black spots on it, indicating some form of deterioration. "Mental degeneration caused by prolonged, gradual exposure to the planet's atmosphere, particularly XM-13. Normally, exposure to XM-13—or Variant, as the humans call it—results in the death of a citizen, but in a few select cases, something else occurs. Rather than dying, the individual is driven mad, experiencing bouts of paranoia, heightened aggression, and both suicidal and homicidal tendencies. They cannot be reasoned with. They cannot be cured."

"That's horrible," said Lena.

Gel nodded. "Indeed it is. Before recently, there were very few cases, but in recent years the number of occurrences has grown significantly. They are becoming more frequent…and more dangerous." He leaned forward. "And the Leadership believes this will only continue, unless something is done to stop it."

A wave of panic coursed through Lena's body. "Is there a plan? There has to be something we can do."

"In fact, there is," said Master Gel. "We even have a cure."

"Truly?" asked Lena.

"You'll recall the boy from Earth that Doctor Curie and her team are looking for."

She nodded. "Yes, sir."

"We believe his genes hold the key to stability. A means of controlling the disease caused by XM-13."

"Because he can breathe the contaminated atmosphere?" Lena asked.

"Correct," said Gel.

"But isn't Doctor Curie providing us with the original genetic research?"

"Indeed, she is," Gel admitted. "We are thankful to her for this, but it is simply not enough. As you can see from the footage, the dangers are very real and present. If we do not find a solution to this problem soon, our entire way of life could be under siege." Gel blinked, and the image of the cell was replaced with the man in the square. "We must find the missing human and analyze his biology for ourselves. It is the only way to stop events like this from happening again."

"Examine?" asked Lena. She didn't like the sound of that.

"Only temporarily," said Gel. "Once we have what we need, he will be returned to his people. Don't worry."

That was a relief. Johnathan and Mei were good people. They deserved to have their friend back, and Lena wanted to help Everlasting. Finding Terry could be good for both sides. "What would you have me do, sir?"

"I'm putting you in charge of your own team of analysts. You will use the Rosenthal satellite to locate the missing human at all costs. Set your people on rotation so that they are working every moment of every day. I don't want any gaps. Once we have the boy in custody, we can focus on finding a cure for this terrible illness. Do you understand?"

"Yes, sir! I'll do whatever I can to help Everlasting."

"Excellent," said the Master Analyst. "You do your city proud."

The Border
February 25, 2351

TERRY LEFT the house in the early morning, snagging a quick bite of bread and cheese on his way. He took his sword with him, ready for another day of practice. He'd spent every single day with his weapon—sometimes under Ludo's guidance, but often on his own. He took long walks in the woods, pausing at various points to work on his stance and form, using the trees as targets.

He found that when he focused and relaxed his mind, the rest came much easier. He did his best to travel with the blade always in his hand, trying to grow accustomed to its weight and feel. In the short amount of time he'd spent with the sword, he found himself quite comfortable with it. Perhaps it was due to having wielded a machete and knife for so many years in the wild, or maybe it was simply his determination that drove him. Either way, he would not rest until he could use this sword to defend his friends from anyone who dared to come.

There would always be dangers on this planet, no matter how safe it might seem. He would always have someone to contend with. The cries from across the wall, which came frequently throughout the night, were a constant reminder of that. Even after he and Ludo's family found their way back home to the farm, he would not relax.

A soft yip came from within the forest—an animal of

some kind, by the sound of it. Terry paused and listened, trying to pinpoint the location. He concentrated on the direction of the cry, filtering the other noises.

A few minutes passed, but he found it—a large beast, breathing heavily, letting out of a soft moan. Was something wrong with it?

Terry took off in its direction, staying light on his feet with his weapon ready. He ran swiftly through the woods, avoiding branches and twigs, making almost no noise, except for the rustling of leaves. The animal's cries grew more frequent, more frantic, as though it were in pain. The scent of blood filled the air as well, causing him to cringe. Whatever was happening ahead of him, it seemed to be the messy sort.

A short while later, a voice erupted in the thick of the woods. Terry stopped immediately, waiting behind one of the larger trees. "Quiet the beast," ordered one. "Quickly, before it wails again!"

"Quiet it yourself, Zika," snapped another. "I'm not your servant."

The voices sounded familiar, but he couldn't place them. Despite his eyes, the trees severely limited his line of sight. He'd either have to wait for them to get closer or—

What sounded like a weapon tore through the flesh of the animal. Its breathing stopped in only a few seconds. "There," said the voice.

"Good. The animal never should have charged at us.

Let's get going. The faster we kill the traitor, the faster we can get out of here."

"Are you sure we're even headed in the right direction? It's been over a week since that merchant saw the cart, and—"

"Do not question me, Tia. I know what I'm doing."

"You always say that, but it was your idea to leave her at the temple in the first place. Look what happened."

Who the hell were these people? They sounded female. Could they be priestesses? If so, this could prove a serious problem. Ysa wasn't healed enough to deal with them, and Terry wasn't sure he could do it on his own. He and Ludo had barely managed to stop Gast when they were in the prison.

Judging by their voices, he could estimate they were nearly a kilometer away. If he left now, he could warn the others. *I need to hurry*, he thought, stepping away from the tree. He turned and ran toward the house. Ludo would be busy in the kitchen by now, and Plead would be sitting at his usual spot near the beach. Their vacation was over, it seemed. Things were about to get a lot more complicated.

Tower of the Cartographers, Everlasting
February 25, 2351

LENA SOL BROUGHT up a holographic display using her

neural implant, requesting an immediate scan of grid 1103-22. The Rosenthal satellite responded with its acknowledgment and proceeded to act as it was programmed, searching each and every biological signature across the grid. It would do this until it discovered entities matching the parameters Lena had given it. In this case, those pertaining to a human male by the name of Terrance, born and raised on the planet Earth, but now presumably living somewhere on Kant. Due to an agreement between the Leadership of Everlasting and the government of Central, efforts were now underway to secure the young man and bring him safely home.

As of this moment, the analysts had been scanning the continent for nearly two days, moving from one grid to the next, cycling their staff through all hours. With any luck, the process would be swift, but there were no guarantees. Despite the strength of the satellite, the possibility of locating a specific individual, particularly without any evidence to their movement, remained unlikely. For this reason, the Leadership had given Lena Sol a team of twenty-six other analysts, each one tasked with the single goal of finding their target. *If only the other satellites were still operational,* < thought Lena. *Just sixty years ago, this process would have taken far less time.*

In truth, the Rosenthal satellite was the product of another age, back before the gas destroyed most of civilization. In those days, Everlasting was one of many cities within the Galant Empire, which spanned the bulk of the continent. Galant was in the midst of an arms race with another country called Andur, which caused a surge in technological advancements, including the construction of several satellites. Andur's efforts were tame, resulting in dozens of failures and deaths, but Galant managed to launch six successful missions. Over time, these satellites broke orbit and were decommissioned, but the Rosenthal was still holding steady with no signs of orbital decay. Even after the Empire had fallen, Everlasting and the Rosenthal satellite lived on.

If only the other satellites had survived longer, thought Lena, sorting through the data from grid 1103-22.

She found nothing of interest, filed the results of the scan, and continued to 1103-23.

This grid took her to a seaside village. The locals called it Capeside. The town was filled with people of varying ethnicities from all along the north coasts, including sailors from across the northern ocean. Scanning so many individuals took longer than expected, so Lena used the extra time to sort through reports from other analysts under her command.

Grid 1104-01. Seventeen humanoids. No matches.

Grid 1105-12. Six humanoids. No matches.

Grid 1105-34. Ninety-seven humanoids. No matches.

Grid 1108-04. Fifty-three humanoids. No matches.

Grid 1113-02. Zero humanoids. No matches.

The list went on, giving similar results each time. With over eighty thousand parent grids, the process could potentially take weeks. Maybe longer, depending on his movements. The Rosenthal satellite began its scanning sequence by examining a central point of interest and expanding outward. In this case, the portal facility in grid 1103-29.

If Terry went underground, the satellite might not be able to find him at all. If he crossed the ocean at any point, the scans would have to go on for months before they reached him. Let's hope he doesn't like to travel, thought Lena.

The hours stretched on as she worked, pouring over scans and data, waiting for reports to come in. At various intervals, her team of twenty-six analysts came and went, replacing one another throughout the day and night.

But Lena Sol continued on, unhindered. She had been given a task and would see it done to the best of her abilities. All was for the good of Everlasting.

Halfway through the night, an alert blinked on her display, indicating another report had been filed. She opened it, expecting the same results.

Grid 1121-87. Four humanoids. One match.

She blinked, wiping her eyes. She took a quick breath and read it once more.

Grid 1121-87. Four humanoids. One match.

One match.

Could this be accurate? She motioned to bring up the full report. Grid 1121-87 was adjacent to the southern wall, near the ocean. It was far removed from any settlements and seemed an unlikely location for someone to go, especially considering how far it was from the portal site. Had Terry truly traversed such a distance on foot? If he was anything like the other humans, particularly the Blacks, then perhaps. They had revealed themselves to be quite adept at survival.

Lena brought up a live feed of the grid in question, magnifying several times until she had the exact location of the match. In an open field on a hill, sitting between a beach and the forest, she found a single building. Outside of it, two figures walked together through the nearby field, while two others waited inside. With a single command, the satellite pinpointed the specific individual and magnified.

A young male with long dark hair walked in the direction of a couple of large animals. He held a thick bag on his shoulder, but dropped it to his side and tore the top open. Petting one of the beasts on its forehead, he proceeded to pour the contents of the bag into a trough. He waited for the animals to begin eating, then rolled the top of the bag and lifted it to leave.

Lena watched him for several minutes, unable to see his face, but nonetheless remained intrigued. The man's ears were short and curved, the same as the other humans she'd met before. The same as Johnathan Finn. Of all the people across the globe, none had ears like them. She leaned in, waiting for a glimpse of the stranger's face, determined not to move until she had it.

At one point, the man tilted his head and she got a brief look at his nose, which extended a short distance, similarly to the other humans. He soon went back inside the house, blocking the satellite from getting a clear view of his face. She could still track his movements, but the details of his appearance would elude the scans. Still, she had enough evidence to take this to the Leadership. The man matched Terry's height, hair color, and general body type, including the ears and nose, making for a remarkable find. While not definitive, it was enough to justify further investigation.

Lena ordered a quarter of her team to focus their efforts specifically on grid 1121-87 and its surrounding areas. The rest of them would continue to search according to established protocol, scanning multiple grids in an effort to discover other matches, should the current findings prove false.

Lena Sol was confident, however, that this would not be the case.

She filed a report directly to Master Gel, stating her hypothesis that the individual in question was indeed the one for whom they'd been searching. Whether or not the master analyst would agree with her findings, of course, remained to be seen.

The Border
February 25, 2351

"Priestesses? They are near? Are you certain?" asked Ludo. His voice was frantic. "We must get Ysa out of here at once! They will show her no mercy."

"We have nowhere to go," said Plead.

"We will take the cart and head south," said Ludo, sounding confident.

"There are checkpoints between here and Capeside. We could go to Edgewater, but it's so close that they could track us there with ease," explained Plead.

"There has to be somewhere," said Terry.

"We can only head south," said Ludo.

Terry thought for a moment. What were they going to do? Plead was probably right about not being able to hide out in Edgewater, and the checkpoints between here and Capeside might be a problem. At the very least, they'd report about suspicious travelers when the priestesses or the temple guards came looking. "There has to be another option."

Plead put his knuckles to his lips, pausing to think. "How far were they, these priestesses?"

"Not very. A few hours, at best. One of them mentioned a merchant giving them directions, but I don't think they knew the whole way."

"I see. It must have been the caravan." Plead cursed under his breath. "The butcher, if I had to guess."

"I thought you were friends," said Terry.

"For a few days, perhaps. Hardly enough to risk one's life. I doubt he would have told just anyone, but a priestess can make a strong case. Thankfully, he didn't know our destination. Only the direction."

Terry knew full well the power a priestess wielded. He'd seen Ysa's strength when she battled Gast on the farm. "What should we do?"

"Whatever is safer for Ysa," said Ludo.

"In that case, I don't think running is in our best interest. The only solution is to hide."

"Okay, I'm listening," said Terry.

"There is a place not far from here, but the location is…problematic," said Plead.

"What sort of place?" asked Ludo.

"This house used to belong to a group of smugglers and poachers. They specialized in exotic goods." Plead looked out the nearby window. "From the other side of the wall."

"The wall? They went to the other side?"

"Right you are, my boy," said Plead. "Dangerous business, but highly profitable. You'd be amazed at the sort of furs—"

"Okay, so that's what we have to do, then," interrupted Terry.

"But we have been to the edge of the wall already," Ludo reminded him. "I never saw a gate or broken section to pass through."

"That's because it's hidden. The smugglers used a tunnel they built themselves."

"I take it you know where it is," said Terry.

"Of course," said Plead, rather proudly.

"Then let's go. We need to move before it's too late."

BETWEEN THE FOUR OF THEM, they managed to load most of the supplies back into the cart before leaving. Ysa and Ludo once again sat in the back, while Terry and Plead took to the front. There was still no sign of the priestesses, no matter how hard Terry tried to listen. With any luck, they'd veered off in another direction.

Plead brought the cart to the northern wall, but stayed with it until it ran into a cliff near the sea. "Everyone out," he told them.

"Is the passage inside?" asked Ludo, helping Ysa off the back of the cart.

"No, not quite," explained the merchant. He motioned toward a set of bushes in the opposite direction. "This way."

With everyone behind him, Plead dug his hands in the ground, searching and flinging up dirt. Plead let out a happy "Aha!" and yanked on a piece of rope, pulling a hidden tarp free.

Dirt scattered into the air, hitting Terry in the face and covering his feet. He wiped his cheeks and spit.

Beneath the cloth and rope, there was a large slab of wood. A hatch of sorts. Plead gripped the handle and, with a quick tug, managed to lift it.

The tunnel inside went straight down, with only a single

rope ladder to hold them. Plead took a couple of torches from the rear of his cart, giving them to Terry and Ludo. He also unloaded a few packs filled with supplies, including some dry food, water, and rope. "Here you go," he said, helping Ludo put it on. "Mind your head when you're down there."

Ysa and Ludo went in first, descending slowly into the dark. The light of Ludo's torch showed the way, revealing the rest of the pit, which curved after about fifteen yards.

"You'll be next, my young friend," said Plead, preparing to give Terry his own pack.

"What are we going to do with the cart and the haddins? Leave them here?"

"There's a cave in the cliff nearby. I'll be waiting for you there."

"Wait, what? You mean you aren't coming with us?" asked Terry.

"Someone has to stay behind to cover the hatch. Otherwise, what's the point?" asked Plead.

"You can't just go running off on your own. Those people are crazy. They'll kill you!"

"Don't fret about me. I'm just a merchant spending some time at the beach." He grinned. "I'll tell them I dropped you off in Edgewater before coming here. They'll believe it. I have a trusting face."

"But—"

"When you get through the tunnel, close the other hatch, then head left and follow the wall. You'll eventually find a little shed. It's not far. That one is far less dirty inside." He grabbed Terry by the shoulder. "And remember not to make any noise if you can help it. Don't leave that building until it's time to return. Do you understand?"

"Why? What's out there?"

"Monsters, maybe. Demons. Guardians. Whatever they are, avoid them. If you see one, you run. You understand me?" His face was very serious. "You run."

Terry stepped into the pit, gripping the rope. "How will we know when to come back?" he asked, beginning his descent.

"Three days," said Plead, getting ready to lower the hatch. "Return here at that time. I'll be waiting for you. Good luck, my boy. Look out for your friends."

"I will," said Terry.

The hatch slammed shut, blocking out the two suns, enveloping him in darkness.

THE TUNNEL WASN'T BAD. A few of the walls had caved in a bit, but not enough to bar their progress by more than a few minutes. The walk was slow, but mostly steady. Terry, Ludo, and Ysa made their way to the other side, locating the second hatch in under a few hours.

This side didn't end with a rope ladder or a pit. Instead, the hatch was within arm's reach. With Ludo's help, Terry managed to crack it open, pushing a pile of scattered dirt and grass to the side.

As Plead had instructed, they hiked west along the wall, looking for signs of another hatch. After nearly two hours, they found it. A pile of unusually shaped stones marked the spot. They looked like the kind Terry had seen on the beach near the cabin, smooth and ovular. Nothing like the jagged rocks found in the woods.

To his surprise, the walls inside the little building were metallic, with a set of stairs leading further in.

"There's no way a group of smugglers built this," Terry said.

The door, metal like the rest, stood next to a device on the wall, which had been bludgeoned at some point and now had guts of wires hanging from within. Beyond the door, which opened with ease, they found a single room, filled with dusty furniture—the same sort Terry had discovered in the underground city, back before he ever met Ludo. The same design and everything.

He didn't know what to say.

LUDO SPENT the first few hours finding a bed for Ysa to rest in. There was hardly any dust or grime, though some weeds had broken through the cracks near the door. Plead had said the poachers came here once a year to work, but he'd expected something far less sophisticated. Whatever this was, it wasn't built by the hunters.

Not by a long shot. Everlasting had made it, probably while building their wall. Had it been an outpost of sorts, long ago? He wished he could ask someone.

There didn't seem to be any working electricity inside, not that he could find. The overhead light was there, but it didn't come on, nor did anything else in the room. Aside from being in far better condition than the underground facility he'd discovered, there simply wasn't much here that they could use. A few furs, disregarded in the corner by the previous tenants, but nothing else. What had this facility looked like before the poachers started using it as a storage locker?

Good thing Plead had given them some supplies. Three days in unfamiliar terrain might have spelled disaster.

Once they had explored the tiny domicile, there was little to do but wait. Ludo had cautioned against going outdoors unless absolutely necessary, so they could only sit and wait out the three days.

Terry kept himself occupied by practicing his form with his sword. Ludo occasionally observed, giving rare advice, but for the most part he left him alone. Terry had come a long way in a short amount of time. Hopefully, his progress would only continue.

As night came, the disturbing sounds of the Guardians returned. They were louder now, and clearer, coming and going until morning. As Terry lay in the corner, still awake, he felt a rumbling beneath him, matching the cries of the monsters outside. They were like footsteps, terrible and furious, shaking the world from far away. Terry imagined a great beast, covered in quills, breathing heavily and watching him. An image of a razorback flashed through his mind—the same one he had fought in the tunnels on Earth, years ago—and he remembered what it had done to Roland, there in that awful place.

Then, for the first time in several months, Terry thought about his home, his friends. He remembered their faces, and he imagined their voices calling to him.

The trembling stopped soon enough, along with the strange noises. Terry let himself relax, closing his eyes, and he drifted. Sleep quickly took him, and with it came the dreaming.

A great light filled him, fading into an image of a field. Green grass waving in the breeze, cerulean skies moving puffy, white clouds.

Near him, a woman stood, clad in a blue dress, and smiling. It was his mother, younger than he remembered, and happier than he had ever seen her.

She took his hand, tugging him along, leading him to a wide and never-ending sea. They found a dock with a boat tied to it. A little one with oars. His mother smiled at him and kissed his forehead, then pointed to the little craft, nudging him into it. He climbed inside without question, then watched as she untied and kicked it free.

His mother waved and blew a kiss as the boat began to

float away. She twirled in her sparkling blue dress, laughing happily.

Terry grabbed the oars and tried to go back, but they slipped into the water below, disappearing. The boat continued to float with the current, moving further away from the beach until nothing was visible. Until the woman in the blue dress had disappeared.

Until the little boy was all alone.

"Ask him again, Tia," said Zika. "Don't be afraid to cut him some more."

"Sorry, little man," said Tia, dangling a small dagger near Plead's cheek.

"I-I already told you, I don't know anything about a missing priestess," he said, sitting with his arms bound and his back against the cave wall. The smell of haggin blood filled his senses. It was so thick he could taste it. The poor animals were still in the corner, their innards strewn mercilessly on the ground.

"We know you smuggled her out. The other merchants described your cart with great detail," said Zika. She took the edge of the knife and ran it along his cheek, breaking the skin. A line of blood formed, dripping from his chin.

Plead had known the risks of staying behind, but now he was having regrets. What had he been thinking? He should have either gone with the others or headed south.

Tried to outrun these people. Tried to get away. He hadn't expected them to track him all the way to this cave. "Please, I don't know. I swear it."

"He swears it," mocked Zika. "Tia, did you hear?"

"I heard," she laughed.

Zika twirled the knife in her fingers. "Shall I cut him again?"

"No, wait!" begged Plead.

"She likes to cut things," said Tia.

"I do," admitted Zika, smiling at the bloody haggin meat pooling blood against the wall. She touched the edge of her blade against his cheek. "It's such fun, you know."

"Alright! Okay! A man and his wife paid me to take them nearby. I don't know who they were," said Plead.

She smiled. "Now we're getting somewhere. What else did they tell you? Did they say where they were going?"

"No, no," he insisted. "All I heard was they had a ship coming to pick them up. Somewhere on the beach. I don't know. I think there's a dock nearby."

Zika stared at him curiously. "You expect us to believe a ship came all the way out here for that traitorous filth?" She laughed like it was a joke. "You take us for fools, little man."

"It's true!" insisted Plead. "Her husband is in league with a wavemaster. I heard him say he knew one. I don't know the name, but they're probably halfway to Capeside by now."

"A wavemaster?" asked Zika.

"A tamer of the sea," said Plead.

"I know what they are!" she snapped, gripping his throat. Her hands were stronger than he expected. "I just find it hard to believe that one would come here for a traitor. Do you understand?"

Plead tried to speak, but couldn't get the words out. He nodded his agreement.

"I heard wavemasters are mostly in Tharosa," said Tia.

"Is that true?" asked Zika, loosening her grip enough for him to answer.

"Yes!" he gasped. "Edgewater gets ships from Tharosa and Lexine all the time. A few are wavemasters. They sail along the coast. It brings them close to here. I don't know where they were picked up, though, or what ship it was. I don't know anything, really!"

"Where did the ship take them?" asked Tia.

"I have no idea! I didn't even see it."

Zika stared at him. "How do we know if you're speaking the truth?"

Plead could feel his hand shaking. He gripped his pocket, trying to calm himself. If only he'd taken the time to study meditation in his youth. Maybe he wouldn't feel so panicked. He'd been lying to her through his teeth, hoping she'd believe it, but the whole thing could come tumbling down at any moment. "I wouldn't lie to you. I'm a follower of the Eye. I'm devout!"

She turned an awkward grin, patting his head. "I bet you are, little man."

"If they're headed south, we'll have to move quickly," said Tia.

"Priestess!" called a man's voice from outside.

Zika turned to the cave entrance. "I told you not to disturb us! Not unless you—"

"We found something! You'll want to come and see."

"Oh, really?" muttered Zika. She looked at Plead. "Did you hear that?"

"I wonder what it could be," said Tia.

The two women dragged Plead out of the cave, carrying him with ease. Even now, scared as he was, he could not help but be impressed. They brought him into the woods, following the soldier who had called for them, finally stopping at—

Oh, no.

"We found some tracks all over this spot," said the guard, standing over the tunnel entrance, which was now open. All of the dirt had been moved to the side.

"Took a bit to find the door, but the indentation in the sand gave us a clue," said another. "Figured it was worth a check."

"What do you think about that?" asked Tia, looking at Plead.

"I don't know anything about this. Smugglers used to run through these woods. It probably has to do with them."

"The tracks are fresh. No more than a day," said the first guard.

"It seems you've lied to us, little man," said Zika, frowning.

"N-No, I didn't," insisted Plead.

"The tracks look like your haggins'," said the priestess. "Look at those big feet."

"That's not—"

"Shall I go and get a piece from the cave to compare?"

"Let's kill him and go after them," suggested Tia, impatiently.

"Oh," said Zika. She swept her fingers through the merchant's hair. "I suppose we're done now."

Zika plunged her dagger into his belly, twisting it in one quick motion. She gripped him by the hair and smiled.

Plead screamed from the pain, unable to move. He opened his mouth to beg, ready to do anything to make it stop. Why hadn't he told her the truth? Why did he have to play the hero? He was never that person. He wasn't noble. He was a trader, a merchant, a talker. Always the man with the goods. What was he even doing here?

"Now, now," said Zika, a kind smile on her. She stroked his head like a doll. "No need to worry anymore. We'll take it from here." She kissed his forehead. "The traitor and her coward husband will be with you soon."

16

Leadership Report 220392.332
Recorded 02.26.884
Subtitled: Rosenthal Analysis

GEL: *Analyst reports confirm the location of a human male in grid 1121-89. We must dispatch immediately.*

KAI: *How certain are you of the identity?*

GEL: *The scans indicate a ninety-six point four percent probability, based on facial and body recognition software. It is very likely that this is the missing human we have been searching for.*

KAI: *You mentioned grid 1121-89, but the earlier report indicated 1121-87. Has something changed?*

GEL: *The individual has since migrated north of the wall. He appears to be taking refuge in one of our abandoned maintenance outposts.*

KAI: *If this is true, then we should proceed with the next phase. Shall we have Master Lao send a ship to retrieve him?*

GEL: *I'm afraid we will need something better than the aircraft. Something with true firepower.*

KAI: *Why is that?*

GEL: *The child is traveling with two associates. One appears to be a priestess, if her tattoos are any indication. You'll recall most of these priests and priestesses have an immunity, which means they must be dealt with in force.*

KAI: *Are you suggesting we send the sentry units?*

GEL: *They've proven efficient in dealing with the natives on the southern wall before.*

KAI: *And what if the boy dies in the fight?*

GEL: *The priestess might be immune, but I don't believe the human is. The sentries can subdue him with the paralyzing agent before disposing of the natives. It should go smoothly.*

KAI: *You'll excuse my reservations. This human is a vital asset. I would hate to lose him.*

GEL: *Don't worry, sir. The sentries can be gentle when the situation calls for it. We'll have him in the lab by the end of the day. I assure you, the mission will succeed.*

KAI: *See that it does, Master Analyst, for all our sakes.*

End Audio File

The Tower of the Cartographers, Everlasting

February 27, 2351

John had spent the last several days meeting with various leaders in Everlasting. They all wanted a chance to talk with the aliens from Earth. He didn't like the attention all that much, but if one of these leaders—Master of this, Master of that—could help him find his friend, he'd put up with just about anything.

Today, he was meeting with Master Gel, the head of Lena's division. The Tower of the Cartographers, they apparently called it. A floating set of buildings above the city.

John could hardly believe it at first. The *Red Door* shuttled them here this morning, taking them hundreds of yards above the ground. They'd told him that the tower was on a kind of floating island, but he didn't quite believe it. Not until he actually saw it with his own eyes, that is.

What a sight it was, too. With this kind of technology available to them, it was no wonder Everlasting ruled the world. Still, John found it a little strange that such an advanced society would ever have a reason to ask Central for help.

Yet, that was exactly the case. Mei was in the city right now, delivering information to Everlasting's scientists on how to solve the Variant problem. Somehow or another, humanity had managed to bypass this radically advanced civilization in this single venture, despite falling behind in everything else.

Lucky us, he thought. *We're not completely worthless.*

"Hey, boss, this is some view, huh?" said Track.

John had heard him coming, naturally. "Pretty fancy. What do you think?"

Track wrinkled his nose. "Eh, it's a little too much for me. I'll take the ground."

"Speak for yourself," said Short. "This place is out of this world!"

"So are we, technically," remarked Hughes, quite proud of himself.

"Funny guy, you are," said Short.

"How do you figure they get this place to float so high?" asked Track.

John couldn't begin to guess, so he said nothing. Everlasting's technology was so far advanced that it sometimes looked like magic. A floating tower in the sky. An invisible shield around their city.

Sure, why the hell not? He didn't have to understand how they worked or why. He only had to know how to survive them. The world could fill with unicorns and dragons, but he'd still manage to keep going and protect the ones he loved. At the end of the day, none of this other nonsense mattered.

Let someone else worry about the wonders of the universe.

"Is everyone ready?" asked one of the attendants. "Master Gel is ready to see you."

John hooked his thumbs into his vest. "Let's do it."

"Good thing, too. I think Mickey's getting sick," said Short.

Mickey was sitting beneath the *Red Door*, leaning against the wheel, rubbing the side of his neck.

"Come on, Mick," said Hughes, helping him to his feet.

The attendant took them inside, through several hallways and around a series of offices. John spotted one room which had several rows of people sitting in slanted chairs, staring at nothing, with empty expressions. Based on what he knew about the implants they had inside their heads, he could only imagine that they were seeing something he wasn't. Some kind of invisible display.

After a short elevator ride, they found themselves on the administration floor. Master Gel's secretary stood to welcome them, dismissing the attendant who'd led them here. "I'm afraid the Master Analyst's office isn't large enough for everyone. Sergeant Finn, do you mind if your team waits here for you?"

"Well, boys?" asked John.

"Have fun, boss," said Short, snickering. "We'll let you handle all the politics."

John gave her a look. "Don't make me promote you," he said.

"Please don't," she answered, raising her hands defensively. "I like being a grunt. It's easy work."

"This way, sir. If you'll follow me."

"Right," said John.

The secretary led him to the nearby office. Master Gel sat behind the desk, sorting through a small box, but stopped when he noticed John. "Welcome," said Gel.

John stepped inside and took a seat across from him. "Thanks for seeing me."

"I understand you wanted to inquire on the status of our search," said Master Gel. "The one involving your associate, Terry."

"My friend," corrected John.

"Right, yes. I apologize."

"Do you have anything yet?" asked John.

"As you're aware, we've placed several teams of analysts on this in an effort to expedite the process. However, we have yet to find anything definitive. The world is quite large. Rest assured, Sergeant Finn, we are doing everything in our power to find him."

"I'm glad to hear that," said John.

"And we are glad to have you with us," said Master Gel. "I believe this alliance will prove most beneficial to both sides, and finding your associate…your friend…is part of it."

"Maybe someone could show us around. Is Lena nearby? It's been a few days since any of us saw her," said John.

"Analyst Sol is preoccupied with another matter at the moment, I'm afraid, but I'd be happy to escort you through the facility, personally. You can see exactly what we're doing and how everything works."

"Is Lena on another project?" asked John.

"Indeed," said Gel. "You likely won't encounter her for some time. I hope it's not an inconvenience."

"I guess not."

"You might be happy to hear that she'll be receiving a promotion soon, due largely to her work in forming this treaty between our two people. A different liaison will be assigned to assist you in her stead, but I assure you they will be highly qualified. Handpicked by Analyst Sol herself."

"That's good. She deserves the promotion. Lena's done a great job."

Gel smiled. "I couldn't agree with you more."

The Border
February 27, 2351

ON THE THIRD DAY, Terry and his friends left their temporary home beneath the dirt, ready to return to the other side of the great wall. The sky was clear at dawn, but brought some overcast by the time they departed, gray clouds moving with heavy wind behind them.

They hurried to the east, keeping by the wall to mind their place. Thunder snapped along the horizon. Terry could already hear the falling rain a kilometer away, moving toward them.

For a moment, he thought he heard another noise,

somewhere far off, but he couldn't be certain. Whatever it was—it didn't matter. They'd soon be out of here and on their way to the cabin. They'd meet Plead, and he'd tell them how uneventful the last three days had been for him. How nothing bad had happened. How everything was going to be okay.

Thankfully, Ysa had regained a bit of her strength during the three-day rest. She seemed to have less trouble with the pain. Perhaps another day or two and she'd be back to normal.

They'd left behind their bags, having used most of the supplies Plead had given them. There was no point in lugging around useless apparel, especially in the rain, not to mention the mud and filth that would come during their tunnel crawl.

Another thunderclap sounded in the sky above, heralding the storm that would soon be upon them. "Let us hurry," suggested Ludo.

As they neared the tunnel entrance, Terry heard the noise again, this time with a little more clarity. It was something resembling a voice, light and melodic, like someone humming. "Hold on," he barked, calling to the others. "Listen for a second. Do you hear that?"

The wind was blowing hard, kicking their clothes. "Is something wrong?" asked Ludo.

Terry pointed at his ear. "Do you hear it?"

Ysa closed her eyes, presumably to listen. She had better hearing than either of them when she was healthy.

Right now, she might not have the range, but it would still be pretty good. Ludo looked across the fields in every direction, darting his eyes around. "What do you hear?" asked Ludo to his wife.

She shook her head. "There is something faint, but I cannot make it out."

"Terry, is someone nearby?" he asked.

"I don't know. It's—"

A roar of thunder boomed, quieting him, and then a drop of water hit him on the forehead. He felt it slide across his nose, cold and fresh. A second later, the rain came down at last, showering them at once.

"We must get to the tunnel!" yelled Ludo.

The wind picked up and slammed the falling drops into them like little stones, pricking Terry's face and chest. They ran through the field, hitting puddles and soft earth. By the time they found the tunnel entrance, Terry's boots were caked in mud and grime, and his clothes were heavy with rain.

Ludo grabbed the hatch and lifted it, casting it against the wind. It slammed into the ground, splashing mud and water all around.

Terry stared into the pit as the rain began to fill it. "Are you ready?" he asked his friends.

"Plead will be waiting," said Ludo. "We must hurry."

"Stop!" snapped Ysa, grabbing her husband's wrist. She grew still and quiet with distant eyes, with a look that suggested she heard something.

Terry tried to listen, too, and at last he heard it clearly. A woman's laughter. It was coming from nearby.

"You hear it?" Ysa asked him.

He nodded. "What is it?"

"A familiar voice," she said. "Prepare yourselves."

Movement in the distance. The sound of splashing boots and grunting men, marching in the rain. They appeared from beyond a set of trees and piled stones. A dozen temple guards with swords and guns…two priestesses in their midst. "At last, we have found you!" cried one of them. "The lost sister. The traitor herself."

"Zika," muttered Ysa.

Ludo looked at Terry. "We must protect Ysa. She is not yet well enough to—"

"Who is that with you?" asked Zika.

"Her husband, it seems," said the other priestess.

"Tia, I know that. I meant the little one."

"Their son, maybe?"

"What an ugly thing. Look at his tiny ears."

"Is it so, Ysa? Is that your child? He seems deformed," said Tia.

"What should we expect from someone like her?"

"Quiet!" snapped Ysa. "You would do well not to speak ill of my family."

"So, it is true," said Zika, laughing. "How perfect. A hideous child for a hideous traitor."

Ysa didn't bother correcting them. "You will pay for your words."

Ludo leaned over to Terry. "Be ready. The fight will be difficult."

"Are they as strong as Gast?" asked Terry.

Ludo shook his head.

"Then it'll be easy."

The priestesses walked closer, about ten yards away. They stood there, staring, waiting. Each of them wore a dagger on their hip—the same type as the sword Plead had given Terry. The same one that had pierced Gast Maldeen's chest and ripped his soul out. Sacred vessels, Ludo had called them.

Whatever the case, Terry couldn't let his guard down... not for a second. He might be able to handle guns and regular swords, but these things were another issue altogether. He'd have to stay on his toes, because one wrong move and—

"I'll tell you what, Ysa," shouted Zika. "If you turn yourself in, we promise not to kill you. You can go right back to your cell. What do you think?"

Tia chortled. "We'll even put your family in the cells next to yours!"

Ludo threw his arm in front of his wife, shielding her. He stepped forward. "Run, Ysa. Get away from here, quickly."

Terry grabbed him by the wrist. "Don't be ridiculous! You can't take them all on by yourself."

"Terry is right," said Ysa, touching her husband's arm. "We must do this together...or not at all."

"No! If you go into battle, you may die. Your wounds are not yet—"

She smiled, her kind eyes staring into his. "It has been many years since we first escaped our fates together, husband, but I have not forgotten my purpose. I was made to fight the Guardians, to shed blood upon this very field. Don't you see, my sweet Ludo?" Ysa leaned over and kissed him. "I was born for this."

She turned from him and leapt forward, exploding into a wild sprint.

Terry watched as Ysa became a blur, a distorted mess of color flying through the rain.

Zika raised her arms to shield herself, but wasn't fast enough. Ysa plowed into her, sounding a snap as loud as thunder.

The collision sent Zika careening backward, flying into the trees, breaking them apart like twigs.

The guards ran at Ysa, their swords raised, but before they could touch her, she was already gone, headed after Zika, a fading blur in the distance.

Tia screamed, then charged at Terry and Ludo, raising her spear high above her head. Rage distorted her face, reminding Terry of some awful beast. The temple guards followed her, setting their sights on the two men.

"I'll take the loud one. You handle the guards," suggested Terry.

"We must hurry. Ysa will not last long on her own," said Ludo. He reached for a handful of throwing daggers. He let the blades loose in a fluid set of gestures, hitting one man in the neck, between his armor, while stabbing another in the eye. Before the group had made it to them, four were already dead.

Terry unsheathed his sword and readied himself. In an instant, he was fully aware, his mind relaxed and his breathing steady. He stepped forward and charged, with Ludo at his side. The farmer continued his barrage of daggers until he'd used them all, then unsheathed his own sword and prepared for the assault.

Terry passed by two other soldiers, sliding the edge of his blade across the neck of the closest one, spilling blood into the rain. In the same motion, he twisted around and plunged the sword into the stomach of the second man, sending him into the puddle beneath his feet. The blade slid free with no resistance, and he raised his eyes, only to be met by the tip of the priestess's spear as it came close enough to nearly touch his forehead. He dodged, watching as the spear slid by him.

He knocked the spear away with his sword, knocking Tia off balance. She steadied herself, then swept her leg back and leveled her weapon. Beads of rainwater glittered on the blade in the dim light of the gray sky.

Terry moved to his side, stepping around her, but the tip of the spear remained fixed and unwavering. As soon as his eyes left it, Tia jerked the weapon toward him, forcing him to take a step back. She laughed.

The sword in his hand was not meant for this kind of

combat. He had to get closer, just as Ludo had taught him. Get in tight and slice.

He stepped closer, clashing his weapon with hers and knocking it away. She moved with it, covering herself.

He tried again, but she pushed the spear at him, keeping back. He deflected it, but barely. "Careful now," she laughed.

He continued to press her, but she kept her distance, always the length of the spear. Here in this open environment, he was at a disadvantage.

She extended the stick in several quick thrusts, managing to cut him in multiple spots, but only slightly. The pain was sharp and brief, barely lasting more than a second, but it was enough to cause him some panic. "Got you," said the priestess, grinning, a hungry expression on her face.

He had to change the rules of this fight somehow. He had to—

Behind her, he spotted a handful of trees. If he could push her there, maybe in close quarters…maybe then, he could win.

The spear thrust at him once more, nearly hitting his side. He took the opportunity to try to grab it, but the priestess was too fast. Again, he looked at the trees. Limiting her mobility was the first step.

He swung his sword at the tip of her weapon, edging his way forward. She snarled at him, inching back to keep her spacing.

He deflected several of her attacks, continuing the slow crawl away from the open field, pushing her. Always pushing. As they moved deeper into the thicket of trees, she surprised him with another lunge, slitting his thigh. Blood ran from the wound, and he nearly stumbled. The woman smiled before trying a second time.

He hit the side of her spear with his sword, knocking it away. Ignoring the pain, he stepped forward, forcing her to take a step back. She collided with one of the trees. A look of panic seized her, and she tried to move, but Terry slid toward her.

She tried to use the spear, but missed.

He grabbed it, raising it over his side. She couldn't pull it back anymore, not with her back against the wood. "Get away!" she yelled.

Terry swung in close and tight, keeping the spear behind him.

He slid the edge of his sword along her stomach, splitting her open like a fish, guts pouring out. The edge of his blade snagged a piece of bone—one of her ribs—catching it. Blood erupted out of her, covering him as he tried to yank the weapon free from her body. Their eyes met, inches from one another, and Terry watched as the life began to leave her face. "No…" she cried as her body fell apart. "I…"

Terry pulled the sword free from her belly, backing away at last, blood on his chest and hips.

The priestess fell to the ground, dead.

He picked up her spear and threw it into the field, then turned his sights to Ludo. The farmer had dispatched most of the guards, with only two remaining. He'd taken a few hits, but seemed to be okay.

Better make sure he stays that way.

YSA FELT the cold mud between her fingers as she pushed herself up from the ground. Zika had separated from her once they hit the trees. Now, she lay in the torn grass of the field, motionless. With any luck, Ysa hoped, the blow had done her in. Perhaps this fight was already over.

Zika coughed, stirring slightly, moving her legs and arms. Of course, someone like her would not be so easily subdued. Ysa was a fool for hoping as much.

Were it so easy.

Ysa got to her feet, wiping the mud from her face and hands. A slight ache in her side caused her to flinch. She lifted her shirt and saw several small scrapes, with splinters sticking out. Her body was not fully healed, it seemed, which meant she would not be able to withstand very many hits. If she'd had a few more days, perhaps her ability to harden her skin would have returned, but there was no sense dwelling on that which could not be changed. She was here in this moment, stuck with this body, about to fight against this woman. That was how it had to be.

Zika struggled to get to her feet, but Ysa ran at her and

attempted to strike. Zika grabbed her leg before it could hit, then threw her to the side. Ysa whirled through the air, landing on her feet.

She took a breath and focused. A micro-meditation. One breath to regain her composure, shutting out the pain in her side.

Focus.

She ran again at her enemy, feigning a blow to her stomach. Zika went to block, but Ysa twisted, carrying the weight of her body toward Zika's throat, slamming her fist into it.

Zika gagged. She drew her dagger and swung it wildly in the air, trying to catch her breath.

Ysa charged, ducking beneath the dagger and wrapping her hands around Zika's legs. She pulled the priestess to the ground.

Zika landed on her shoulders, kicking into a backward roll, and kicking Ysa in the face. She stood, then ran at her, raising the knife, and straddling Ysa.

Ysa caught the woman's wrist, holding her back. The knife inched closer. Zika pushed harder. The blade touched Ysa's cheek, cutting the skin. She felt a surge of pain, but didn't let go. "Just let it happen!" said Zika, grasping the weapon with both hands.

Using her weight, Ysa twisted her body, causing the two of them to roll to the side. Zika kept the knife on her. They fumbled together until they hit a large rock. Zika was on top again, but the weapon had moved. It was inside of

Ysa's stomach.

She screamed at the pain.

"Almost there," whispered Zika.

Ysa tried to move the dagger—to pull it free—but Zika would not allow it. She could already feel her strength fading. She had to do something quick. She held her screams and clenched her teeth, then clawed at Zika's eyes.

Ysa dug her thumbnails deep into the priestess's eye sockets, tearing a scream from Zika's throat.

Zika loosened her grip, allowing Ysa to push herself free, kicking the woman off of her. She gripped the handle of the weapon buried in her gut, blood soaking through her shirt. Closing her eyes, she yanked the dagger out, a red mist spraying from the wound.

Zika started to come at her again, but Ysa wouldn't have it. She leapt at her, taking Zika by the jaw and slamming her into the mud. In the final act, Ysa raised the blade and readied the strike, prepared to do what was necessary. Prepared to kill the witch at last, to do whatever she—

The ground shook.

"ZHAA, ZHAA, ZHAA!" she heard a thunderous voice declare. "ZHAA ZHAA KAA!"

"Ysa!" cried Ludo. She looked to see him running toward her with Terry at his side. They were waving their arms and screaming. "Ysa, get away from there!"

The ground shook again.

"ZHAA ZHAA ZHAA!" came the awful sound. "ZHAA ZHAA KAA!"

A shadow grew tall over her, beginning from behind. It grew until it covered several steps in front of her, still rising. She turned to see a giant thing, a *moving* thing, with metal limbs and swords. It stood as tall as the wall itself.

A Guardian of Everlasting, come to smite them all.

THE GUARDIAN TOWERED over Terry like a skyscraper, its metallic body drenched in the falling rain. It had the shape of an armored man, almost like a samurai from ancient Earth, with strange designs across its body, similar to the tattoos on Ysa's head. On each arm, it bore two massive swords, very similar in form to the one Terry carried in his hand.

Near the titan's feet, Ysa struggled with the other priestess, attempting to pin her to the ground. Ludo was already running toward her, waving his arms and screaming. "Ysa, get away!"

She was on top of Zika with the knife to her throat, when she finally saw her husband. The monster raised its weapon high, bringing it down on the two bloodied women as they sat, gawking. Ludo barreled into his wife, knocking her clear. They hit the ground, sliding.

Zika screamed as the blade came down on her, burying her entire body like a twig in mud. All at once, she was silenced, crushed and broken.

The Guardian raised the sword again, pulling it from

the mud. Its metal edge was covered in red and brown, blood woven together with mud. "ZHAA ZHAA ZHAA," sang the hulking beast before turning its sights on Ysa and Ludo. "ZHAA ZHAA KAA."

"No!" screamed Terry. He dived forward, running as fast as his legs would allow, sprinting like a demon toward the Guardian's back. Without thinking, he slammed his sword into its leg, but the blade deflected off the metallic armor. The Guardian swept one of its weapons at him, like it was trying to swat an annoying fly, but Terry dodged to his side and avoided it.

The Guardian continued in the direction of Terry's friends, but they were already running.

Terry grabbed a part of the monster's leg as it walked, holding on with all his strength. He started to climb, trying to make his way to the head. The Guardian quickly noticed.

It stopped, and Terry heard a loud clank coming from its backside, like a vent opening. Almost immediately, there was a rancid, foul smell, like a dead animal, filling and burning his nose and lungs. He coughed repeatedly, but kept his grip on the Guardian's leg.

Terry's whole body went numb, all the feeling in his limbs draining out. He lost total control over the next several seconds before finally letting go of the armor plating. Sliding off the monster's leg, Terry fell into the mud, rolling helplessly before landing in the trench left behind by the sword.

He fell into the remains of the dead priestess, bones and shredded flesh mixed with dirt. Rain continued to fill the crevice, pooling inside. Pieces of Zika's body lay all around him.

Terry tried to move, but couldn't. The water from the storm continued to fill the trench, and he feared he might drown before much longer. He had to get out of here. He had to help his friends before they were killed. *Get up*, he told himself. *Get up, before it's too late.*

He concentrated, focusing his energy and relaxing. From deep within his mind, he pulled from his hidden well of strength. He imagined himself at the farm, standing in the autumn sunlight, listening to the birds as they flew overhead. All the rain was gone now, wiped from his reality. All the blood and mud inside this crevice gone and forgotten. Only the dream remained. He stood there in his mind, focusing his thoughts, collecting all the power left in him, every ounce there was to take. He would use it all if he had to. He would give it freely.

Terry felt his foot jerk, and a bit of feeling returned. He moved his fingers next, and then his arms. A few seconds later, he was pushing himself up, the dizziness of the drug finally dissipating.

The pain of his wounds from the other priestess's spear throbbed intensely. He pushed the feeling back inside himself, focusing instead on the task ahead. He couldn't slow down, not until the job was done. Not until his friends were safe.

He grabbed the side of the pit. With mud and blood on every inch of his body, he raised himself up, finally standing in the heavy rain.

The Guardian was a hundred meters away now, pursuing his friends. He had to get there, quick.

He started running, rain hitting him in the face, following in the massive footprints of his foe. He reached the titan soon enough, spotting his friends just ahead. Without another thought, he leapt onto the monster's back and gripped its metal casing. Like before, the Guardian tried to cast him off, but Terry dodged the giant arm and its blade. As it neared him a second time, he anticipated the swing, jumping to the arm and wrapping himself around the hilt. As it brought its hand around to the front, he caught a glimpse of the chest and head. Between them, there was a crevice with enough room to pierce, if he could reach it.

The Guardian's eye, which had until now been fixated on Ludo and Ysa as they ran, took its focus to Terry, following his every movement. With the full force of its body, it slammed its hand into the ground, nearly dismounting him. He buried his sword between the cracks of the plating, holding on for his life.

With each attempted dismount, Terry felt his wounds sear with pain, pulling him briefly out of his trance. He tried to push the sensation to the back of his mind—to bury it—but every strike brought him further away. If he didn't do something soon, he'd lose himself to it.

Terry pressed his foot against the hilt, breathing heavily, and with a rising heat in his chest, pushed himself off.

He flung himself toward the Guardian's chest, hitting it with the full force of his weight, and drove the weapon into the gap between its armor plating. The titan reached for him, but he raised his legs, dodging it, and then buried the rest of the blade inside the crack.

The Guardian's glowing eye grew bright with white and yellow light, and it cried an awful scream. "ZHAA ZHAA ZHAA!"

Terry pulled the sword from the crack, ripping wires and tearing metal in the process. The beast wailed in protest, slowing its movements, seemingly unable to cope with what was happening. If he could just get inside of it, maybe the fight could be over.

Holding the outer casing, Terry pressed his feet against the neck, and with all the remaining strength he could gather…he pushed.

The chest piece snapped and fell to the ground, landing with a thud in the dirt. The Guardian wavered, nearly stumbling.

Terry could barely hang on anymore, so he let himself fall. He landed on the ground and rolled, then turned to watch the Guardian as it began to scream.

Instead of a mechanical cry, however, there came the voice of a man, erupting from within the Guardian.

Terry stared at what appeared to be a pilot, strapped inside a pod. He had a mask on his face with a tube extending out, but there were several rips in it. The man grasped desperately at the tubing, trying to seal the tears, but it was no use. His face was already losing its color. For whatever reason, he was choking to death.

The pilot's entire body began to spasm. His eyes rolled back in his head, and he vomited inside his mask. After a few seconds, he stopped moving, dropping his head.

The Guardian froze, too, and the light in its eye faded into nothing. It only stood there, motionless.

Terry stared at the sight before him with absolute bewilderment. What in the hell did he just see? A Guardian with a person inside? But the man was suffocating on the air.

On Variant. Did that mean—

Terry felt a sudden throb of pain in his arm, and then another in his leg. The heat in his stomach was rising. *I need to sit*, he thought. *Just for a second.*

He hit the ground with a slight thud, slouching and breathing heavily. He started to close his eyes, tired from everything. So tired.

Another noise came from behind him, snapping him awake. "ZHAA ZHAA ZHAA," it sang. "ZHAA ZHAA KAA!"

The soil beneath him quaked.

"Terry!" called Ludo from afar.

He looked to see his friend running toward him, leaving Ysa behind. She'd made it safely inside the tunnel hatch. *Good*, thought Terry, barely conscious. *At least they'll be okay. At least I was able to...*

A shadow appeared, swallowing him in darkness. He twisted around, already knowing what he'd find.

Another Guardian of Everlasting, watching with its single, glowing eye.

17

Leadership Report 221602.521

Recorded 02.27.884

Subtitled: Target Apprehended

GEL: The mission was a success. The young man from Earth has been taken into custody.

KAI: He was nearly killed. Success is hardly the word I would use, Master Analyst.

GEL: The toxin was ineffective, so a more direct means of containment had to be applied. There was no other way.

KAI: A more direct means? The child managed to kill one of our pilots with nothing but a sword. How do you account for such a thing?

GEL: With any luck, we will know the answer soon. The boy's physiology, coupled with the research Doctor Curie has provided us, will greatly accelerate our own work. I'm certain of it.

KAI: *Perhaps, but the mission was still sloppy. We lost a sentry unit, which is sure to anger Master Lao. There are only twelve in active service, and you know how difficult they are to reproduce. Our engineers only have so many fusion cores to work with.*

GEL: *The other Leaders will understand. The loss of a sentry is worth the knowledge we will gain—*

KAI: *If the boy is still breathing. The report says the second pilot didn't even have to attack him. The boy was so exhausted that he collapsed on his own.*

GEL: *He has several wounds, but they weren't caused by the patrol. The pilots were specifically ordered to avoid lethal force unless absolutely necessary. Containment was their only goal.*

KAI: *If the sentries didn't cause the damage, what did?*

GEL: *Orbital feed showed an altercation taking place moments before our arrival. We don't know who started it, and speculation would accomplish little at this stage, but his wounds are consistent with that of a small blade. After a few days of treatment, he should be fully recovered.*

KAI: *I should hope so, Master Gel. The rest of the Leadership will not be pleased if your plan was all for nothing. Do you understand?*

GEL: *Yes, sir. However, despite the stumble, our objective was achieved. The boy will be monitored and analyzed, and whatever secrets his biology holds, we will uncover them in due time. Let us stay the course, Master Kai, for the sake of our future.*

KAI: Save the false patriotism, Analyst. Remember who you are speaking with.

End Audio File

Tower of the Cartographers, Everlasting
February 27, 2351

Lena Sol could hardly believe what she had just witnessed on the monitor. Two sentry units had been tasked with securing a single individual near the southern border —the human male named Terry—only to enter into a heated encounter. The confrontation not only resulted in the death of a pilot, but nearly got the target killed as well. *Was this my fault?* she wondered, replaying the footage for the seventh time. *Am I the one responsible?*

She was the one who discovered Terry's whereabouts. It had started here, right at this very console. If she'd never filed that report, the pilot would still be alive…and Terry wouldn't be—

She stopped herself. What was she doing, questioning her actions like this? She knew better than that. Everything she did was for her city. All was for the good of Everlasting…wasn't it?

It had to be, yes. The city came above everything else,

every individual's needs. Every desire and want. She could not question herself. Not now. Not ever.

Still, Lena could not escape the feeling in the back of her head. She hated herself for it…for whatever this was. *If only I'd never found that facility in the quarantine zone,* she thought, not for the first time. *None of this would have happened to me.*

A light appeared, blinking red to indicate a message. It was from Master Gel, requesting her presence in his office. Could it be about the footage she had just watched? Perhaps he'd been monitoring her activity and found it strange that she'd rewatch the same thing so many times.

Quietly, Lena deactivated her terminal and left. She made her way through the tower to Master Gel's office, passing a few familiar faces, but saying nothing.

When she arrived, the door was already open, and the secretary told her to go ahead.

The Master Analyst sat behind his desk, looking as though he'd been waiting. "Welcome," he said, motioning for her to take a seat.

"Good afternoon, sir," she answered, trying not to show her nervousness.

He gave a slight nod. "Please sit."

She did as he ordered, then waited anxiously. Was he going to send her to get a memory cleanse? A rush of panic filled her stomach. She wanted to leave. Run away and hide inside a box somewhere. Not sit here and be punished. *I knew I shouldn't have looked at the footage. What was I thinking?*

"There's something I need to discuss with you," said Master Gel, pulling Lena from her thoughts.

"Sir?"

"You have done a remarkable job with the work I've given you. As a result, I'm promoting you to level-eight. You will be a vice-administrator starting tomorrow."

Lena blinked. Did she hear that right? Level-eight analysts were typically twice her age, with years more experience. "Excuse me, sir, but did you say——"

"Level-eight," he confirmed. "That's right. You will be placed in charge of your own subdivision, answering only to the resident level-nine. The work will be demanding, but it's also essential. Congratulations."

The sudden promotion caught her off guard. Was she dreaming? She'd wanted her own subdivision ever since she was in training. How could this be happening? "May I ask what subdivision, sir?"

"Of course. I'm putting you in charge of the Argos outpost in the Bell Ring Isles. We're researching a certain type of natural gas beneath one of the islands, which is only found in a handful of other locations on the planet. We believe it holds significant value."

"Argos," she said, letting the name sink in. She remembered reading about it during one of her briefings last year. Argos was an inconsequential facility located far to the south, about as far removed from Everlasting as one could get. "But sir, I don't have any experience with——"

"Please, no need for modesty. You've proven yourself quite

capable. I believe you will adjust quickly. The current administrator will oversee your work and training, and will assist you with the transition process. His name is Nudin Kur, and he's expecting your arrival sometime tomorrow afternoon."

"Tomorrow?" she asked. "So soon?"

"Is that a problem?"

"N-No, sir," she answered, regretting her previous response. She had to be careful about questions. Too many of them implied noncompliance, and such habits would not be tolerated. "I-I am very thankful."

"I'm happy to hear that," said Master Gel. "Please go and pack your things. My assistant has your orders prepared. Medical first, I believe, followed by Supply. You'll receive everything you need, so there is no reason to return to your home. The shuttle departs tonight." He raised his hand toward the door. "I expect good work from you, Analyst Sol. Don't let me down."

Lena paused, debating whether to ask if she'd done something wrong, but stopped. *No questions,* she reminded herself. She got up from the chair and proceeded to leave.

She headed down the hall toward the transport bay, but stopped when she rounded the first corner. A wave of panic had taken hold of her, and she felt herself being pulled in multiple directions. She wanted to run home and away from this moment, this feeling. What had she done to deserve this? Argos was the kind of place they sent incompetent workers. Working there would only kill her career. It was little more than punishment. Why would the Leadership do this to her?

Are they trying to get rid of me? she asked herself. *Did I do something wrong?* Maybe they believed she'd grown too close to the visiting humans, or perhaps she'd made her reservations on Terry's capture a little too obvious.

She buried the feeling, knowing she had to do what her superior had told her, knowing she had to fulfill her purpose. No one refused an order from a member of the Leadership, no matter how much they might disagree. Transferring to the middle of the ocean was the last thing she wanted for her life, but there was no getting around it. The city relied on the sacrifices of its citizens to survive. Not the other way around.

Everything is for the city, she told herself. *Capturing Terry, letting the pilot of the sentry die, lying to Doctor Curie and Johnathan Finn, moving to Argos. All was for the good of...*

She felt sick to her stomach. An upset in her chest and throat. Walking quickly through the hall, she stepped into one of the bathrooms and headed to the nearest stall. Lena lifted the seat cover, then fell on her knees as her stomach seized up and returned her breakfast.

Afterward, with shaking hands, she flushed, and felt a lingering heat on her face. Sweat dripped from her forehead, and she fell back against the wall, trying to catch her breath.

Lena had only ever been loyal to the Leadership. She

had done everything they'd ever asked. Why, then, were they so eager to throw her away?

A White Room
February 27, 2351

TERRY OPENED his eyes to a bright light. He was on his back, strapped to a slab of cold metal. Above him, there were several rods pointed down at him. They were attached to some sort of machine, which seemed to be interconnected with the ceiling. He tried to move, but felt the sudden sting in the spot where the spear had pierced his flesh. He was still weak from the attack, it seemed, incapable of his full strength.

Footsteps echoed from the other side of the room. A man cleared his throat. "He's awake," said the stranger.

"Shall we begin the first procedure?" asked another voice.

The first one gave a confirmation. "Careful with him. He's all we have for now. Biopsies only."

Terry tried to move, but the straps were tight around his wrists and legs. "Who's there? Hey, where am I?"

The strangers didn't answer. Instead, the machine above his head began to move, twirling the rods with some mechanic rhythm. They stopped, and one of the rods extended, splitting in half to reveal a thick needle. It lowered to his chest, and he screamed.

Fifth Medical Building, Everlasting
February 27, 2351

AFTER PICKING herself off the bathroom floor, Lena made her way to Medical. Despite how she felt about her current situation, she had no other choice but to follow Master Gel's orders.

One of the doctors greeted her and told her to sit. She did, and waited patiently to be seen. One last checkup before tomorrow's journey to Argos. Once she received confirmation of her good health, she'd be on her way. Go here, go there. Medical, Supply, Argos. Never where she wanted. Always where they told her. All she had ever tried to do was serve Everlasting, yet this was her reward.

A quick image of the video footage flashed in her mind —the sentry lifting Terry's limp body off the ground, preparing to bring him back to the city. Upon seeing this, one of the natives had charged the unit with a weapon, trying to stop it. The sentry knocked him away with ease, disabling him. Was that man a friend of Terry's? Was he trying to save him? She pushed the memory from her mind. It was better not to think about such things.

Better to forget it altogether if she knew what was good

for her...but Lena could not forget. No matter how hard she tried, she couldn't shake the guilt.

The doctor arrived with an injector in his hand. "Put out your arm," he told her.

She did, and he pressed it against her skin. She felt a cold sensation as the device injected the substance into her arm using electrophoresis. It was completely painless.

"That's all from us. You can go," he said, removing the needle.

She nodded. "Thank you."

She let herself sit there for a few minutes, not wanting to leave. If she did, it meant going on to the next location. Another link in the chain, pushing her further toward Argos and away from her life in the city.

Using her implant, she called up an image of the city. It materialized into a hologram that only she could see, floating above her lap. Using her fingertips, she zoomed in and out, twirling the three-dimensional image around like a toy. After a moment, she tapped the building she was currently sitting in. The Fifth Medical Building on the eastern half of Everlasting, nestled between four other medical facilities. She wondered which one contained Terry, the alien from another world. John and Mei's friend. The one she'd watched on the screen, who'd very nearly perished.

But what if he *was* dead, after all? The question lingered in her mind, dancing with her fears. How would she live with herself, knowing she was responsible? An anxious flutter ran through her stomach and chest. She had to find out before she left for Argos. She had to know, at the very least, if the boy from Earth had survived.

She went to the access hub and entered her authorization code, which allowed her to browse the logs. She ran a quick search through the database for any mention of Terry, but found nothing. She tried again, this time using the terms *alien* and *Earth*. Several entries appeared, but they were all associated with Doctor Curie's people and the information Everlasting had learned about their planet to date. Finally, she searched for incidents involving the southern border.

Several appeared, mostly referring to the ritualistic practices of the tribespeople who made a habit of sending their females through the wall. According to one report, this had happened a few weeks ago, resulting in several of the natives' deaths at the hands of two sentry units.

Lena continued to scroll through the list, but stopped when she saw something mentioning a downed unit, which had to be recalled. It was currently being repaired. The deceased pilot was briefly referenced as well. A link to another report was tagged at the end of the article. It had red lettering, indicating a highly classified report. Only a handful of citizens would even be able to see this link, let alone access it. No doubt, someone in the Leadership would notice if she continued.

I shouldn't, she thought, hovering her finger above the holographic text. *I could get into trouble. I could—*

She stopped herself. She was already in trouble. She was already going to Argos, wasn't she? Besides, she was leaving tonight. By the time anyone noticed her search, she'd already be on a ship, heading to the middle of nowhere. If anyone asked, she'd tell them the truth—that she was only concerned about his well-being. The Leadership might watch her for a few months, but since she'd be in Argos, nothing would ultimately come of it. All Lena wanted was closure, so why couldn't she have it?

She took a breath, and then accessed the link. Another report appeared, this time with all the information she'd hoped to find. Images of Terry fighting the first sentry were there, along with some information on his medical status. It said he had been in critical condition, having received several severe lacerations, but was now recovering. Lena searched for his current location. The database showed he was in one of the medical buildings nearby. Not here, exactly, but right across the square outside.

She could walk there in under a minute if she wanted to, but could she really do it? Investigating through the network was one thing, but actually going there was something else. She might receive a memory therapy session if things went poorly. Maybe it was okay to stop here.

She got to her feet and proceeded outside. Dozens of citizens walked in the open square, talking and laughing with one another, largely oblivious to everything around them. She took a seat on the nearest bench, facing the Sixth Medical Building.

She stared at the front door for a long time, still not wanting to leave. Still debating what to do. Terry was in there, somewhere. If only she wasn't so weak and afraid.

When it seemed like she might never be able to go through with it, she heard a scream coming from across the square. "Bomb!" cried someone from within the crowd.

Lena had almost no time to react when the explosion occurred. It sent a shockwave throughout the square, knocking her to the ground and scattering the mob.

A White Room
February 27, 2351

TERRY FELT the shock when it happened, then watched as the men in white coats scrambled in a panic.

"What was that?!" snapped one of them.

"Look! There's smoke!" said another. He took a mask and covered his face.

The first one did the same. "What's going on?" he asked with a muffled voice.

"Another attack, maybe?"

Terry squirmed to get free, but the straps were still too tight. It would be a while before he was strong enough to break them. "Hey, let me out of here!"

But the two men ignored him. "We're safe as long as we stay here," one said to the other.

The nearby door slammed open, and someone entered with great urgency. It looked like a soldier of some kind, dressed in a protective suit, with a mask to shield his face. "What are you doing in here?" he asked the two doctors. His voice was odd, almost computerized. He held a rifle of some kind in his hands. "This building is getting attacked! You need to leave. Now!"

"What about him? Leadership has orders not to leave him alone," said one of the doctors.

The armored stranger glanced at Terry. "Don't worry. I'll escort him personally to the Eighth Medical Building and secure him there. I have orders to get every citizen out of here first, so you need to leave."

"We understand," responded one of the doctor. He looked at his friend. "Come on."

"Keep your masks on at all times," explained the soldier.

"Yes, sir," said the doctor. He scrambled to put on his mask. "Thank you."

The two doctors quickly left the room.

The suited individual approached Terry from the side, stopping to look at him. They examined each other. "Who are you?" asked Terry.

The man only stared at him, tilting his head. "So, you're the alien, are you?"

Terry didn't say anything.

"I didn't mean to insult you. I've just never seen anyone like you before."

Another explosion rang in the distance, shaking the facility. Terry squirmed, trying to get out of the straps. "This is crazy! What's going on out there?"

"Nothing dangerous," answered the stranger. "It's only a distraction."

"What are you talking about?"

"Do you even know where you are right now?"

"Everlasting, right?" asked Terry.

"That's right. Do you know what those men were planning to do to you?"

Terry didn't answer.

"They're trying to extract genetic information from you. Then they're going to kill you."

Terry blinked. "What?"

"You have something inside you they want," said the soldier.

"No, I don't. That's not—"

"You can breathe the atmosphere outside," said the stranger. "That's a valuable commodity."

"You mean Variant? The gas?"

"We call it XM-13. It's deadly to everyone in Everlasting. Their goal was to replicate the process through which you attained immunity. The people in this city aren't like the natives outside. They'll die if they're exposed."

Just like the pilot inside the Guardian, thought Terry. "If that's true, why didn't they bother with anyone else? There's plenty of others who can breathe it."

"Your genes were altered. They didn't evolve this way. Someone changed you. It makes you unique."

How in the world did this person know about how Terry was created? What else wasn't she telling him? "Who are you?"

The stranger gripped the side of the helmet and pulled it off, letting down a bundle of brown hair. Two female eyes stared back. "My name's Jinel Din," she said with a grin, "and I'm here to rescue you."

THE WOMAN in armor unstrapped Terry's arms and legs. As he got to his feet, he felt the heat on his chest from where the machine had pierced him. Between this and the wounds he received at the border, he wondered if the pain would ever stop.

"Are you alright?" asked Jinel, staring at him.

"I will be," he said.

"We have to get going. Here, take this." She handed him a mask. "It will filter out the toxin."

"What toxin?"

"The one the Leadership will release. It's a paralytic, which means you won't be able to move. We can't have that, can we?"

"Right," said Terry, remembering the fight with the Guardian. The giant machine had released some kind of gas, paralyzing him. He could probably withstand another dose if he had to, but it was better not to take the chance.

"Follow me," she said, leading him through the nearest door. "Oops. I nearly forgot." She reached behind, taking the pack off her back and opening it. "You'll need something to hide those ugly ears of yours."

"You said these people want to use me to find a cure to Variant, but you live here, right? Why are you helping me?"

Jinel covered her face with her own mask, sealing it with a soft click. "Whoever controls the cure controls this city," she said in a synthetic voice. "If the Leadership gets their hands on you, they'll use that cure as another form of subjugation."

"So, this is some kind of rebellion?" he asked, placing the shawl around his ears and neck.

"Of a sort, yes. We're giving Everlasting back to the people. If you understood what goes on here, you'd agree that something has to be done."

Terry glanced back in the direction of the lab they'd just left. "If it's anything like what I saw in *there*, I'm sure it's awful."

"Believe me when I tell you, it's worse than you can imagine."

Worse than drilling a hole into his chest? Worse than taking little pieces of his body for their own experiments? "Who exactly do you work for?" asked Terry.

"An organization called Garden. We've spent the last decade and a half fighting the Leadership's grip on this city." She looked at him, her whole face shielded by the mask. "You're in a war now, Terry," she said, simply. "And this is only the beginning."

Hall of the Leadership, Everlasting
February 27, 2351

"WHAT DO YOU MEAN, there's been an attack?" asked John. He'd only just arrived, expecting to meet with the Leadership. As it turned out, though, hell was breaking loose all throughout the city.

"It's as I said," resumed Master Trin. "Several assaults have been made on Everlasting over the last hour. One in the Medical Quarter. Another in Manufacturing. Another near this very facility."

"Is it still going on?"

"The Master of Arms is the one in charge of Civil Protection."

"So, you don't know?" asked John.

Trin's eyes dilated momentarily. "Forces have been distributed throughout the city," he said, as though he was reading something. "There have been several casualties, but we are driving them back."

"That's a relief, but who are they? Where are they coming from?"

Master Trin hesitated. "I...don't know."

"You don't know who's attacking you?"

"They call themselves Garden," said a voice from behind him. John turned to see Master Gel approaching. "Radical extremists. We believe they've been infected by the atmospheric gas, corrupting their minds in the process, though we can't be certain."

Corrupting their minds? John had never heard of Variant doing that. Then again, these people weren't exactly human, either. If what Mei had said was true, their DNA was slightly different. Who knew what kind of effect it could have on them? "How can you be sure they're not just really pissed off?"

"I'm sorry, I don't understand your meaning," said Gel, who apparently had never heard the word "pissed" before.

"Nevermind," said John.

"Hey, boss," called Mickey. "Everything alright?"

"Ain't you been listening?" asked Short.

John ignored them. "Look, if we're talking insurgents or whatever, let me and my boys help. We've got the gear and the experience to deal with this sort of thing."

Gel and Trin looked at each other. "No, I don't think that's a good idea," said Trin. "We can't have you murdering people in the streets. You're outsiders."

Gel nodded. "Agreed. The Master of Arms is handling the situation. His response must be made with great precision. He wouldn't appreciate it if we—"

A sudden explosion erupted from outside, followed by a series of screams. An alarm sounded throughout the floor, flashing yellow lights. "Well that can't be good," muttered John.

"Boss, I think this place is under attack!" shouted Hughes, trying to speak over the noise.

Several people went running through the hall, passing them. "I'd say that's probably right," said John. He looked at Gel and Trin. "You two might wanna get out of here."

"We can't leave the building," said Master Gel.

"The only entrance is at the front end," said Master Trin.

"Do you have any troops nearby?" asked John. For the first time today, he was glad that Mei had stayed behind at Bravo Point.

Trin paused, staring at the air above him. "It looks like Master Tao's forces are occupied. He says he'll send them as soon as possible. We should take cover until they arrive."

"There's a safe room. I suggest we use it," said Gel.

Another explosion, this time much closer. John could sense them coming down the nearby hallway. "You need to move!" he snapped. "We'll stop them here."

Master Trin looked panicked. "That's not—"

Master Gel grabbed his arm. "Let them do as they want! We have to get out of here!"

John watched as the two men made their escape. He didn't blame them for being afraid. They weren't soldiers. None of these people were.

Hughes readied his rifle, checking the magazine and grinning. "About time we got some action."

"Alright, boys," said John, unlatching his gun. "It's time to show these folks what it means to carry a big stick."

Medical Quarter, Everlasting
February 27, 2351

SMOKE WAS RISING from the side of the Seventh Medical Building as hundreds of citizens ran screaming in every direction. A panicked office worker knocked into Lena and sent her tumbling to the ground.

Several people ran through the square, nearly trampling her in the process. She rolled beneath the bench, holding her knees together with both hands. The mob's screams were so loud it made her ears hurt, but it didn't take long for them to dissipate.

Lena's chest pounded, and her tongue went dry. She was breathing so heavily, flinching at any sound she heard.

She climbed out from under the bench, lifting herself onto her feet. She looked at her hands as they shook violently, then reached behind her head. She felt bits of dirt all through her hair and tried to wipe them away.

The Sixth Medical Building's doors were only a dozen steps away. She could run inside and wait this out. That was better than running blindly through the streets, wasn't it? Who knew what sort of danger those people would encounter out there. What if another bomb went off?

What if the Leadership released the toxin in the streets, paralyzing everyone in the process? Those people would just be helplessly lying there, unable to avoid another attack. At least inside a building, she could hope for some kind of protection.

The doors opened with ease, although the lights inside were flickering. The explosion must have damaged one of the lines.

She leaned against the wall and slid down to the floor. The whole first floor of the building seemed to be empty. Everyone must have evacuated as soon as they heard the explosion. I wonder if Terry's in here somewhere, she thought.

Probably not anymore. The doctors had likely already moved him to safer location. Either that, or he was under lock and key and inaccessible. Lena called up her display to look at the report she'd found. It said he was in room 229b. The basement, right beneath this floor. By the look of the blueprints, the stairs were pretty close. If she wanted to, she might be able to find the room.

Whatever was going on outside, the Department of Civil Protection would respond with due force fairly quickly. They'd never notice her taking a peek in the basement.

Really, what harm could it do?

She kept the map up and began following it. It led her past several desks and terminals. Various office supplies had been knocked to the floor, no doubt from the panicked workers as they fled. In the rear, a few yards behind the office administrator's unit, she found a set of doors. *Right through here*, she told herself. *I can do this.*

She reached out to touch the handle, swallowing her fears, but stopped.

There was a voice on the other side. Someone was coming.

JINEL DIN OPENED the door and immediately drew her weapon. "Halt!" she commanded.

Terry glanced over her shoulder to watch as a woman fell backward onto the floor. "Wait!" she begged, holding her arms above her head. "Sorry, sorry, sorry!"

Jinel looked down at the girl, tilting her head a little and staring. She lowered her weapon.

"What is it?" asked Terry.

"This woman," muttered Jinel.

The girl kept her eyes closed, keeping her head against the wall. She was trembling. "I was only here to get away from the explosions. Please! I'm sorry."

Terry reached for Jinel's arm. "Hey, let's leave her alone and get going."

"She's a high-level analyst," said Jinel.

"You've met her before?" asked Terry.

Jinel looked at the girl on the floor. "Lena Sol, analyst."

Lena, still shaking, peeked up at them sideways. "Y-Yes, that's me."

"Get out of here," said Jinel. "It's dangerous."

Lena scrambled to her feet, taking a few steps back. "Thank you, sir."

Jinel and Terry stepped out of the stairwell. "See that you get home quickly."

Lena stared at Terry, noticing him for the first time. She looked surprised, raising her finger at him. "Y-You're…"

"What?" he asked, expecting her to say something about how strange he looked.

"You're Terry," she finally said.

He stopped at the sound of his own name. "How does everyone know who I am around here?"

"She knows a lot of things," said Jinel.

Lena stared at both of them. "You're taking him out of here? But he's not restrained. That's not procedure, is it?"

"Didn't I tell you to go home, Analyst?" asked Jinel, lifting her weapon a little.

"Hey, easy," said Terry. "There's no reason for that. Look at her. She's not dangerous. Let's just get out of here."

Lena's eyes narrowed a bit, and she looked out the nearby window in the direction of the smoke. Terry could sense the gears turning in her head. She was putting it all together. "You're not with Civil Protection, are you?"

"There's the level-five analyst in action," said Jinel.

"Level-seven," corrected Lena, her voice shaking. She swallowed. "S-Soon to be level-eight. Your records are outdated. Are you logged into the network?"

Terry tried to focus on her heartbeat. Injured as he was,

he could still sense it beating quickly. She was terrified. "How do you know who I am?" Terry asked.

Lena held her hands in front of her. "I met your friends. They came here to find you."

Friends? Was she talking about Ludo and Ysa? "What do you mean?"

"Doctor Curie and Sergeant Finn," she said.

The names meant nothing to him. "Who?"

"You don't know your own friends?" she asked.

"We don't have time for this," barked Jinel. "We have to go, Terry. Civil Protection will dispatch a team soon. No doubt they've already landed close by and are investigating the explosion."

Terry nodded. "Okay."

"Wait, what about the others? You can't go!" demanded Lena.

"Watch us," said Jinel, starting to leave.

Terry reluctantly followed. He wanted to find out what this analyst was talking about, but he also couldn't risk getting caught again.

Lena started after them. "Terry, wait a moment! Please!"

Jinel was already outside, waiting with the door open. Terry could smell the smoke from the nearby building as it continued to burn. He grabbed the handle, pausing to look back at the girl. "It's too dangerous for me. Sorry." He turned to leave.

"John and Mei!" she yelled.

He stopped. Did she just say—

"Your friends are waiting for you, Terry," said Lena Sol. "I've seen them. I met them. They came through the gate to look for you. They're here!"

"But," he started, fumbling with the words. "But that's not possible."

"I said, let's go!" shouted Jinel.

"She said John and Mei are here," said Terry, almost dizzy. The shock of the news had hit him with the strength of a bull. He could barely react…barely process what this woman had said. How could his friends have come all this way? How could they have followed him? It wasn't possible, was it? It couldn't be. No, there had to be a mistake.

A siren erupted from across the square, near the destroyed building where the bomb had hit. The noise filled the area with a piercing, overwhelming screech. They all covered their ears. "It's starting!" cried Jinel Din, readying her rifle. "The Leadership's pets have arrived."

Hall of the Leadership, Everlasting
February 27, 2351

JOHN SQUEEZED the trigger and unloaded a barrage of fire-power into the oncoming forces. In a single spread, he managed to injure three of them, crippling their attack.

The Blacks took the usual formation. Mickey, Track,

and John took positions near the front and middle, while Hughes and Short stuck to the rear.

The fallen enemy soldiers reached for their guns, despite being shot, but Mickey and Track made quick work of them. John preferred not to kill these people, but when a bullet to the leg doesn't stop a man, there's only one option left.

Another wave came through the narrow set of doors, but they fell to the floor almost immediately, stopped by two sniper shots and a well-placed knife throw. The sound of Hughes reloading his rifled echoed through the facility.

"Should we keep this party going?" asked Track.

"Let's push them out," said John.

With his team at his side, John led the way forward. They stepped over the fallen enemy fighters and made their way through the double doors.

As soon as John entered the following corridor, he was beset by three more enemies, too close to target. A round of metal zipped through the air and into one of the men's necks, courtesy of Hughes. He fell onto the floor, bleeding out.

John withdrew a knife from his side, slid beneath another target, and cut the ankles deep. The man screamed and dropped to his knees, right before Track drove another blade into the soldier's temple. It was all done in a single, fluid attack.

The Blacks pushed forward, slaying one insurgent after another. Several civilians had already been killed and now littered the hallway floors with their blood. "Double time it!" barked John.

They rounded another corner, coming into the tower entrance. The foyer was largely empty, but screams could be heard outside. John gave his team the signal to progress, but to do so cautiously. When they reached the outer door, he spotted several armed individuals. "Everyone set? Let's clear the yard!"

"Right beside you, boss," said Track.

The Blacks deployed through the entrance doors using a standard SWAT pattern, alternating left and right. John was the first outside, and he spotted several targets in the streets nearby.

Track and Mickey let loose a storm of firepower, tagging three in the head, two in the chest.

Hughes came out last, along with Short, quickly propping his rifle on a stone block, using the structure to shield himself. With his finger steady on the trigger, he fired at an oncoming target further down the street, shattering the man's forehead.

John threw a knife, hitting one of the last intruders in the chest, then ran for the man's gun, disarming him. With the enemy's weapon in his hand, John kicked the corpse to the ground, tossing the weapon behind him. Using his own, he took aim and fired, hitting two more with direct shots. Out of the corner of his eye, he spotted a moving shadow approaching from a nearby alley. Without another thought, he unlatched a small grenade, held it briefly, then threw it along the ground and into the opening. It bounced off one of the walls, frightening the men inside before finally exploding, sending a cloud of dust into the open street.

In under a minute, the Blacks had the area secure, with most of the combatants on the run, heading deeper into the city. "Should we go after them?" asked Track.

"Let the government handle the rest," said John.

Another shot erupted from Hughes's rifle. It hit a target in the distance, over a hundred meters removed from them. "Sorry!" called the sniper. "He was getting away."

John watched as the target fell, but noticed the bullet had only snagged his gut. He'd have to get closer to finish the job. "Mickey, with me," said John. "The rest of you, hold this position."

Mickey and John jogged to the injured survivor as he struggled to crawl. The soldier had left his weapon behind in a desperate move to flee, so John motioned for Mickey to grab it. As John approached, he found the soldier trailing blood behind him, grunting as he tried to get away. "That's enough," said John, once he was a few meters from the man.

The soldier stopped, raising his hands.

John turned him on his side, then frisked him for any weapons. He found a few knives, but nothing else. Mickey kept his weapon aimed on the soldier the whole time. "You wanna tell me what you people are doing?" asked John as he loomed over the bleeding stranger.

The man swallowed, but said nothing.

"The people inside told me you've been infected by the gas. They said you're crazy."

"*Vennisr,*" muttered the soldier. "*Onn vennisr.*"

"Oh, yeah? Hey, Mickey, you hear that? He's talking," said John. He leaned forward, gripping the extremist's collar. "You came in here and murdered a bunch of people today. You understand what I'm saying? Do you?"

"*Nioqitheg er csoth,*" he said, breathing heavily.

John looked at the wound in the man's stomach. It was covered in thick blood. There was no way he'd make it, not without some immediate medical attention, and even then...

"*Onn vennisr, caa,*" said the dying man. "*Posqil benn tniolri shij...*" He coughed, and blood came out.

John let go of his shirt, staring into the stranger's eyes as he released a final sigh of relief. He could only watch as the man grew still and empty, letting go of the pain.

"What do you think that was about?" asked Mickey, after a moment.

John shook his head. "Wish I knew, Mick. This whole planet's nothing but a mess."

Medical Quarter, Everlasting
February 27, 2351

TERRY WATCHED AS AN AIRCRAFT ARRIVED, hovering over

the area across the square. Several soldiers dismounted and ran into the smoke. "Quick, we have to go!" said Jinel. "Before they figure out there's no one over there."

Terry looked back at Lena. He couldn't leave her here, not without finding out more about John and Mei. "Are you staying or coming?" he asked.

She stood there, darting her eyes back and forth between Terry and the aircraft. "Okay," she finally said, catching up to him.

They headed out through the nearby square. Jinel led the way, taking them in the opposite direction of the aircraft. As they neared the back of one of the buildings, she dropped to a knee, then lifted a flap on her wrist, revealing a screen. "I'm pinned behind Medical Eight with the asset," she said. "I need a diversion while we make our way out."

A short pause.

"Got it," she said.

"Who was that?" asked Terry.

Jinel got to her feet and readied her weapon. "Friends."

"Who are you people?" asked Lena.

"Garden," answered Jinel. "That's all you need to know."

Terry could sense Lena's tension. She was rubbing her arm, breathing heavily through her mask. If she didn't stop, she'd probably end up hyperventilating. He put his hand on her shoulder. "Relax."

She nodded, still taking heavy breaths. "Sorry."

"As soon as we're clear, we have to move," explained Jinel. She looked at Lena. "You're staying here."

"We can't just drop her in the middle of a warzone," explained Terry.

"She can't be trusted," said Jinel.

"You don't even know me!" snapped Lena, who had had enough, it seemed.

Jinel lowered her gun and tapped the side of her mask. The dark material faded away, becoming transparent. Her entire face was now visible. "I do know you, Analyst."

Lena blinked, staring at Jinel. "You're—" Her mouth fell open. "You're supposed to be dead!"

"Lies from the great and powerful Leadership, I can assure you," she said. "In fact—"

A scatter of gunfire unloaded from nearby. "We have intruders! They're coming from the east!" shouted one of the soldiers. "Take them down!"

"That's our signal," muttered Jinel.

Terry grabbed Lena's hand. "Stick with me, okay?"

She nodded, a confused look on her face.

Jinel, with Terry and Lena behind her, burst into the street, dashing between the two buildings. Terry pulled Lena Sol along, slowing so she didn't stumble. Jinel aimed her sights on a few who had taken notice of them, and fired, clipping one in the leg and the other in the chest. Before they could return the shots, she leapt into a small alleyway. "Through here!"

Terry came behind her, but he was trailing. Lena could hardly keep up. "Come on!"

"I can't! You're going too—"

Terry turned to help her, but spotted the injured soldiers on the ground, positioning themselves to fire. One was struggling with his weapon, cradling it in his arms. He took aim at them, trying to steady himself, and in a single, deafening moment, fired.

The bullet hit Lena, sending her off her feet. She screamed as it pierced through her forearm before continuing on and hitting the nearby wall. Terry caught her right as he entered the alleyway, and they both fell on the ground.

Jinel helped lift Lena off of him. "Did she get hit?"

"She's bleeding!" said Terry.

"Get out of the way," ordered Jinel. She felt on her side and took out a small canister. Popping the top of it, she shook it a few times, then sprayed the wound.

"What are you doing?"

"Sealing it so she doesn't bleed out," she explained. "It hit an artery."

"We have to get her out of here!" said Terry.

Jinel took a piece of cloth and wrapped it around Lena's shoulder. "We've done what we can, but she's staying here."

"What are you talking about? We can't do that!"

"There's no time to argue!" shouted Jinel. "We can't—"

A bullet hit the side of the building, chipping part of

the wall. Suddenly, one of the soldiers came running into the alleyway. He collided with Terry, knocking him over. The two rolled until they hit the wall. The soldier grabbed at Terry's neck, but he snagged the man's wrist and pulled it away.

The soldier reached for a knife, getting ready to attack. Terry watched his eyes, trying to anticipate the angle. The man jerked forward, swiping right and then left, missing each time.

A bullet hit the man directly in the forehead, and he fell to the ground, motionless. Terry looked behind him and saw Jinel standing, her rifle still aimed on the dead man.

Terry's ears rang from the shock of the gun. "You just—"

"We don't have time for this. Come on!" ordered Jinel.

"What about Lena?" he asked.

Jinel ran to the edge of the alley, staying behind the wall. She fired blindly in the direction of the enemy troops. "Leave her here!"

"You can't be serious," said Terry.

"She's a potential security threat," said Jinel.

"I'm bringing her with us and that's all there is to it," said Terry. He placed his arms beneath Lena. "It's either that or you leave us both behind."

Jinel glanced at the gathering forces in the square. "Fine, but we have to go right now."

"Lead the way," said Terry.

Jinel motioned for him to follow, then ran out the other

end of the alleyway. She called her associates as they went, letting them know when they were clear from the area.

In that moment, a single, monumental blast exploded from behind them, shaking the ground in a heavy display. Terry nearly fell, but Jinel caught him by the side. He managed to keep Lena steady in his arms. "What the hell was that?!"

A swell of fresh smoke filled the sky above the area they'd just left. "That would be the second bomb," said Jinel.

18

Leadership Report 221885.021
Recorded 02.28.884
Subtitled: Aftermath

KAI: *Half of the Medical Quarter is in ruins. Buildings Six, Seven, and Four are either destroyed or heavily damaged. Several Civil Protection personnel are dead. Oh, and the alien was taken right out from under us. How exactly do you propose we deal with this?*

    GEL: *We'll get him back, I can assure you.*

    KAI: *How? We have no idea where these Garden individuals even are, let alone how to contact them. They're a band of traitors and degenerates.*

    GEL: *Surveillance caught a glimpse as they were fleeing. It seems they had some assistance from one of our analysts. A woman named Lena Sol.*

KAI: *Ah, yes. She was on the team that discovered the aliens in the first place. What was she doing in the Medical Quarter?*

GEL: *She was scheduled to depart for Argos a few hours later. It's standard routine to have a medical checkup beforehand. We aren't certain if she knew of the attack or simply encountered the rebels during their assault, but judging from what the video showed, it seems she has joined them.*

KAI: *If that's true, the boy will likely learn that his friends are looking for him. What happens when he finds them? Everlasting has not been engaged in a war for centuries.*

GEL: *That's not going to happen. We'll stop this Garden before it has a chance to flourish. I already have a team of analysts scanning the city for evidence of their movement. Master Lao also has several of his squads patrolling the city.*

KAI: *The Master of Arms? He can't be pleased with how this situation has unfolded.*

GEL: *Certainly not, but he understands. Don't worry, sir. We will find the alien, whatever it takes.*

KAI: *Of that, I have little doubt, but I'm afraid you will not be involved in this any longer.*

GEL: *Sir?*

KAI: *You have mishandled this at every turn. I'm sure you can see the failure in your actions. You are the Master Analyst, after all. Please, analyze yourself.*

GEL: *I will be the first to admit there have been mistakes, sir, but—*

KAI: *No more excuses. I am tired of your words. Return to your floating tower and wait for my orders. Master Lao will handle this* *investigation, moving forward. You are fortunate I do not have you replaced.*

GEL: *Yes, sir. I...I'm sorry. Thank you, sir.*

KAI: *Save the apologies, Gel. Earn my respect by doing your job. Use the satellite to scan the city and the surrounding countryside. Locate the alien and report his location. Do not come to me with anything less.*

GEL: *Yes, sir.*

End Audio File

Hall of the Leadership, Everlasting
February 28, 2351

The day after the assault on Everlasting, John stood before the assembled Leadership, along with his team. Mei had asked to come as soon as she heard news of the attack, but John insisted she remain at the portal. He couldn't let anything happen to her, no matter how angry she might get.

"Johnathan Finn, Mason Hughes, Alicia Short, Peter Track, and Arthur Mackenzie, we thank you for your assistance and service," said Master Trin, standing next to the other assembled leaders.

Short snickered. "Haven't heard Mickey's full name in a while."

"You kept this building secure and were more than essential in safeguarding several lives, including mine. I thank each of you for the courage you displayed."

"You're welcome," said John. He was never very good at these things.

Master Lao motioned for Trin to sit, then stood to be recognized. "I can assure you that the bulk of the invading forces have been extinguished. Thanks to our combined efforts, this battle was quick and decisive."

John thought about the man he'd killed in the street and the look on his face as the life drained out of him. "I appreciate the gratitude, but it was nothing. I'd actually like to get back to my people. If you guys can provide us with a ride, it would mean a lot."

"Of course, Sergeant Finn," said Master Lao. "There will be a vessel waiting for you in the docking bay as soon as you're prepared."

The meeting concluded soon after, and John and his team made their way immediately to the *Red Door*. "What's the hurry, boss?" asked Track, right as they were leaving the atrium.

"A lot is happening here. Better we stay out of it for now until we talk to Central," said John.

"You think Command is gonna have us pull out?"

"Don't know," he answered. "But it sure does seem like something's going on. Something more than what we're seeing. You get me?"

"I get you, boss," said Track.

"I just think we need more intel before we can get behind this mess."

"Whatever you decide, you know we'll back you," said Short, who was following behind them.

"All of us," said Hughes.

They entered the hangar where the *Red Door* was docked and waiting.

Despite leaving, John knew he'd be back. With so much on the line, Central would insist upon it. Still, he had to be with Mei for now. He had to take a breather. He'd felt uneasy ever since he arrived in this city, but never quite like when he was standing over that dying soldier. He didn't pity the man, because he'd never been a fan of extremism, but there was something about him…something more than violent hate. He'd been driven by a deeper motivation, John knew. A righteous cause that could draw a man to kill or die.

It would have been a lie to say John didn't suspect something was wrong in the great city of Everlasting. Something the Leadership didn't want him to see, perhaps.

Whatever it was, he had to get away from it. At least for now. John had come to this planet with a single purpose in mind: to find his oldest friend and bring him home. The Leadership had promised to help, and he would continue to remind them about that commitment, but he also wouldn't stop searching on the ground. He'd follow the clues Terry had left, however difficult the search might prove. If he had to visit every village on Kant, he'd do it without question.

Ask them if they'd seen a scrawny kid with round ears and green eyes.

He'd find a trail and follow it. John had traveled universes to get here, and he wasn't about to stop now.

The *Red Door* left the hangar bay, heading in the direction of the quarantine zone. It passed above the Tower of the Cartographer, and John gleamed a quick view of the floating island's surface. He imagined Lena Sol inside, working diligently. Maybe she was trying to locate Terry right at this moment. John would do the same. He wouldn't give up.

Not yet, he thought, leaning against the glass. *Not now. Not ever.*

Somewhere Underground
February 28, 2351

LENA AWOKE TO A PIERCING LIGHT. She turned away from it as her eyes slowly adjusted.

"Easy," said Jinel, sitting beside her. "You took a dive."

They sat inside a small room, hardly any bigger than a closet. A pile of medical supplies had been crudely tossed into the corner, while her bed and Jinel's chair took up the bulk of the room. Lena tried to move, but the sharp pain in her shoulder made her yelp.

"I wouldn't move around too much," said Jinel.

"Where…am I?" asked Lena.

"A Garden outpost. One of many."

"A Garden…outpost?" asked Lena, still a bit disorientated. "I'm not in Everlasting?"

"You don't need to worry about that," said Jinel. "For now, you're staying in this bed. You need to recover."

"Where's Terry?" she asked.

"He's right outside."

The door cracked open. "Here," said a voice. Lena looked over and saw Terry's face appear. "I heard my name."

"I need to talk to you," said Lena. "I need to—" A cough stopped her. It hurt to breathe.

Terry eased his way into the tiny room, then sat at the edge of the bed. "Hey, relax," he told her. "You need to rest. We can talk later."

"No," she said. "Your friends are out there looking for you."

"You said that before," said Terry.

"Doctor Curie and Sergeant Finn. They told me—"

"You mean John and Mei?" asked Terry.

"Yes," she answered. "You don't know their full names?"

"We didn't have last names when we were children. You don't get them until you graduate and you choose them. I never got an official graduation." His eyes fell on the bed, and he smiled. "It sounds like they found good names."

She nodded. "Very good names."

"I can't believe they're here. This means I can see them."

"Easy, now," said Jinel. "No one's going anywhere right now. None of us are. Civil Protection has the entire city locked down, which means we're stuck where we are."

"There has to be a way," said Terry.

"Give it a few days. I promise, I'll get you to your friends in time, but right now you need to stay put. You're still wounded, remember?"

"I haven't forgotten," he said, glancing down at his arm.

A quick image of the fight at the border flashed across Lena's mind. She recalled how Terry had disabled the sentry unit right before collapsing and passing out from his injuries. "I'll help you find them, once you're ready," said Lena.

Terry looked surprised. "You'd do that for me?"

"Sergeant Finn and Doctor Curie were very kind to me. I owe it to them to help." That was only partially true, she knew. The guilt of the border incident was still fresh in her mind.

"Sorry, Analyst, but you'll have to stay in this room for now. I can't have you looking around," said Jinel.

"Are you afraid I'll find a secret and share it with the Leadership?" asked Lena. "They were about to send me to Argos, halfway around the world, just to get rid of me. I'm not going back, especially now that they've seen me with you."

"What do you mean?" asked Terry.

"Civil Protection has surveillance all over the city. We were in the open, so I can assure you they were watching. If they follow protocol, and I'm certain they will, I've already been marked for a full conversion."

"A full what?" asked Terry.

"It's when they wipe your memory clean," said Jinel. "They erase your whole brain."

"Seriously?"

"The Leadership does not take kindly to dissidents," said Lena, glancing at Jinel.

Terry grimaced. "This planet is insane. Slavers, priests, giant robots, and now conversions. One nightmare after another."

"I expect it hasn't been easy for you, but I promise things will get better," said Jinel.

"What's better for one person might be worse for another," answered Lena.

Jinel rose, clutching the rifle at her side. "That's how it is with war. There's always a winner and a loser."

"That's where you're wrong," muttered Terry, staring at the barrel of her gun.

"How's that?" asked Jinel.

"No one wins in the end. Even after the fighting is over and the dust has cleared…even when you've wiped it all away, you've still got blood on your hands, and half of you are dead," he said, looking at each of them. "And then it starts all over again."

EPILOGUE

NEAR THE GREAT wall of Everlasting, far from the coast, a ship sailed through a moonless, quiet night. On most days, the ship carried a crew of twelve, but tonight it had two new passengers on its deck.

A man and a woman. A husband and a wife. A farmer and a priestess.

Ludo stared out across the sloshing waves, toward the city of Everlasting, or where he imagined it must be. The wavemaster Hux had told him of a way through the wall, an opening so large a passenger boat could fit. Now they went to find it.

Beside him, Ysa stood with quiet resolve, saying nothing. She had insisted on coming with him, her life owed to the lost boy on the other side of that wall.

Together, Ludo and Ysa had fled as Terry sacrificed

himself to save them from the Guardians of Everlasting. They owed him their lives.

For centuries, the people worshipped the Eye. For years, they believed their gods were waiting in the holy city on the hill. Perhaps it was true, and the two of them sailed toward their own destruction.

But they would not be denied.

Together, Ludo and Ysa had defied the gods before for love. Now, it was no different. Now, they did it for Terry, their chakka-kin. Their family.

Ludo gripped the hilt of Terry's sword, its shimmering blade reflecting starlight. He had found it in the field after the fight, and had not allowed it to leave his side since. With his other hand, he squeezed his wife's fingers. "The air is cold tonight," he remarked.

She nodded. "We are far in the north now. Farther than I have ever been."

"We have our wings to guide us," he assured her. "They will carry us to him."

"Strong as they are," she answered.

He squeezed her hand once more and smiled. "Strong as they are."

TERRY, MEI, and JOHN will return in THE VERNAL MEMORY, available right now exclusively on Amazon.

STAY UP TO DATE

Chaney posts updates, official art, previews, and other awesome stuff on his website. You can also follow him on Instagram, Facebook, and Twitter.

Search for **JN Chaney's Renegade Readers** on Facebook to join the group where readers can come together and share their lives and interests, especially regarding Chaney's books.

For updates about new releases, as well as exclusive promotions, sign up for the VIP mailing list. Head there now to receive a free copy of *The Other Side of Nowhere*.

https://www.subscribepage.com/organic

Enjoying the series? Help others discover the Variant Saga by leaving a review on Amazon.

ABOUT THE AUTHOR

J. N. Chaney has a Master's of Fine Arts in creative writing and fancies himself quite the Super Mario Bros. fan. When he isn't writing or gaming, you can find him online at **www.jnchaney.com**.

He migrates often but was last seen in Avon Park, Florida. Any sightings should be reported, as they are rare.

Hope Everlasting is his fourth novel.

Made in the USA
Middletown, DE
18 November 2019